Hazel Green Series

ONE FINE DAY

CINDY KIRK

WAVERLY HOUSE

CONTENTS

Prologue	1
1. Present day	7
Chapter 2	18
Chapter 3	28
Chapter 4	34
Chapter 5	40
Chapter 6	50
Chapter 7	59
Chapter 8	71
Chapter 9	81
Chapter 10	92
Chapter 11	103
Chapter 12	112
Chapter 13	122
Chapter 14	132
Chapter 15	144
Chapter 16	153
Chapter 17	163
Chapter 18	173
Chapter 19	184
Chapter 20	196
Chapter 21	204
Chapter 22	213
Chapter 23	224
Chapter 24	235
Chapter 25	245
Chapter 26	254
Epilogue	259
Sneak Peek of One Step Away	263
Also by Cindy Kirk	277

PROLOGUE

FIVE YEARS EARLIER

My first impulse is to run. To jump up from the leather chair in a room that smells faintly of disinfectant and take off. I have no idea where I'd go. Anywhere has to be better than this office in the physicians' wing of Springfield's Arborview hospital.

I remain seated. Unlike my dad, I'm not a runner. I face the difficult stuff with my head held high. Whether it's a father walking out the door or a doctor telling me the baby I felt move for the first time only yesterday, might be—would likely be—born with severe abnormalities.

Jonah and Veronica are seated to my right. The child I'm carrying is theirs. This is the baby they tried to have for years. Out of money and nearly out of hope, they came to me, their good friend.

"A meningocele is rare, but if it's that type of spina bifada, especially located in the lower spine, well, that would be best case scenario."

Rare. Which would mean we hit the jackpot as far as birth defects go.

I didn't feel particularly lucky about our odds right now.

From the looks on Veronica and Jonah's faces, they weren't ready to head out and buy a lottery ticket, either.

"What's the more likely scenario?" Jonah spoke quietly, his voice deep with only the slightest hint of a quiver.

This tall, broad-shouldered man with wavy blond hair and kind blue eyes has been my best friend for as far back as I can remember. Of course, once he married, Veronica became his bestie.

She's blonde, too, but instead of hair the color of sun-ripened wheat, hers is a silvery shade that looks like it came straight from a bottle. I think it's natural. At least, I've never seen dark roots. But then, the advertising exec always looks picture perfect.

The silence lengthens until it begins to pulsate off the moss green walls. The air grows heavy. I force myself to breathe. In and out. In and out.

Veronica and Jonah's fingers remain tightly intertwined.

I grip the highly polished wood arms of the chair.

"Depending on severity, the child may have very little feeling, if any, in her legs and arms. She may not be able to move those parts of—"

"She'll be paralyzed." The color drains from Veronica's face, leaving it ghostly white.

"That's a possibility." The doctor answers in an easy manner but the twitch by his left eye tells me he doesn't like being interrupted.

"What else?" Veronica demands in a tone I'm sure she never uses with her advertising clients.

"Let the doctor say—" Jonah pauses when his wife jerks her hand from his.

Veronica's chest rises and falls as if she's coming to the end of a long and difficult race. "I want the truth, not pie-in-the sky hopes."

"Mrs. Rollins." Even as the doctor began, the tilt to Veronica's jaw tells me the man doesn't stand a chance.

The emotion rising inside me settles in my throat. I say nothing. I'm not sure I could force out any words, even if I had something important to say.

My hand rests on the belly that had begun to swell low in my abdomen. The gesture is meant to reassure the tiny one growing inside me that I won't let anyone hurt her.

"My cousin Tiffany's doctor told her that her baby's head was smaller than normal, but said everything would likely be okay. Well, it wasn't okay. That baby was horribly malformed and never left the hospital. I was with her when he died." Veronica blinks rapidly. "Forgive me if I'm not interested in best case scenarios."

"What other problems do these children usually have?" Jonah clears his throat. "Other than, ah, other than paralysis."

"Bowel and bladder problems. Hydrocephalus, which is fluid build-up in the brain. Even when treated with a shunt, it may cause seizures." The doctor pauses. This time it's his turn to clear his throat. "As well as learning or vision problems."

"Well." Veronica huffs out the word then turns and skewers me with her pale blue eyes. "It seems the baby you're carrying will be paralyzed and unable to control her bowels and bladder. If that isn't enough she could have seizures, be blind and mentally retarded. Oh, and let's not forget the clubfoot. That's a definite."

"Yes. The baby has a clubfoot." The doctor pauses, then turns silent.

"How are you feeling about all this, Abs?" Jonah shifts his gaze to me, his eyes dark with concern.

I saw the foot on the ultrasound, once the doctor pointed it out. The spine defect wasn't as clear. I'd also seen her heart, beating strong and fast.

I loosen my death grip on the chair. "It isn't the best news, but it seems there's room for hope."

"Hope?" Veronica screeches the word and lunges up from her

seat. She might have gone for me but Jonah places a hand on her arm and pulls her back down.

"Haven't you been listening?" She's yelling and crying at the same time. "My baby is a freak, destined for a life of pain and suffering."

"We don't know that. You heard the doctor. Not for sure." I clamp my mouth shut before I remind Veronica that no part of this baby is genetically *hers*. Jonah's sperm and an egg donor formed this child. I agreed to let it nest inside me, to nourish and protect it while it grew.

"What I know, is I can't take any more. The miscarriages, the failed adoption and now this. It's too much." Veronica clasps her hands together in an obvious attempt to still their trembling.

My heart aches for Veronica. She's endured so much in her quest to become a mother. Before I can reach over and give her arm a comforting squeeze, her gaze returns to the doctor.

"How soon can you schedule an abortion?" Veronica's tone might sound matter-o-fact but the strain edging her mouth and the fact that her knuckles are now as white as her face, give her away. "I'd like this done and over with as soon as possible."

"Vee. We should take time to think about this." Jonah's low tone, obviously intended to soothe, has the opposite effect.

Like a rabid wolf, Veronica bares her teeth. "What is there to think about?"

The question is greeted by frozen silence.

The doctor opens his mouth then closes it.

Jonah expels a heavy breath. "Today's news isn't what any of us were hoping to hear."

The abject misery on his face reminds me of how he looked the day his beloved dog, Ranger, died.

"I'm sorry, Jonah. I was wrong to snap at you." Veronica's eyes fill with tears once again but she blinks them back before they can fall. "When the AFP test came back high last week, we knew spina bifada was a concern. We agreed that quality of life is important. It's obvious this child's prognosis is grim."

Butterfly wings flutter low in my belly.

After several erratic heartbeats, I find my voice. "There will be no abortion."

Caught off guard, Veronica turns to me, her eyes wide.

Jonah regards me thoughtfully, his expression inscrutable.

"Perhaps you'd all like to take some time to think about this." The doctor's gaze slides to Jonah. "Right now, we're at sixteen weeks' gestation. There is still time. Not a lot, but still time to consider."

I lift my chin. "I will not terminate this pregnancy."

"You don't have a vote." Veronica appears more puzzled than angry by my vehement assertion. "It's in the contract you signed."

"I don't think there's a court in the state of Illinois that would order a woman to have an abortion she doesn't want." Veronica isn't the only one who did her research. Once the test for genetic anomalies came back with the AFP elevated, I did some digging of my own. I like being prepared.

Veronica's nostrils flare. Though her face remains bone white; two high red blotches now color her cheeks. "If you refuse, you'll be in breach of the contract. The payments will stop. Is that what you want?"

None of this is what I want. But I learned long ago we don't always get what we want.

Before Veronica can say more, Jonah wraps an arm around her shoulders and murmurs something in her ear. Whatever he says has her sagging against him.

I look at Jonah, hoping for…well, for what I wasn't sure. Perhaps, confirmation that I'm not in this alone. Maybe a sign that he'll be there for me as he was when that bully in fourth grade knocked me to the ground.

Can't he see I'm on the ground and bleeding?

When we began this journey, he promised the three of us

would be in this together, all the way through. But instead of reaching out and pulling me into the fold, he consoles his now sobbing wife.

As his gentle hand strokes her hair, his gaze meets mine. I see sorrow and regret in the blue depths.

My heart sinks. Without any words being said, I understand.

This time, I'm on my own.

1
PRESENT DAY

Five years ago, if someone told Abigail Fine she'd be living in Hazel Green, Illinois and running her own business, she'd have said they were crazy. If they told her she'd be cleaning toilets, well, that she would have believed.

Thanks to the generosity of a great-aunt she hadn't known existed, two years ago she became the proud owner of a boutique hotel. Abby inched the metal snake into the bowels of the bowl and continued to fish. While she hadn't yet managed to catch what was clogging up the toilet in room 201, giving up wasn't in her nature.

"I'm sorry about this, Abby."

Abby paused to look back into the freckled face of Nevaeh Nichols, the high school girl she employed during the summer to clean rooms. As she usually did when she worked, Nev had pulled her auburn hair back in a high pony. Her brown eyes, large in her thin speckled face, reminded Abby of a sweet spaniel.

"You have no reason to be sorry." Abby turned back to the bowl, keeping her voice matter-of-fact. "In fact, you deserve a gold star for noticing this bad boy wasn't flushing properly."

"It emptied, but slowly." Nev absently straightened a slightly off kilter plush ivory towel draped over a thick brass bar.

Room 201 had been the final stop for Nev as the couple who'd occupied the room last night had requested a late departure. Abby checked them out personally and they'd raved about the room. Not one mention of a slow-to-empty toilet.

When Nev had reported the issue, for one brief moment Abby considered calling a plumber. But if she'd learned anything in the two years since inheriting the hotel from her great aunt, it was that money flowed out far faster than it flowed in. Which meant, she needed to attempt to fix problems herself before calling in the pros.

The snake bumped up against something squishy. Abby gave a shout.

Nevaeh stumbled backwards. "What's wrong?"

"It's all good." The knowledge she wouldn't need a plumber was sweeter than any French pastry. "Bring the bucket over here."

The girl held the container out as Abby slowly pulled back on the snake. The careful, deliberate movement reminded her of reeling in a fish. But Abby could guarantee whatever she caught today wouldn't be on any menu tonight. The metal tape slowly retracted, the hook buried deep in a bloated sanitary napkin.

Abby locked the snake then lifted and positioned the soggy mess over the bucket. "Here's the culprit."

"Yuck."

With a grin, Abby released the pad and let it drop.

Wrinkling her nose at the smell, Nev stepped back. She held the bucket at arms' length. "That's disgusting."

"Yes, it is." Abby's tone remained cheerful as the cash register in her mind tallied how much she'd saved by fixing the problem herself. "I'll take the bucket down with me. You, my dear, are officially off-duty."

With a spring in her step, Abby descended the stairs to the

utility room at the back of the hotel's first floor. Once she finished there, she hurried to relieve Iris Endicott at the front desk.

Eight of the ten rooms were already booked for the evening. Six was the break-even point. Her cheer meter inched up a notch when she saw Iris checking in a guest.

As Abby stepped forward, she mentally congratulated the newcomer on making such an excellent choice.

Standing two stories tall, The Inn at Hazel Green was the only hotel in the town's historic district. From the gleaming hardwood floor to the exposed brick wall in the entry, the hotel radiated warmth and welcome. While there were larger and more modern hotels out by the interstate, many visitors preferred to stay here. Not only because of its proximity to all the quaint shops but because of the hotel's appealing ambiance.

And, Abby reminded herself, because of the personalized service she, and every one of her employees, offered to guests. Stepping to the desk, Abby bestowed a warm smile on the forty-something woman dressed smartly in tailored navy pants, a sleeveless white silk top and heels.

"Welcome to The Inn at Hazel Green." Abby glanced at the name on the computer screen as she extended her hand. "Ms. Grimsby, I'm Abigail Fine, the proprietor. I'm happy you chose to stay with us. If there's anything we can do to make your stay more pleasant, all you need to do is ask."

"You look too young to be in charge." For a second, the cool assessment in Charlotte Grimsby's pale blue eyes triggered memories of Veronica in that stuffy doctor's office all those years ago.

Different person, Abby told herself. Different situation.

"Thanks for the compliment." Abby had turned thirty last year and being called young was now a reason to rejoice.

"I'll give you another. I love your dress." Unexpectedly, Charlotte reached forward to rub the soft sable-colored fabric with ivory polka dots between her fingers. "A bit old-fashioned for my tastes but the perfect foil for your dark hair and eyes."

"It's what we in Hazel Green like to call vintage-wear." Living in a community that billed itself as a place where history comes alive, where dressing in period pieces was not only accepted but encouraged, had given Abby the freedom to experiment with all sorts of styles. "This is a cotton swing dress, popular in the 1950s."

Turning, Abby studied Iris, the pretty blonde history teacher who worked for her during the summer. Iris had gone stylishly casual today. She'd coupled a royal blue skirt with tiny boats etched around the hem with a stretchy red and white striped top.

Abby tapped a finger against her lips. "If I'm not mistaken, Iris is wearing a 1940's era high-waist Hoover swing skirt."

"Ding, ding, ding." Iris winked. "Give the woman a cigar."

"I'd prefer a donut." Laughter bubbled up and spilled from Abby's lips like a joyous waterfall.

"You two are beyond adorable. It's as if you don't have a care in the world." Charlotte's gaze narrowed and she studied the two women as if they were bugs under a microscope.

Her acerbic tone had Iris's smile fading and tiny frown lines forming between her brows.

Abby regarded her guest thoughtfully. "I think we can both agree it's a rare person whose life is free of challenges."

Charlotte's gaze shifted.

"You have a beautiful place." The care the woman took in assessing the furniture in the lobby reminded Abby of a pawn broker contemplating an offer. "I adore exposed brick."

"The Inn was built in 1884. Been in the family ever since." Abby let her gaze linger on the hand-tooled maple banister leading to the second floor. The wood gleamed as if it had been freshly polished that morning.

Which it had been. By her. Abby was continually amazed by what Renaissance wax, a soft cloth and lots of elbow grease could do.

"Ms. Grimsby." Iris's tone remained pleasant. "I've checked you into our William Jennings Bryan suite."

Charlotte cocked her head, appearing to not recognize the name.

Abby understood her confusion. She hadn't known anything about the man until she'd moved to Hazel Green. "Following his defeat in the Presidential election of 1900, Mr. Bryan became the most popular orator on the Chautauqua circuit. It's rumored he spent the night in room 110 when the hotel first opened for business. Apparently, he continued to stay here whenever he was in the area."

Ignoring the impromptu history lesson, Charlotte studied the large metal key Iris pressed into her hand. She rolled it between her fingers. "I haven't seen one of these in ages."

"Adds to the nostalgia in a way a keycard never could."

Iris's comment prompted a smile of approval from Abby and garnered a reluctant nod of agreement from their guest.

"While I'm in town, I'm hoping to do business with Jocelyn Valentine. The Milliner." Charlotte added the last bit, as if concerned they might not recognize the name.

Abby had no idea how it worked on Michigan Avenue but in Hazel Green all the merchants not only knew, but supported, each other.

"Her shop is super close, just down the block and around the corner." Iris pointed west. "It takes less than two minutes to walk from our front door to hers."

"Jocelyn is extremely talented." Abby thought of the gorgeous hats featured in The Mad Hatter's decorative window. "If you're looking for one-of-a-kind hats, either to feature in your shop or for personal use, she's your gal."

"You've been most helpful." The woman gestured with the hand holding the key. "I assume my room is down that hall."

"It is." Abby rounded the stand and gestured to the leather overnight case at the woman's feet. "May I help you with your bag?"

Charlotte flicked the offer away with a swipe of her hand. Though she gave the appearance of a woman in a hurry, she didn't immediately reach for the bag. Curiosity filled her eyes as her gaze lingered on the colonnade which separated the lobby of the hotel from the restaurant.

"If you get hungry, you should consider Matilda's. They serve fabulous farm-to-table food. Trust me. You can't go wrong with anything on the menu." Even if the restaurant hadn't been under her roof, Abby would have still have recommended the place. In Hazel Green, no one out-cooked Matilda Lovejoy.

Charlotte's expression turned thoughtful. "Thanks for the suggestion."

Once the woman disappeared down the hall, Abby shot Iris a questioning look. "Nine rooms filled?"

"Your math skills are impressive." Iris flashed a smile. "201 is the only one still available. Since your fishing expedition was a success, that room is ready to book."

For a second Abby wondered how Iris knew the outcome of her trip to the fishing bowl, then realized Nev must have told her on her way out the door. Her handful of employees were a tight-knit crew. But then, so were the townspeople. Kind and generous to a fault, they were what made Hazel Green special.

Abby had arrived in this northern Illinois community two years ago shortly after a winter storm dropped two feet of snow. She'd been apprehensive and unsure whether she'd made the right decision in moving here from Springfield. It hadn't taken long for her to realize she'd hit the jackpot.

The second Abby stepped through the front door of the hotel, she'd been greeted by Matilda, who'd been managing the hotel until the estate was settled. One touch from the woman's hand was all it had taken. Abby remembered the moment vividly. It was as if someone had wrapped a warm, soft blanket around her and her daughter and said welcome home, weary ones, welcome home.

From that second, the support she'd received from, well, everyone had been astonishing.

Until then, Abby had felt as if she'd been on her own her entire life. Her father jumped ship early in her childhood and her mom had passed away after being hit by a car shortly after Abby graduated from college.

Thanks to a stranger's decision to leave everything to a great-niece she'd never met, Abby and her daughter now had a forever home and more good friends than she could count.

"I'm glad I'm not working this evening."

Abby blinked herself back to the present in time to see Iris jerk her head toward the hall.

"She's going to be a demanding one."

"I thought Charlotte was pleasant enough." Abby kept her tone even, not wanting to get drawn into gossiping about a customer.

She didn't hold out much hope of Iris letting the subject drop. Since her husband's death, Iris had turned into a glass-half-empty gal. Not that Abby blamed her. Seeing your husband shot in front of you could turn anyone bitter.

"Did you see the way her lips pursed?" Iris pulled her bright red lips into something that resembled more a pout than a pucker. "Like she'd just sucked on a lemon."

Abby thought of the pale band of skin she'd spotted encircling Charlotte's left ring finger. Could she be recently separated? Divorced? Perhaps her husband had recently died. "What's that saying? People are fighting battles every day that we know nothing about."

"True." Iris gave a grudging nod. "You certainly were right on target last week with Katie and Tom."

Thinking about the couple brought heaviness to Abby's heart. When the two first arrived, they'd been taciturn and a bit abrupt. After a couple of days, she'd learned the heartbreaking truth.

The two, who'd recently celebrated their third wedding anniversary, were in Hazel Green to plan Katie's funeral. Simply recalling the conversation had tears stinging the backs of Abby's eyes.

While she couldn't change Katie's terminal cancer prognosis, Abby had done all she could to make their stay in Hazel Green as comfortable as possible.

Iris unlocked one of the drawers behind the counter and pulled out her purse. "I don't see how you do it. How you keep such a good attitude."

"I believe we offer more than warm beds to weary travelers. We offer joy, hope, love."

"I suppose."

The reluctant agreement had Abby fighting back a smile.

"I'm heading out." Iris touched her shoulder. "Are you sure you'll be okay alone?"

"I'll be fine." You'd have thought Iris had asked for a huge favor instead of simply requesting the rest of the afternoon off to do some shopping.

Abby walked with Iris to the front door with its glass insert. The name of the hotel was etched in a bold, yet elegant, font. Reaching around Iris, she opened the door. "And, I'm not alone. Roselle is in the kitchen doing the prep work for dinner and Eva Grace should be dropped off in the next hour or so."

"I can't believe the munchkin is old enough to go to a birthday party." Iris's expression softened the way it always did when she spoke of Abby's daughter.

The teacher loved children but hadn't been able to have kids of her own. Iris had mentioned once that she and her husband had been looking into adoption when he was killed.

"It's crazy to think she'll be starting kindergarten next week." When she had the embryo transfer, Abby hadn't planned to raise a child. Now, she couldn't imagine her life without Eva Grace.

She followed Iris out into the sunshine and gave her friend a playful shove. "What are you doing still hanging around here when there's shopping to do?"

Even after Iris disappeared around the corner, Abby remained on the sidewalk. There was no reason to hurry inside. If any of the guests called for assistance, her cell would ring. Lifting her face to the sun, Abby soaked in the energy that permeated the business district.

Locals and tourists mingled on the sidewalks. Flags and banners, advertising various upcoming activities that would culminate in the Hazel Green Birthday Bash, hung from old-fashioned light posts. Instead of concrete sidewalks going all the way to the curbs flanking the cobblestone street, the city had left openings that were now filled with blooming flowers.

Abby narrowed her gaze on a black-and-white awning half a block away. The striped canopy made a bold statement over the front window of the antique shop. She swore it hadn't been there last night when she and Eva Grace made their nightly trek to the park.

Glancing back, Abby studied the green dome awning over the hotel's front door. While it looked good with the red brick, she wondered if she should consider something bigger? Or perhaps try a different color?

"Mighty pretty day."

Abby recognized the deep, cheerful voice even before she turned. When the rotund man with the white beard standing before her wasn't playing Santa Claus, he delivered the mail.

"Hi, Frank. You're looking chipper."

Frank Partridge rubbed a hand over his fluffy beard. "Got myself a haircut and a beard trim yesterday."

"I can see that." Instead of reaching his waist, the beard stopped mid-chest.

"Where's the little one?"

"At a birthday party." Abby glanced at her watch. "She should be home any minute."

"Give her this." Frank took a sucker peeking out of his shirt pocket and handed it to Abby.

"Hey." She shot him a teasing smile. "Don't I get anything?"

"This is for you." Frank reached deep into the cloth bag slung over his shoulder and pulled out a thick wad of mail.

Abby's smile froze when she saw what was at the top of the stack.

She knew the envelope. Recognized the scrawl.

"Everything okay?"

"Everything is fine. Thanks." The concern in Frank's voice had her adding a smile. "You have yourself a good day."

"That's the plan." Whistling between his teeth, he sauntered down the sidewalk.

An unexpected tap on her shoulder had Abby whirling. The top envelope slipped from her grasp and fluttered to the ground.

Before Abby could react, Matilda bent over, the sweeping folds of her paisley caftan, circa 1975, fluttering in the breeze. She scooped up the envelope in one easy motion.

Abby held out her hand but Matilda merely studied the writing. "Just like clockwork."

Impatience had Abby wanting to play snatch and grab. She reined in the impulse. "It's from Jonah. I told you about the money he sends every month."

"You also mentioned the notes he includes for Eva Grace." Matilda inclined her head. "Have you read any of them to her?"

"I will. When she's older." *Maybe*, Abby added silently to herself.

"What about the notes he sends you?"

Abby blinked, resisting the urge to snap that anything Jonah had to say was of no consequence.

When it mattered most, he hadn't been there for her. Or for Eva Grace.

That, she would never forget.

CHAPTER TWO

As Abby wiggled into the form-fitting silk dress, she thought of the awkward moment with Matilda earlier. She was grateful her friend had let the subject of the ridiculous note Jonah had written, drop.

Seriously, who above the age of ten wrote, "Please read my letter. It's important," on the back of an envelope?

Important or not, his enclosed missive ended up in a large bag where the rest of his notes were "filed." The ones addressed to Eva Grace went into a box. Both bag and box sat on the top shelf of her closet. The cash went in the bank.

Despite Veronica's threat to cut her off years ago, the money and letters continued to arrive each month. The first time, Abby had been so angry she'd nearly ripped up the letters and cash and sent the pieces back to Jonah. Only the knowledge that this was *his* baby growing inside her, had her hesitating.

In the end, she'd put away the letters and kept the money.

Pride, her mother once told her, doesn't fill an empty stomach or put a roof over your baby's head.

Pregnant and broke, Abby hadn't needed a crystal ball to know her life was about to get very hard.

Anger surged. She would not give one more thought to Jonah Rollins. If giving money assuaged his conscience, so be it. But the income, however welcome, wasn't what she'd needed most during those difficult, early years.

Years when she did good to get five hours of sleep a night. When worry and fatigue had her hair falling out in clumps. When Eva Grace cried and screamed and pleaded each time the casts came off to be replaced by the dreaded braces. Braces that had to be worn twenty-three out of twenty-four hours.

"Mommy? May I come in?"

Eva Grace eased open the door to Abby's bedroom and peered inside. She was a petite pixy with bright blue eyes and a mass of golden curls. Her facial features were delicate, but Abby saw Jonah in the shape of her eyes and the single dimple in her left cheek.

"Of course."

The words barely left her lips when the little girl bounded into the room and flung her arms around Abby.

"You look be-u-ti-ful." Eva Grace rubbed her cheek against the silky fabric of her mother's dress. "I wish I could go to the party tonight. I like parties."

"You had your party this afternoon," Abby reminded her. "Celebrating Bristol's birthday."

"We had cake." Eva Grace's face brightened. "And ice cream."

"There may be cake tonight." Abby fingered her daughter's soft curls. "But I'm practically positive there won't be any ice cream."

"No ice cream?" Eva Grace leaned back, her blue eyes wide with disbelief. "Poor Mommy."

As Abby stroked her palm over the child's hair, her heart swelled with love. How blessed she was to have this amazing girl as her daughter. "There may be petit fours. If there are, I'll snag a couple for you."

Eva Grace's eyes brightened. She stepped back and began to

twirl again. "I like the ones with the little flowers."

"I'll do my best." Following her daughter's example, Abby whirled, the skirt of her dress flaring out. But the air on her back told her she wasn't quite as ready for the evening as she thought. She stopped and turned. "I need a favor from my favorite daughter."

Eva Grace giggled. "I'm your *only* daughter."

It was a familiar game and the happiness on her child's face arrowed straight to Abby's heart. "Would you please zip me up, only daughter?"

Eva Grace scrambled onto the dressing table chair, eager to help. Gazing at their reflections in the mirror, Abby admired the shiny pink shoes her daughter had worn to the party. It had only been within the past six months that pretty shoes had even been an option.

She'd come so far. *They'd* come so far.

Abby vividly recalled the worry-filled days in the NICU following her child's birth and surgery to repair the meningocele. Then, the years of serial casting and bracing to deal with the club foot.

She exhaled a ragged breath. Sometimes, it was hard to believe those days were behind them.

"All done." Eva Grace sing-songed the words and hopped down from the chair.

With their hands clasped together, she and Eva Grace surveyed Abby's reflection.

Though Abby sometimes felt ancient because of all that had happened in the past five years, tonight wasn't one of those times. Perhaps, because the dress was cherry red, which was her favorite color. Or maybe because she'd gotten back to her "fighting" weight. For the past year she'd been getting up early to lift weights and sneak in a cardio workout before Eva Grace started her day.

Abby might be starting her third decade but she was in the best shape of her life.

"You have brown hair." Eva Grace cocked her head. "I don't look like you."

This wasn't the first time Eva Grace had pointed this out. She knew why she and her mom didn't resemble each other. The tale of how a tiny fertilized seed had been planted in Abby and grown into Eva Grace was a favorite story.

Lately, Eva Grace's questions had been more focused on her "daddy." She didn't seem interested in the mommy portion because in her mind, she had a mommy. But a daddy, well that was a mysterious creature.

Though Abby never brought up Jonah, when Eva Grace asked, she kept her answers honest but vague.

"You have light hair. I have dark hair." Abby smiled. "Neither of us have red hair."

Abby flipped the Satoir necklace around so the tassel at the end hung not in the front, but down the back. When doing her research on 1920's era jewelry, Abby had discovered the decade had been one of experimentation. Cheaper pieces and colors that clashed were part of the fun. As well as long strands, like she wore tonight, that drew attention to the open back of her dress.

"Bristol looks like her daddy." Appearing bored, Eva Grace once again began to twirl, arms outstretched. "They both have red hair."

Abby sat on the bed and slipped on her shoes. "When I was a little girl, I wanted striped hair, like a zebra."

If she'd thought—hoped--to get her daughter off-topic, the child's next question confirmed it hadn't worked.

"Did my daddy have hair like mine?" Eva Grace pinched a strand of hair between her finger and thumb and let it dangle.

An image of Jonah as a little boy with a thick mop of blond curls, flashed before her.

"I seem to recall he did." Abby kept her tone casual and off-hand.

Abby pressed her lips in a tight, thin line to keep from adding she didn't know him all that well. She'd never believed her old friend would leave her hanging in the wind. Or, been willing to sacrifice his own child to keep his wife happy.

"Did he—?"

The doorbell's ring stopped whatever question Eva Grace had been about to utter.

"Nev-a-eh is here." Eva Grace raced from the room to answer the door.

Saved by the babysitter, Abby thought as sweet relief surged.

As time went on, there would be more questions about Jonah. Specific questions. Eva Grace was a smart, curious girl and the only one of her friends without a father in the home.

Abby needed to be prepared to answer those questions.

But that wasn't something to worry about on this beautiful late August evening.

Jonah Rollins was a thousand miles away.

He was her past and she was firmly grounded in the present.

The party, sponsored by the Hazel Green Foundation—fondly referred to as the Green Machine—was being held at the Pomeroy mansion. The home, designed by Richard Green and built for his friend, Jasper Pomeroy, had been erected in 1923. Recently, the house had passed to real estate developer Leo Pomeroy, a direct descendant of Jasper and current mayor of Hazel Green.

As tonight's event was being held in a relatively small venue, a limited number of civic leaders, business owners and volunteers had been invited.

It was far different than the bigger, more elaborate, Birthday Bash that would be held in October. That soiree, open to everyone, would be held in the Civic Center ballroom the night of Hazel Green's birthday.

Abby gave her keys to the valet before climbing the steps to the front door. She was greeted by a young man dressed in a dark tuxedo and wearing shoes so shiny Abby could have used them as a mirror.

With a grand flourish, he opened the door and gestured her inside. Abby let the beauty of the home envelope her as she moved deeper into the house. The Art Deco influence was everywhere; from the silver-leaf ceiling to the bold, geometric patterned rug overlaying a black-glossed floor.

Abby paused at the sight of the chandelier. She remembered the silver-plated light fixture from previous parties. Original to the home, it was a work of art with distinctive long glass prisms at the top. This was the first time she'd seen it festooned with plumes of ostrich feathers.

It appeared as if a huge bird had given its wings a good flap and smothered the lights in feathers. Abby had no doubt if Eva Grace was here, she'd be begging for "just one" of those fluffy feathers.

Abby barely had time to swallow a chuckle when she was hit by the sweet scent of calla lilies. Her heart lurched. These lilies had been her mother's favorite flower. At the funeral, the fragrance had been overpowering.

Blocking out the smell as best she could, Abby concentrated on her surroundings. She wove her way through the crowd. The realization that she knew most of the people attending tonight's event both baffled and comforted. In just over two years she'd become a part of this vibrant community in ways she'd never dreamed possible.

Every few feet Abby found herself stopped by someone with a

question about the "big" birthday bash. Though she'd been apprehensive about not only overseeing all the pre-events but chairing what many considered the most important planning committee, seasoned volunteers had made her job easy.

As she smoothed her skirt and prepared to dive into the crowd once more, Abby realized her hand was trembling. The sense of unease that had her nerve endings pulsating, puzzled her.

There would be no surprises tonight. She was among friends. The only wild card was the new police chief, hired when Harold Strum had quit to care for his ailing wife.

While the man would take Harold's place on her committee, Abby didn't plan on him being an active participant. No doubt settling into his new position would keep him very busy, especially at first.

Abby understood difficult transitions. Not counting the changes in her personal life, she'd made a huge leap when she moved here and took over the running of a ten-room hotel.

At times, it was still hard to believe her dream of owning a business had come true. There had been so many moments when it looked as if she'd never reach that goal. For every step forward, she'd been pushed two steps back.

Then, Jonah and Veronica had offered her $50,000 to carry a child for them. Even that hadn't worked out quite the way she'd thought it would…

A knot formed in the pit of Abby's stomach. She figured this jitteriness must stem from her earlier conversation with Eva Grace. Relax, Abby told herself. She inhaled deeply, then slowly released her breath. She was here to have fun. It had been months since she'd hired a sitter and had the opportunity to socialize with friends.

"You're looking pensive. Pretty. But pensive."

Abby swiveled, a smile already on her lips. "Nell."

Cornelia "Nell" Ambrose brought two fingers nearly to Abby's red lips before pulling back. "Not Nell. Hazel Green."

Dressed in a shimmery, intricately beaded dress, circa 1925, Nell fit the image of the town's patroness to a "t."

"You look fabulous."

"The twenties were an exciting time period." The cocktail length flapper dress hugged Nell's lithe figure like a glove. "I absolutely adore the fashions."

Nell wasn't the only one who loved the decade. The era was popular, which in Abby's mind caused it to be over-used. "I was surprised Rachel and her committee decided on 1920's attire."

"Considering where the party is being held, I'd say it makes perfect sense." Her friend waved a hand and eight painted bracelets on her right arm clinked together.

Nell's hair--or rather Hazel's--spilled from under a silver mesh cap in thick waves. The dark walnut color suited her fair complexion, dark brows and high cheekbones. Then again, most styles and colors suited the beautiful Cornelia.

When she wasn't playing Hazel, the attorney wore her own silvery blonde strands in a stylish pixie.

Tonight, Nell *was* Hazel Green.

It wasn't simply that she matched the town's namesake in stature and confidence. If that were the only criteria, any number of women in the community would be suitable impersonators.

Due to an uncanny ability to transform herself into popular actors and lecturers of the time—both male and female—Hazel Green had been one of the most popular performers on the Chautauqua circuit. Which was why, impersonating her at special community events demanded skill and innate talent.

Two things, Cornelia Ambrose had in abundance.

Nell, confident and self-assured, appeared to be the picture of a woman with answers to all life's toughest questions.

But how could that be? As a child advocate attorney, her

friend saw the pain and heartbreak every day. If anyone, Nell should be constantly questioning whether true love exists and whether giving your heart to someone is ever worth the risk.

Abby learned that lesson at a young age when her father walked out the front door one day and never came back. Her mother, well, she'd died, leaving her only daughter alone in the world.

And Jonah. Up until she'd gone into that delivery room alone, Abby had held out hope he'd come through for her.

She wanted to ask Nell if she'd ever been betrayed. If she'd ever had her heart ripped from her chest by someone she trusted.

But, as close as she and Nell were, the questions remained unspoken. Though Abby was curious, she didn't want to be put in a reciprocal position of sharing her own thoughts and feelings.

Instead, Abby grabbed two crystal flutes of champagne from a passing waiter and handed one to Nell.

Abby sipped the bubbly, finding the taste of this particular champagne very much to her liking. "Have you met the new police chief yet?"

A gleam filled Nell's baby blues. "Not yet."

Abby took another drink. "Rumor is he's a real hunk."

Nell cocked her head, looking vaguely amused. "Don't tell me *you're* interested?"

Though Abby had no desire—or time--to get involved with anyone, something about Nell's dismissal of her, rubbed Abby wrong. She gestured casually with one hand. "I may be."

Nell's expression turned thoughtful. "In my experience those who pursue a career in law enforcement can be a mixed bag."

"You'd know."

For a second startled surprise flickered in Nell's cool blues eyes.

"As an attorney, you deal with police all the time."

Nell offered her what Abby thought of as the woman's Mona Lisa smile. It was ridiculous for the two of them to even be discussing the man. As far as they knew, the guy could be married with three kids. But Abby didn't think so. She swore she'd heard someone mention he was single.

"To Chief Whateverhisnameis." Nell lifted her flute in a mock toast, her blue eyes glittering. "May he be one of the good ones."

CHAPTER THREE

"Just who I was looking for."

Abby smiled as Liz Canfield strode up. The journalist managed to look cool and professional despite an outrageous amount of fringe hanging from the hem of her flapper dress.

Still, it wasn't the fringe but the white and plum Coquille feather hair clip in her friend's dark hair that had Abby's smile widening. She gave Liz a quick hug.

Nell and Liz exchanged smiles.

"I didn't expect to see you tonight." The comment was out before Abby could stop it. She blushed, realizing how rude that sounded. But she *was* puzzled. She'd personally reviewed the guest list. Liz hadn't been on it.

"Hank was supposed to come but he wasn't feeling well. He asked me to take his place." Liz jerked a thumb in Nell's direction. "I'm supposed to interview this one and write up a story on the soiree. Though it meant getting a sitter for Sawyer, I couldn't pass up the opportunity to use my journalistic skills."

When Liz had lost her reporter job in Chicago last year, the only job she'd been able to find was as a Circulation Analyst with a rival newspaper. This was the first Abby had heard of her working for the local paper. "When did you start working for Hank?"

Henry "Hank" Beaumont, was the owner and editor-in-chief of the *Hazel Green Chronicle*.

"I'm just freelancing. It's a terrific assignment." Liz flashed a quick smile and gestured with her head toward the buffet table. "Free food, drink, and the company of good friends."

"I'm happy it worked for you to be here. I know how busy you've been." Abby gave Liz's arm a squeeze. "How's your mom?"

Though her smile never wavered, the light in Liz's eyes dimmed. "She's a trooper. After the surgery and chemo, she insists radiation is a walk in the park."

The surgery and chemo had been anything but a walk in the park for Sandra Canfield, whose diagnosis of metastatic breast cancer had taken them all by surprise.

Abby's grip tightened on her friend's arm. "If there's anything I can do to help, please don't hesitate to ask."

"That goes for me, too," Nell told her.

"Hazel Green offering her assistance." The dimples in the reporter's cheeks winked. "Mom will be honored."

Nell raised an elegant hand. "I'd love to stay and chat with you peons, but I must mingle."

When she turned to go, Liz stepped forward. "Not so fast, HG. You need to answer a few questions first."

Two perfectly arched dark brows winged upward. "What kind of questions?"

"Easy and quick ones." Liz spoke rapidly as if fearful her interviewee might vanish into the crowd. "I promise."

Nell gave an almost regal nod. "What would you like to know?"

How did the woman do it? Abby wondered. The tone, the mannerisms, the…look. As they watched, she'd morphed into Hazel.

Liz pulled out a phone from a purse shaped like a scallop shell. "Do you mind if I record the interview?"

Once Nell, er Hazel, gave her assent, Liz launched into a flurry of questions.

"Readers will want to know how a platform reader and impersonator of well-known actors first crossed paths with the prominent—and obscenely wealthy--architect, Richard Green."

Hazel took a sip of champagne. Her eyes took on a distant look and her lips curved. "I was living in New York when Richard came with a friend to a Chautauqua performance. He arrived just as I took the stage as Susan B. Anthony." Hazel gave a throaty chuckle. "He told me later he was instantly smitten. I asked for clarification. Was it me who had him smitten, or Miss Anthony?"

"If you were as good as they say, I have no doubt it was a little of both." Liz glanced down, as if making sure the phone was recording. "What was your first impression?"

"The man dazzled. He literally swept me off my feet. In less than six weeks we were wed. After our honeymoon, I found myself living in this delightful town." Hazel's eyes turned luminous. "My darling Richard made it his mission to get the town's name changed as a special wedding gift. Of course, he succeeded. My husband was very tenacious. I became the only one I knew who had a town named after them."

"Quite an honor," Liz agreed. "I imagine it was an adjustment going from being a performer to being a wife."

"For the first few months, Richard and I kept very busy." Hazel's eyes sparkled mischievously. "We were, after all, newlyweds."

Abby felt a pang of envy before remembering none of this had happened to Nell.

"Then, I threw myself into getting my new home town on the Chautauqua circuit." Hazel's gaze swept the room before refocusing on Liz. "It was a challenge, but I persevered. Like my husband, I can also be tenacious. I've always believed the arts an essential part of a vital community."

The interview continued. Liz asked so many questions Abby was surprised "Hazel" didn't ask the reporter if she was writing a newspaper article or a book.

Abby wandered over to a table holding enough petit fours to fill a stadium. Folding a napkin over two flowered ones, she slipped them into her tiny bag before returning to her friends.

She arrived just as Liz slipped the phone into her bag.

"Look to your right." Nell was back in her own skin for the moment, her husky voice a whisper. "Rachel brought him tonight."

No need to say who. Rachel Grabinski and Marc Koenig had been a twosome since Christmas. Though Abby was concerned about how the smooth-talking investment guru treated her friend, for Rachel's sake, she and Liz had tried to like him.

Nell, on the other hand, had absolutely no use for the man. Abby wondered if her friend's attitude had anything to do with Marc having made a play for her while he was still married.

"No surprise there." Liz kept her voice equally low. "They're always together."

Abby sincerely hoped things weren't heating up between the two. After her parents were killed in a car accident when she was eighteen, Rachel had devoted herself to raising her siblings.

Only in the last two years, once the last sibling graduated from high school, had she been able to live her own life. If Marc supported her dreams, that would be one thing. But he appeared to be one who liked calling the shots.

"If she marries him, it will be the biggest mistake of her life." Nell's voice rang tight with conviction.

"You know something." Abby gripped her arm. "Tell me."

"I know lots of things." Nell offered a tight smile. "Including that it's past time for Hazel to mingle."

Wiggling her fingers in farewell, Nell slipped away.

"What do you think she knows?" Two lines of worry furrowed Liz's brow.

"You're the reporter," Abby reminded her as they watched Nell give the mayor's younger brother a hug. "I'd say it's time you do some digging and find out."

~

Mingling was the name of the game.

Hazel went right.

Liz went left.

Abby went straight to the gorgeous black and chrome bar staffed by a bartender who looked barely old enough to drink legally. He offered Abby a polite smile. "What can I get you, ma'am?"

Ma'am? Surely, she didn't look *that* old.

Stifling a sigh, Abby studied the drink list. The party organizers had gone authentic. Reading names like "Gin rickey," "Bee's knees," and "Southside" was like taking a trip back in time.

"I'll take a Mary Pickford." White rum with pineapple juice, maraschino liqueur and grenadine appeared the perfect choice for this out-of-the-ordinary evening.

The party was one where strange cocktails, feathers on chandeliers and beaded headbands were de rigueur.

While Abby normally enjoyed socializing, right now she'd give anything to be sprawled on the floor at home playing a board game with Eva Grace. While waiting for her drink, the uneasy feeling that dogged her earlier, returned.

The bartender handed her a cocktail glass filled with crushed ice and liquid the color of ruby red grapefruit. A cocktail stick skewered a maraschino cherry. "Here you go, ma'am."

Once again Abby tried not to cringe. She reminded herself the boy was simply being polite. "Are you having a nice evening so far?"

Surprise skittered across his handsome features. "Why, yes, I am. Thank you for asking."

She took a sip, smiled. "This is good."

"It's very popular." The boy/man offered her a perfunctory smile before turning to the next customer.

"There she is. The woman I was looking for."

Though the voice came from behind her, Abby instantly recognized Leo Pomeroy's voice. Deep and cultured, it radiated command. Leo, one of the partners in a successful family-owned real estate development and investment firm, was silver-spoon born. His brothers now ran the company while Leo ran the town. Last year, at thirty-four, he became the youngest mayor in Hazel Green history.

Though widely admired for his business acumen, some considered him stand-offish and arrogant. That had never been Abby's impression.

She hurriedly pulled two crumpled bills from her bag and stuffed them into the tip jar before turning. "What is it you want from me now, Mr. Mayor?"

Her tone was teasing, her smile friendly. Last week she'd told Leo she was going to quit answering his calls because every time they spoke, she ended up chairing another committee.

"The committees are all filled." Amusement ran through his voice. "I just wanted to introduce you to our new police chief. He'll replace Harold on your committee. Over here."

Leo made a come-on motion to a man weaving his way through the crowd. Abby shifted her focus, a smile of welcome on her lips.

Her smile wavered. Her heart gave a solid thump against her chest. She swallowed convulsively. Introductions were hardly necessary.

Not when the man standing in front of her was Jonah Rollins.

CHAPTER FOUR

"Hello, Abby."

"Jonah." His name was all Abby managed to push past frozen lips.

Leo's surprised gaze flicked between them. "You two know each other?"

Jonah cleared his throat. "Abby and I grew up down the block from each other in Springfield."

"I had no idea." Leo opened his mouth as if to say more then stopped, his gaze drawn to a member of the catering staff waving wildly. "Excuse me. It appears we have a problem. Enjoy reconnecting."

Abby wished she could simply turn and walk away from Jonah liked he'd walked away from her all those years earlier. But she couldn't move. Her feet felt heavy, as if weighted down by a thick block of ice.

For the moment, it appeared she was stuck. She lifted her chin and gazed into familiar blue eyes. "What are you doing here?"

~

Five Years Earlier

"We need to deliver the baby today." Dr. Moser, the perinatologist who'd been following me throughout my pregnancy, is a blunt man. Though he has kind eyes, he doesn't pull punches.

Tiny beads of perspiration pop out all over my body and a rivulet of sweat slithers down my spine. I shift my bulk and wish for my mom. I desperately need someone's hand to hold.

The doctor's piercing gaze, focused directly on me, gives me nowhere to hide. He won't say more until I respond. That's how he rolls.

I lift my hand to my neck and pretend to be contemplating the unexpected announcement. What I'm really doing is fighting the fear clawing at my throat.

I'm barely thirty-six weeks. I thought I'd have more time.

I drop my hand to my belly. Eva Grace kicks against my palm and I relax. As long as she's inside me, she's safe.

Dr. Moser studies me.

I keep a tight rein on my emotions. I feel as if he's assessing me, looking for any signs of weakness. He won't see any. When I give into my fears, it will be in the privacy of my own apartment.

"Why today?" I nearly cheer when my voice comes out steady and firm.

"Your blood pressure is high." His gaze remains fixed on my face. "You're spilling protein into your urine. Your ankles are swollen."

"It's August and the humidity is off the charts." I keep my voice light, hoping he'll crack a smile.

Instead, he rubs his chin. "You have preeclampsia."

I nod as if I understand. I should ask what that is, but I don't want to know. Not now. Not when my emotions are close to the surface and I feel as fragile as an egg in a toddler's hand.

Somehow, I manage to summon a smile. "What's the harm in waiting a couple more weeks?"

"Not advisable." He waves a dismissive hand. "Your condition can easily--and quickly--move into full-blown Eclampsia. If that happens, you risk seizures, even death."

I swallow hard against rising panic. "But her lungs—"

"She should be fine."

Should be. Over the past months, I've grown to despise qualifiers.

"Tell me the plan."

To his credit, he doesn't skimp on details. Though he speaks clearly, my heart beats so loudly it drowns out his voice. I do hear that the epidural will help lower my blood pressure.

"Abby." His voice softens to an almost grandfatherly tone. "If you want to call someone to be with you during the delivery, this would be the time."

I give a jerky nod.

As soon as he leaves the room, I pull the phone from my bag. I stare at it for several heartbeats. Who is there to call? The friend from college who promised to be with me is on vacation in Hawaii. Even if she was willing to fly back, she wouldn't make it in time.

Jonah. A tiny voice in my head whispers his name.

I can't believe I'm even considering calling him. Not after he turned on me, on us. Not after I made it clear what I thought of someone who didn't have the balls to stand up for their child's life.

He didn't fight back. Which pissed me off even more. I made it clear I was done with him and Veronica. Me and the baby, we would do just fine without either of them and their money.

Still, I stroke my belly and consider. Despite cutting him out of my life, he sends cash every month. There are letters too, addressed to me and the baby. I don't read them.

My teeth sink into my lower lip and I taste blood. I scroll through my contacts and find his name. I've come so close to deleting his contact information but haven't been able to bring myself to cut that final cord.

Call me weak. Foolish. It isn't anything I haven't called myself.

I hit the number. My breath hitches at the sound of a voice. But the voice is tinny and slightly bored.

"The person's mailbox you are trying to reach is full. Please try again later."

Give up, I tell myself, *consider this a sign.*

I think of being alone in that delivery room and I text him. I tell him what's happening and ask him to be with me for the birth.

I hit send and the message shows as delivered. I'm still waiting for a response when the nurse steps into the room. I can barely concentrate on the instructions. I keep glancing at my phone, my ears on high alert.

When she leaves, I gather my things but remain in the office. My legs are shaking so hard, I'm not sure I can walk. Even as I sit there, my mind races.

Wednesday used to be Jonah's day off. Perhaps he's at home. I try his land line and curse when I get the recording. I leave a message.

"Hi, Jonah." I pause to clear my throat. "It's Abby. The doctor is going to deliver the baby this afternoon at Arborview. My, ah, my blood pressure is up and he seems to think it's necessary."

I attempt a laugh but it pitches high and scares me, so I hurry on. "I tried your cell but the mailbox is full. My friend can't be there and I wondered if you might like to come. I'm kinda scared and…"

Tears slip down my cheek. I swipe them away with the pads of my fingers and take a steadying breath. "It would be nice to have someone with me. But you need to come now."

I try to think of something else to say, but my mind goes to a blue screen. "Well, hope you can make it."

After making sure the volume is up, I shove the phone into my pocket.

The Jonah I knew, the boy I once loved with youthful abandon, would never miss the birth of his child.

I cling to hope he'll come, even as the phone remains silent.

Veronica played the message a second time.

Abby. Though she'd once liked the woman, all positive feelings had disappeared when she refused the abortion. Didn't she realize the hell she'd put Jonah through? The strain she'd put on their marriage?

How many times had he mentioned his desire to contact Abby and "make things right?" Too many to count, that was for sure. Her husband didn't seem to comprehend the simple fact that a "special needs" child would ruin their lives.

Veronica wished things could be different. Dear God, she wished things were different. If they were, she and Jonah would be at the hospital now, welcoming a baby girl into their lives.

But once again, her dreams of a perfect family had collapsed.

She thought of the years she and Jonah had spent trying to conceive. Then, the miscarriages. After the first one, she'd stopped getting excited. Even when the doctor had gently told her that her egg quality was poor, she'd wanted to keep trying.

Jonah had been the one to suggest adoption. For a second, her lips curved recalling the day they'd gotten the call that Kayla, a college student, had chosen her and Jonah.

The baby boy the college student carried was to be theirs.

The nursery was readied, each piece of furniture carefully considered. She'd had the room professionally decorated in a Peter Rabbit theme. As Kayla's due date approached, the bureau drawers grew crowded with impossibly cute baby boy outfits from four baby showers. Everything had been ready.

She and Jonah had been with Kayla in the delivery room. But, instead of the baby being handed to Veronica as planned, the doctor handed him to Kayla.

It was a simple mistake. The doctor wasn't Kayla's regular OB. He didn't know the baby was to come to Veronica. But when she stepped forward to take him, Kayla's arms had tightened around her son.

Veronica pinched her lips together to still the sudden trembling. Jonah had wanted to try again, but she couldn't face another birth mother changing her mind. They'd looked at surrogacy but couldn't afford it. Until Abby had laughingly mentioned, when they'd been discussing the $100,000 price tag for a surrogate, that she'd do it for half the price.

Another disappointment.

Veronica's gaze dropped to the ridiculous landline Jonah insisted on keeping. A few taps deleted the message.

She moved swiftly to the kitchen, to the phone her husband had left on the counter that morning when he'd left to shoot hoops with friends.

She knew his password. Jonah had no secrets from her.

It took Veronica only a second to delete the text.

Abby had chosen to continue the pregnancy.

Now, she had to live with that choice.

CHAPTER FIVE

Despite his friendly smile, the tense set to Jonah's shoulders and the watchful wariness in his eyes told Abby he'd suspected this reunion wouldn't go well.

At least the man was smart enough not to expect her to fling her arms around him in welcome.

Abby tightened her jaw. Jonah still hadn't answered her question. What was he doing in Hazel Green parading around as the new Chief of Police?

Abby's eyes met his unwaveringly. Though she desperately wanted to put some distance between them, she wasn't going anywhere without answers.

A muscle in Jonah's jaw jumped. He shoved his hands into his pockets and rocked back on his heels. Dressed in a dark suit and standard blue striped tie, he obviously hadn't gotten the memo about vintage fashion.

He didn't fit in.

He shouldn't be here.

Abby pressed her lips together. If she started talking, she might not stop.

"I, ah," Jonah paused to clear his throat, "in my letters, I told you I applied for the position as Chief of Police. I told you I'd gotten the job. You never replied."

"Is the position temporary?" She pushed out the question, prayed for the right answer.

Puzzlement filled his blue eyes. "It's permanent. I explained that in my letters."

She shrugged. Abby had tossed them in a box and never read them. Now she wished she had, especially the last one. Then again, the job and the move had likely been a done deal by that time. How was she going to bear having Jonah and Veronica in the same town?

Done deal, Abby reminded herself. With a population of twenty thousand, Hazel Green was big enough that their paths should rarely cross.

Abby glanced around. "Where's your wife? I can't believe you left her at home."

"Veronica is back in Springfield." He frowned. "Our divorce was final three months ago."

Abby opened her mouth to say she was sorry his marriage failed, but stopped herself in time. She didn't care enough to be sorry and wasn't going to be a hypocrite.

"You didn't read my letters."

The incredulous look in his eyes surprised her. Surely, he didn't think she'd spent the past five years hanging on his every word.

"Not a one." She lifted her lips in a tight smile.

"It seems we have a lot to talk about."

The last thing Abby expected was for Jonah to reach out and place his hand on her arm. In her haste to put distance between them, she jerked back so violently she stumbled. Might have fallen except for steadying hands on her arms.

"I was hoping to bump into you this evening." The voice was smooth as cream. Matilda reached around Abby and extended her hand to Jonah. "I don't believe we've met. I'm Matilda

Lovejoy."

He gave the offered hand a shake. "Jonah Rollins."

"Oh." Matilda's gaze shifted from him to Abby then back again. "Abby's friend from Springfield."

Something sparked in Jonah's blue eyes and his shoulders relaxed. "We grew up down the block from each other."

Abby wanted to punch Matilda through the silky gold jacket covering her arms. This man hadn't been her friend for years and Matilda knew it. She was the only one of Abby's friends who knew Jonah's name, knew what he'd done—or rather hadn't done—five years ago. So, why was she greeting him like an old friend?

"Sorry that took so long." Leo strode up, gazing with interest on Abby before shifting his gaze to Matilda. "Everyone is raving about your parmesan stuffed mushrooms."

"They are delicious." Matilda winked at Abby. "I've already had three. Just to check on the quality, you understand."

She'd forgotten Matilda and her staff had done the catering tonight. No doubt the buffet table was filled with enough food to feed a small army. "I haven't had a chance to check out any of your wonderful appetizers. I'm going to remedy that situation right now."

She hadn't taken a step when she heard Jonah say, "I'll go with you. I'm a little hungry myself."

Abby's eyes met Matilda's. Something in the woman's direct gaze had her straightening her shoulders. Matilda was right. She had to speak with Jonah, sometime. It'd be best to lay out the ground rules now.

"Suit yourself." Abby spoke without glancing in Jonah's direction. They were nearly to the tables when she veered off course.

"Have you seen the terraces?" She continued toward two French doors embellished with geometric patterns without waiting for his agreement. Abby let out the breath she held when she stepped onto the brick terrace and noticed the area was deserted.

Despite the slight chill in the air, Abby had no doubt that in an hour or so, the crowd would grow so large revelers would spill outside. For now, she and Jonah had the area to themselves.

Once the doors closed behind them, Abby walked until she stood at the edge of the terrace. A mermaid statue with a bright blue tail stretched out beside a backyard pond. Abby took a second to gather her composure then slowly turned, confident if he looked at her face, he'd see nothing she didn't want him to see.

Abby studied him for a moment, conscious he was doing the same.

The years had been good to him, she noted dispassionately. His hair, the color of winter wheat, held no trace of grey. His six-foot frame, what she could see beneath the dark suit, was as fit as ever. Only his eyes were different.

While still the color of the sky on a clear summer day, the eyes she remembered always had a spark. Sometimes of mischief, often of good humor. Tonight, those eyes that had once sparkled with life were watchful.

"Why are you here, Jonah?" His name rolled too easily off her tongue. Abby didn't like it that even after all this time it felt familiar.

When he opened his mouth to answer, she held up a hand. "Please don't insult us both by saying you applying for a job in the same town where I live was a coincidence."

Her voice trembled just a little at the last. Abby cursed the fact. It had to be the citrusy scent of his cologne, a fragrance he'd worn since high school. One, she recalled, Veronica never had cared for.

"Moving here was deliberate."

She clasped her hands together, waiting for his explanation.

"Four years ago, I was elected Sheriff of Lincoln County. It's not as big as Sangamon but it was a good opportunity."

Springfield, where they'd both grown up was in Sangamon,

one of the largest counties in Illinois. Lincoln County was one of the smallest.

"I'm familiar with the size of the county." Her tone remained flat and well-controlled. "I'm from the area, remember?"

When she saw something flash in his eyes, Abby cursed herself for adding that last word. She didn't want any trips down memory lane.

"Of course." Jonah paced to the edge of the flagstone terrace then back again. He didn't look at her again, which was for the best. "After that day in the doctor's office, I put all my efforts into my career. It was easier that way, less painful that way."

He raked a hand through his hair, the look of misery on his face at odds with his matter-of-fact tone.

There wasn't one ounce of sympathy for him in Abby's entire body. Not even a drop.

Jonah lifted his hands, let them fall. "I don't know what else to say."

He didn't know what else to say? Abby's blood went from a simmer to a full out boil. *This* was the extent of his explanation for his behavior?

"What happened with you and Veronica?" Abby didn't know why she was asking since she didn't much care what had sent their marriage into a tailspin.

She told herself it was simple curiosity. Jonah and Veronica had appeared to have a solid relationship. If they hadn't, she'd never have agreed to carry a baby for them. But apparently that had been just been one more thing she'd been wrong about.

Incredibly weary, Abby dropped down on a metal settee with a fan back. Folding her hands in her lap, she waited.

Jonah hadn't stopped pacing since he stepped onto the terrace, Abby's heart picked up speed when he unexpectedly commandeered the chair beside the settee. The faint scent of citrus wafted on the evening breeze.

Dispassionately, she took note of the lines around his eyes that hadn't been there five years ago.

"Veronica still wanted a baby."

The comment punched like a fist straight to the heart. She inhaled sharply, then covered it with a cough.

"We'd barely left the doctor's office that day when Veronica started pressing for us to find another surrogate. It was as if she blamed your womb for the baby's anomalies." Jonah's gaze remained focused straight ahead, into the darkness just beyond the soft glow of the terrace lights.

She expected him to continue, but he only continued to stare into nothingness. "What did you say to her?"

The edge to her tone, as tough as high tensile steel, had him facing her.

"I said no." His gaze turned pleading, as if expecting her to… what? Understand? Forgive? Pat him on the back?

"I couldn't think of another baby, not when—"

"When you already had one on the way? A baby you'd walked away from after I refused to end her life?" Saying the words brought a profound ache to Abby's heart. But her eyes remained dry and her voice gave no indication of her inner pain.

"It wasn't that way. I never stopped thinking of her. Or of –"

"Stop." She spat the word. "I don't want more lies."

Jonah expelled a harsh breath. "I told Veronica we should wait. But, time passed, and I couldn't bring myself to--. I finally told her I didn't want another surrogate. Not then. Not ever. She was crushed. For her, that was the last straw. Having a child was so important to her."

"Having a *perfect* child was important to her."

He said nothing.

So, they'd split over Veronica's obsession with motherhood. How ironic that the one thing they'd stood together on, had been the thing to tear them apart.

"I understand why Veronica isn't with you." Abby inclined her head. "Now, tell me why you're here."

Jonah had wondered what seeing Abby again would be like. He recalled vividly that day in the office when the doctor had given her the news. Her face had been ghostly white, her dark eyes too large in her worried face.

When Veronica suggested they move ahead with scheduling an abortion, Abby had looked at him. It had been the same way she'd looked at him when Jared Shuster knocked her down in fourth grade. That time, he'd been there for her.

But in the office, he hadn't come to her rescue. He'd wanted to, but all the years of infertility treatments followed by a failed adoption had taken their toll on Veronica's emotional health.

Then, she'd been in the room when her cousin's baby—born with anencephaly—had passed away. Veronica had been still reeling from that experience when they'd gotten the news about the baby Abby had been carrying for them. The news had turned her relentless, fiendish about having a "perfect" baby.

"Tell me why you're here."

The demand, spoken in that cold tone, had Jonah jerking his thoughts back to the present. Back to Abby, who had once been his closest friend.

She looked like a woman who didn't have a care in the world. Though her dark hair was longer than it had been the last time he'd seen her, it was still a glossy mahogany with hints of red. He'd thought her eyes, big and brown and full of life, were her best feature. When she'd seen him they'd gone from warm to cold in a heartbeat.

Jonah had watched her for several minutes from across the room, before Leo insisted he meet Abby Fine. Only then did he learn he would be serving on a committee she chaired.

When he crossed the room with Leo, Jonah hadn't known what to expect. Abby hadn't responded to any of his letters. He'd let her know he was considering moving to Hazel Green, mentioned when he'd gotten an interview, and asked what she thought when he'd been offered the position.

Radio silence.

He hadn't been dissuaded. The recent birth of his nephew had fueled a smoldering longing to connect with his daughter. His parents had been startled when he'd told them of his plan to move to Hazel Green. Harold's retirement had come at the perfect time.

He'd accepted the position and told Abby when he'd be arriving. But she'd been shocked to see him. Though she had a stellar poker face, he'd always been able to tell what she was thinking.

"I'm here because I'd like to get to know Eva Grace." After a moment, his lips tipped in a slight smile. "You named her after my mother."

It had been several months after Eva Grace's birth that he'd ran into a woman who once worked with Abby. She hadn't even known Abby was pregnant. For Jonah, hearing what she'd named the baby had been bittersweet.

Veronica had resisted the idea of naming their child after a family member. Then, again, his ex-wife and his mother had never been particularly close.

"I like the name Grace."

So, she wasn't going to admit that his mother, Nancy Grace Rollins, who Abby once adored, played any part in her decision. He remembered the day his mother had stopped over and mentioned she planned to go to Abby, to see how she could help.

Veronica had gone ballistic. She'd told his mother and him that if they had anything to do with their former "surrogate" she would take Abby to court for breach of contract. She didn't care if she won, only that Abby would know the full fury of her displeasure.

His mom had kept her distance. As had he.

Family loyalty had cost all of them.

"I'd like to get to know Eva Grace. I'd like it if you and I could be friends again." Jonah coupled the pronouncement with a slight smile. "I could help you out—"

That was as far as he got before she slapped a hand down on the table. Hard.

"Let me make one thing clear." Her eyes were as dark as obsidian, her jaw set in a hard line. Waves of icy air rolled off her to slap him in the face. "You will stay away from my daughter."

The finality in her words had his own temper rising. "I'm her father—"

"You're a sperm donor." Her eyes narrowed to slits. "A father is there for his child. When she cried because the braces hurt, a father would have been there to comfort her. When she had bad dreams, a father would have been there to soothe her fears. You've *never* been there for her."

He couldn't argue the point. He hadn't been there for Eva Grace or for Abby. But he was here now. And he would not let them down. Not again. Never again.

"I've made mistakes." Jonah struggled to find the words. Talking about feelings and emotions never came easy. His mother teased he was like his dad who showed his love through acts, not through flowery words.

If Abby would give him a chance, he'd show what a good dad he could be to Eva Grace…and what a good friend he could be to her. First, he had to convince her to give him that chance.

"I want to make up for the past." Jonah swallowed hard. "Please give me that chance."

"You want to drop into our lives, now that it's convenient for you. Now that the not-so-perfect child has survived all the trauma and pain, you're ready to accept her."

"I was ready to accept her back then." He clenched his hands into fists at his side as emotions roiled and raged inside him.

"You had a funny way of showing it, Rollins." Abby's laugh held no humor. "You didn't even show up for the custody hearing."

Before he could tell her he knew if he didn't show up she'd be awarded joint custody, she sliced the air with her hand.

"Let me tell you how it's going to be." Abby clipped the words, her expression stony. "You're going to stay away from Eva Grace. You come around, I'm calling the police. I don't care if you are the chief."

"I'm her father." Keeping a tight rein on his emotions, Jonah reminded her of that one indisputable fact. "She's five- years-old. You can't tell me she doesn't ask about me."

Something flashed in her eyes that gave him the answer.

"She wants to know me."

"She's a child. *My* child." Abby met his gaze. "I will do what's best for her."

Incredulous, he could only stare. "How can you say that not knowing me is what's best for her?"

"You'll hurt her."

"I won't."

"You chose your wife over your child's *life*." Abby's voice shook with emotion. "When her very existence was on the line, she couldn't count on you to have her back. Why would I ever let you get close to her now?"

CHAPTER SIX

Abby made it clear Jonah was to keep his distance from her and from Eva Grace. But he'd waited five years to see his daughter.

"I've been impressed by Hazel Green's school system." Though his insides hummed with anticipation, Jonah's tone remained even. "I've spent a good part of this week personally checking out each school."

"I heard you'd been making the rounds." Gage Sutter, the principal of Helen Potter elementary, shot him a sideways look as they strolled down the hall.

Underfoot the linoleum gleamed and the air had that new school smell. Which made sense considering Helen Potter opened last week. It brought the number of grade schools in Hazel Green to nine, eight of which Jonah had already visited. Along with six middle schools and three high schools.

Though he'd wanted to drop by Eva Grace's school the instant school began for the year, he knew how crazy those first few days were, not only for students but for teachers. It had also been his first week on the job.

He'd bided his time and set up appointments at each of the schools, saving Eva Grace's for last. The principals had been open

ONE FINE DAY | 51

to the visits, eager to explain how their school complied with Standard Response Protocols for hazards or threats to their students and staff.

Jonah had done some research on the guidelines before moving to Hazel Green so could discuss incidents where law enforcement might need to be involved.

"I've enjoyed the tours." Jonah kept his tone casual. "There's a big difference between a high school classroom and say, a kindergarten one. I assume there is, anyway."

Gage shot him a quick grin. "Well, let me show you one of ours."

"How many sections do you have?"

"Only two."

Which meant there was a fifty-fifty chance Eva Grace would be in the class they visited. If she wasn't, Jonah figured he could think of a reason to check out the other room.

As Gage opened a brightly decorated door, Jonah had a moment to wonder if he would recognize Eva Grace. He assumed she'd have blonde hair and blue eyes, since both he and the woman who'd donated the egg had that coloring. He hoped that at this school, the name of the child would be on their table in front of where they sat.

Following the principal into the room, he was immediately struck by two things. The quiet and the color red. The teacher, a grandmotherly woman with salt-and-pepper hair wore a bright red shirt. The students were all dressed in varying shades of the same color.

"Today is red day for the kindergarteners." Gage spoke softly, in deference to the little boy who stood in front of the room. "They're encouraged to wear red and to bring something red for Show and Share."

Jonah wasn't familiar with Show and Share, but assumed it was an updated version of Show and Tell.

"This is Clifford." The boy had dark brown hair, a long face and an earnest expression. He thrust out an arm, his fingers tight around the neck of a red stuffed dog. "Clifford is in books. He's a good friend."

The boy continued speaking in halting sentences about Clifford, the red dog, while Jonah's gaze scanned the classroom. There were three little girls with blonde hair. From where he stood, he couldn't see their names.

He was considering how to make his move when the boy sat down and the teacher glanced at her list.

"Eva Grace, would you like to share?"

Like a Jack in a Box, one of the three girls with blonde hair popped up from her seat. She had curly blonde hair pulled back from her face in a tail and tied with a bright red ribbon.

She danced her way to the front of the classroom in a cherry red top and black tulle skirt.

"She's a dynamo." Jonah murmured. He didn't realize he'd spoken aloud until Gage chuckled.

"That's Eva Grace Fine." The principal's tone was indulgent. "She's smart as a whip. Her mother owns the Inn downtown."

"The Inn at Hazel Green." Jonah's eyes remained fixed on his daughter. With her upturned nose and wide mouth, she looked just like his twin sister. "What *is* that in her hand?"

"I don't know. You never know what the kids will bring for Show and Share." Gage glanced at his watch. "We can stay for a few minutes and find out. Unless you need to get back to the station?"

This couldn't have worked out more perfectly. Jonah kept his tone off-hand. "I have time."

Like the boy before her, Eva Grace thrust out her hand, palm up. "These are red wax lips. They were first made over a hundred years ago. Not these lips."

The quick clarification, made when some of the girls wrinkled their noses, brought a smile to Jonah's lips. Unlike the boy,

Eva Grace appeared comfortable standing in front of her classmates.

"They're fun to play with." Quick as a snake, she popped them into her mouth and the class erupted in laughter.

A lifting of the teacher's hand silenced them immediately.

"Thank you, Eva Grace. Now—"

"That isn't all, Mrs. Leininger," Eva Grace gave the teacher a charming smile. "You can also chew these lips like gum."

"They taste like cherries." Her little mouth struggled to chew the big lips into a manageable wad.

"That's very interesting, Eva Grace." The teacher pulled several tissues from a square box on her desk and held out her hand. "Unfortunately chewing gum isn't allowed in school, so I have to ask you to spit it out."

After a momentary hesitation, the child complied.

Jonah wasn't prepared when Eva Grace's curious gaze shifted from the principal to settle on him. His breath hitched as their eyes locked on this child who had come from him.

A wave of regret hit like a tsunami. He'd made so many mistakes, lost so many years. Abby was right. He didn't deserve a second chance.

Then Eva Grace flashed a brilliant smile and love flooded him.

Right then, Jonah knew that while he might not deserve that second chance, he was going to take it.

One way or another, he was going to know his daughter.

Hearing a soft tap at the door, Abby rose from the sofa. She padded across the hardwood, her feet encased in her favorite UGG slippers. After she'd put Eva Grace to bed, she removed her make-up and topped yoga pants with an oversized top.

The thought struck her as she gazed through the peep hole

before opening the door, just how different her life was from most thirty-year-old single females. Instead of clubbing and drinking martinis with friends, the highlight of her Friday night had been playing the Sneaky Snacky Squirrel game with Eva Grace and now, having a glass of wine with a friend.

Abby stepped aside to let Matilda enter. "I wasn't sure you'd make it. From all the people standing in the lobby, it appeared business was booming tonight."

"We were on a wait until nine." Matilda still wore the Victorian attire she preferred when overseeing the dining room which told Abby her friend had come straight from the restaurant.

The trim black skirt went nearly to her ankles while the white Weddington blouse with its white stand collar edged in lace presented a perfect picture of demure Victorian elegance. Matilda had swept her auburn hair up into a Gibson Girl inspired bouffant bun.

The style suited Matilda's strong, yet feminine features and drew attention to her cat green eyes.

Matilda glanced at the kitchen table where the game still sat open. She arched a brow. "Who was the first to fill their log with acorns?"

"Eva Grace won the first game. I edged her out on the second. I should have picked up but I got involved doing some ordering." Abby gestured carelessly toward her laptop. "The new soap we've switched to has been very popular. I'm ordering extra and making it available for purchase in the hotel and online."

"Smart." Matilda nodded. "Always good to have an extra revenue stream."

"Since the soap is locally made, I'll be helping out another small business. Win-win." Abby picked up the bottle of wine she'd had breathing on the counter. "Will you have a glass with me? It's Country Red from Galena Cellars."

"Absolutely. I've heard good things about their wines." Matilda accepted the glass Abby poured and handed to her.

Instead of sitting on the sofa, she sat at the table and spread the colorful acorns over the board. "I love this game."

"Do you want to play?" With the bottle in one hand and her own glass in the other, Abby took a seat on the other side of the table. "I'll let you go first."

"You're so kind. And, I love you to death." Matilda flashed a smile that had a dimple in her left cheek winking. "But be warned, I play to win."

"Me, too. I had this neighbor who loved games even more than her kids. We'd play—" Abby stopped abruptly. Jonah's unwelcomed appearance had to be the reason she'd thought of his mother.

When Nancy Rollins had ignored the birth of her grandchild, Abby had pushed the woman out of her mind. Pushing her out of her heart had proven more difficult. Abby had loved Jonah's mother. Nancy, neighbor and stay-at-home-mom, had affectionately dubbed Abby her fifth child.

Considering Abby had spent more time in the Rollins house than her own, it made sense. Jonah's home had been far more comfortable than the duplex she and her mom shared after her father took off.

"My mother and I played a lot of games." Matilda picked up several acorns and shook them like dice.

"My mom was too busy working." Abby glanced toward the hall leading to her daughter's bedroom. "I work to put food on the table, but spending time with Eva Grace is a priority."

"As it should be." After returning the acorns to the board, Matilda's finger poised above the spinner. "Ready?"

The warmth in Matilda's smile had the tension easing from Abby's body. She took a gulp of wine. "Game on."

Four spins later, Abby groaned as she landed on the furious storm, which according to the rules blew away all the acorns she'd gathered.

"So close." With a resigned sigh, Abby dumped the acorns from her log back on the board.

Matilda gestured with a handful of candied almonds, Abby had sitting out on the table. "Isn't that how it is in life?"

Abby cocked her head.

"You get close to a goal," Matilda explained, "only to have some outside force—in this case a furious wind—knock you off course."

Abby glanced unseeing at the board. "I may be down, but I'm not out. Don't underestimate me."

Matilda shook her head. A smile tugged at the corners of her red lips. "I would never make the mistake of underestimating you."

"Jonah did."

Instead of spinning the wheel, Matilda leaned back against the colorful cushion of the white kitchen chair and lifted her wine glass. She studied Abby over the rim for several seconds then sipped.

Abby wasn't sure what had gotten into her. Matilda hadn't brought up Jonah, though the woman knew he was Eva Grace's father.

As Matilda often watched Eva Grace, she needed to know where things stood between her and the Police Chief. The last thing Abby wanted was for him to stop by to see her daughter when Matilda was alone with the girl.

"Seeing Jonah at Leo's party was awkward. I suppose it could have been worse." Abby popped a nut into her mouth and chewed. "Though I'm not sure how."

Matilda's finger swiped the spinner. Frowned when it landed on the sad squirrel. "Drat. I miss a turn. Looks like your luck is turning."

Abby stared down at the board. "I don't like why he's here."

"Why *is* he here?"

Abby remembered how he'd looked on the terrace. Her finger

swipe had the spinner circling as if on steroids. When it finally slowed to a stop she picked up the squirrel tweezers and grabbed an acorn with a turquoise top and put it in the slot. "He wants to get to know Eva Grace."

"Ah." Matilda's gaze searched her face.

Abby was thankful she didn't need to hide her emotions from her friend. She raked a hand through her hair as her heart began to ache, the way it always did when her thoughts drifted back on that horrible time. "I told him no way in hell. Actually, I can't remember the exact words I used. That was the gist."

Matilda reached over, gave Abby's hand a squeeze. "Seeing him again must have been difficult."

Abby gave the spinner another push. She watched it rotate and felt the tightness in her chest ease. "He thought he could simply step back into our lives."

When Matilda raised a brow, Abby continued. "He says he wants to make things right, not only with Eva Grace but with me as well."

Abby glanced down and noticed the spinner had stopped. "I get to choose two."

Confusion blanketed Matilda's face. "He wants you to choose to…?"

"What? Oh, not Jonah." Abby laughed. "The game. I get to choose two acorns."

"Your luck has taken a serious turn in the right direction."

"In regards to the game, maybe." Abby picked up the squirrel tweezers. "I don't for one second believe Jonah will back off. I haven't seen the last of him."

"By virtue of his position, he's on your committee."

"I'm hoping he'll blow it off." Abby pursed her lips. "Somehow, I don't think I'll be that lucky."

"I believe he's planning to attend."

Abby's gaze sharpened. "What makes you think that?"

"Hazel Green's new police chief is a hot topic. Especially since he's handsome, young and single. More than one woman told me she met him at the party." Matilda sipped her wine. "Several asked if I knew where your committee was planning to meet. They'd heard Jonah was planning to attend and wanted to casually stop by."

"Why didn't you say anything to me before this?"

"I figured if you wanted to talk about him, you'd bring him up." Matilda sipped her wine, inclined her head. "Now you have."

"The committee meets tomorrow." Abby looked down at the squirrel tweezers in her hand. She could pick two acorns.

As Matilda predicted, her luck had turned. Something told Abby that tomorrow her luck would take another turn, and this time not in the right direction.

CHAPTER SEVEN

Jonah didn't hear a peep from Abby about the committee planning meeting. He went anyway.

When he'd met Leo for lunch last week, the mayor gave him the date, time and location. Though Jonah wasn't particularly interested in party planning, he was interested in getting to know Abby and his daughter.

The line outside the Engine House Café, an old fire station-turned-diner, stretched out the door. He spotted Rachel Grabinski, another committee member. They'd been introduced at the party and he'd since discovered she and Abby were friends.

Jonah remembered Rachel's date as pleasant but slick. Instinct told him Marc Koenig was not a man to be trusted.

"Rachel."

She whirled at the sound of her name, smiled. "Chief Rollins. How nice to see you again."

"Please, call me Jonah."

Rachel was an attractive woman, if you went for the hot librarian look. Her dark eyes, behind a pair of tortoise shell frames, were a startling contrast to her hair, which reminded

Jonah of Café Au Lait. Today, that cream-colored hair was pulled back from her face with a low clip.

"I hope Abby has reservations." Rachel glanced down at her phone and checked the time. "My boss is giving me an extra half hour for lunch, but that will go fast if we have to wait."

"You work at the Food Bank."

She smiled, appearing pleased. "You have a good memory."

"I do." Sometimes too good, Jonah thought. He remembered every word of his last exchange with Abby back in Springfield, when she'd told him to stay the hell away from her. He cocked his head. "Are the restaurants in town always this busy on Wednesday?"

Rachel expelled a breath. "Today is Dine In. The restaurants in this area each come up with a multicourse menu for ten dollars."

"I'm sorry I kept you waiting." Abby hurried up, her gaze focused on Rachel, ignoring him completely.

Nell sauntered up, as if hurrying never crossed her mind.

Jonah had been introduced to 'Hazel Green' at the party. She was an intriguing woman. Something told him there was more beneath this woman's surface than she wanted anyone to see.

"Chief." Nell offered an easy smile.

"Ms. Ambrose." Jonah inclined his head. "Or should I call you Hazel?"

"Today, it's Nell."

"Jonah."

"Now that you two have gotten each other's names down, we need to discuss our next step."

Nell merely lifted a brow at Abby's abrupt tone. "I understood lunch and committee updates were on the agenda."

"I forgot today was Dine In." Clearly agitated, Abby blew out a breath. "I didn't make a reservation. I'm sorry."

Jonah remembered Abby as the picture of calm, but she wasn't today. Was it the screw up with the reservation? Or his presence?

Surely, she'd expected him to show up. If for no other reason than he'd been appointed to head the Security Committee by the mayor.

Used to being in charge and making decisions, Jonah resisted the urge to step in and move things along. Instead, he rocked back on his heels and waited to see how Abby dealt with the situation.

"I'm sure any restaurant downtown will be packed." Rachel shot Abby an apologetic look. "Things at the Food Bank are hectic. I promised Tom I'd be back in ninety."

"Rachel's right. We aren't going to find anything in this area." Nell's gaze settled on Abby. "Driving somewhere will take time and Rachel's ninety-minute lunch hour is already down to eighty."

Abby nodded with obvious reluctance. "I guess we'll have to resched—"

"I've an idea." Rachel's hand shot straight up, like a school girl in a classroom. "We can meet at your place, Abby. We'll put in a take-out order at Matilda's. She can let us know when it's ready and one of us can pop down the hall and pick up the order."

"Works for me." Nell's silvery blonde hair was a startling contrast to Hazel's dark hair. "Whatever Matilda has on her menu is bound to be fabulous."

When Abby continued to hesitate, Jonah sensed her friends' puzzlement. Rachel's solution made sense. Nell agreed. He had no comment.

Why was she hesitating?

She doesn't want me inside her apartment.

"Sure, we can do that." Abby turned toward the hotel and Nell fell into step beside her.

That left Jonah to walk with Rachel.

"What do you do at the Food Bank?" He'd always had a high respect for entities who gave back to communities.

"I'm the Volunteer Coordinator." Pride filled Rachel's husky voice. "For years I was one of the volunteers. Then I got my degree and this position opened up. Tom hired me."

"I bet you do a great job." He slanted a sideways glance. "You have the positive personality you need with volunteers, but you're no pushover."

"Why, thank you." Two bright spots of color appeared on Rachel's cheeks.

"My parents encouraged all of us kids to give back," Jonah confided. "I did my share of volunteering for various agencies so I know the skills needed in a coordinator."

"In my job description they listed," Rachel lifted a hand and ticked off the attributes one by one, "good communication skills. Patience. And, a good attitude. Those were the essentials they felt someone in my position needed to possess."

Jonah nodded. "I'd add two more. Strong leadership skills and organization."

With a few questions, Jonah found Rachel had held her position nearly two years. Before that, she'd completed college while raising five brothers and sisters.

"I can't imagine how difficult it must have been for you to not only lose your parents but find yourself in charge of your younger siblings at eighteen."

"You do what you need to do." Rachel shrugged. "Life isn't always fair. Or easy."

"No, it isn't." Jonah's thoughts wanted to drift to the past, but he resisted, reminding himself his presence in Hazel Green was about moving forward. "I imagine you're enjoying having time to do what you want now."

Rachel took a second to answer. A pensive look crossed her face before she agreed.

If Jonah wasn't a trained observer, he might have missed her hesitation.

They followed Nell and Abby into the hotel lobby, which was filled with people waiting for an open table in the restaurant.

"Look." Nell pointed to a chalkboard displaying the menu. "Half a sandwich with soup. Salted butter tart for dessert. "Much better than what the Engine House was serving."

Nell shifted back to them. Abby did the same with obvious—at least to him--reluctance.

"I'll give Matilda our order while the rest of you get settled in Abby's apartment." Nell glanced at Abby. "Does that work for you, Abs?"

Abby nodded.

It was interesting, Jonah thought, watching Nell take charge. He wondered if that's how it would be during the meeting. Nell was on the roster as Vice-Chair, which he'd learned meant next year she'd be in Abby's spot.

Pulling a pad and pen out of her bag, Nell stood poised and took their order like a waitress. Other than Abby who chose the Market Veggie sandwich, Jonah and the other two picked the Roast Beef with Havarti. They all went with the Butternut Squash soup.

"I like Chicken Noodle," Jonah said to Rachel. "But I haven't had Butternut Squash soup in years."

"You're in for a treat." Rachel patted his shoulder. "Nobody does soups as well as Matilda. Am I right, Abby?"

Abby, who'd just finished unlocking the door, turned and nodded.

An almost imperceptible frown furrowing her brow told Jonah she'd noticed the easy camaraderie between him and Rachel and didn't like it. Not one bit.

"It's excellent soup." Pushing the door open, Abby gestured them inside.

As he stepped past her, Jonah recognized the familiar scent of cinnamon laced with the faintest hint of vanilla.

A wave of sadness at this distance between them washed over him. This woman had once been his best friend. Someone in whom he'd confided his hopes and dreams. He would have done anything for her and she for him.

Once he'd married they hadn't been as close, but that was to be expected. As his parents had often said, when you married your spouse becomes your best friend. Somehow that had never happened with him and Veronica. No matter how close they became, his ex-wife had never moved into best friend territory.

Perhaps because they were simply too different. But he'd loved Veronica, though sometimes he wondered if he loved the woman he thought she was or the person he wanted her to be.

Jonah pulled back his thoughts. What had gotten into him? It had to be the fragrance. He'd heard scents could take you back years.

Instead of analyzing why, Jonah focused on the apartment at the back of the hotel where Abby and Eva Grace lived. While the living room and kitchen were small and combined, the space was too big to be called an efficiency. If he wasn't mistaken, when taking the width of the hotel into account, there were probably two bedrooms down the short hallway, not one.

"Did you get those new curtains hung in Eva Grace's room?" Rachel asked, confirming his two-bedroom supposition.

"I did." Abby's smile lit her whole face. "She loves them."

Rachel turned to him. "Do you have sisters?"

Conscious of Abby's eyes on him, Jonah nodded. "I have two."

"Then, you'll appreciate this room." Rachel glanced at Abby. "Do you mind if I show it to—"

"I do mind." The words held a harsh edge which Abby attempted to cover with a laugh and an airy wave of her hand. "It's a mess right now."

Rachel flushed. "I'm sorry."

"Nothing to be sorry about." Relief flooded Abby's face when the doorknob turned and Nell stepped inside.

"Matilda will text me when the food is ready. Since they're swamped, I told her one of us would pick up." Nell glanced at

Abby for confirmation and received a nod. "At the table or in the living room?"

"Let's do the table." Abby lifted a pot of daisies from the center and placed it on the counter. "It's a good thing Kyle had to miss. I wouldn't have enough seats for everyone."

"Kyle?" Jonah cocked his head.

"Kyle Davidson. He's overseeing the Marketing, Advertising and PR functions," Rachel explained.

"He sent in his report." Abby gestured for them to take their seats. "I'll give you his update when it's his turn. Before we get started, what can I get everyone to drink?"

After a pitcher of ice water was placed on the table, Abby fixed cool brown eyes on him. "I believe you mentioned something about needing to leave early, Jonah. You can give your report first."

Jonah lifted the glass of water. "Actually, I've blocked out two hours from my schedule."

He knew what she was trying to do. Abby was making it clear she wanted him out of her apartment as soon as possible. If he were her, he'd likely feel the same. But he wouldn't be leaving early. He had a duty to this committee and to Eva Grace.

And, to his old friend. Even if, in Abby's mind, their friendship had ended five years ago.

"I'm the one who needs to leave," Rachel flicked her wrist, glanced at her watch, "in exactly sixty minutes."

"You'll be done then." Abby's voice was as warm as her eyes. "I promise."

"Do you still want me to go first?" Jonah asked.

"I do want you to go," Abby hesitated for several beats before adding, "first."

Jonah stood.

Hope flared in Abby's eyes. "What are you doing?"

Nell glanced up. Her curious gaze shifted from him to Abby then back again.

"I'm used to giving reports standing. I trust it won't be a distraction."

Abby waved a hand, gesturing for him to begin.

"I reviewed the plan that was set up and I'm impressed." Jonah began to pace the room as he spoke. "A risk assessment was done early on to identify possible security issues. The committee looked at the number of guests anticipated, including any special high-profile events, as well as where the Birthday Bash will be held."

As Jonah reached the other end of the living quarters, he gave the contents of the table his full attention. Pictures of Eva Grace from infancy on up filled the small side table. Just seeing the child in braces brought his heart to his throat.

"Is that all?" Abby demanded.

"We've compiled detailed job descriptions for all staff during the Bash. I sent those to Abby's email this morning." Jonah slid his gaze around the table, focusing on Rachel and Nell now. "If either of you would like copies, I'll be happy to send them to you, as well."

"I'm impressed," Nell gazed thoughtfully at him. "You've gotten up to speed quickly."

"It's been relatively easy since much of the work was done before my arrival." Jonah walked to the window and glanced out while stealing another glance at the pictures. "Appears the rain predicted for today is holding off. Oh, one more thing. The Security committee also prepared an evacuation plan in case of emergency, mapped out all emergency exits, looked at access for paramedics and have a contingency plan in place in case of power outages."

Nell's phone buzzed. She glanced at the screen. "Food is ready."

She started to rise but Jonah waved her down. "Since I've already given my report, let me get it."

"Thank you, Jonah." Nell's smile was warm. "And thank you and your committee for all their hard work."

"Yes," Abby echoed. "Thanks."

When he returned, Jonah discovered Abby had already read what Kyle had submitted and was ready to move to Rachel's report.

Jonah passed out food which looked delicious and smelled heavenly. As he'd only been on the job a few weeks, he probably should have taken Abby's cue and left. God knew there was plenty of work waiting for him back at his office.

The problem was being around Abby wasn't as easy as he imagined. Today was the first time their paths had crossed since the party. This was an opportunity and he wouldn't cut it short.

"Rachel." Abby smiled at her friend. "Would you like to eat first and give your report after you've finished? Or give it now? Either works for us."

Rachel, who'd just finished cutting the half of her Roast Beef and Havarti sandwich in two, looked up. "I prefer to get the report out of the way."

"When you're ready." Abby slipped her spoon into the soup. "No rush."

She was nice to her friends, he realized. Which didn't surprise him. That giving, nurturing nature was one of the reasons she'd agreed to be a surrogate for him and Veronica in the first place. That, and the fact that the $50,000 she was to be paid would go a long way toward helping her get a business loan for the coffee shop she was determined to open.

Abby had been hesitant at first, even when the money had been offered. The fact that she hadn't ever had a child, normally a requirement for being a surrogate, hadn't concerned them. She was young and healthy.

They hadn't even been worried about her wanting to keep the baby. Back then, Abby hadn't been certain she ever wanted children.

Veronica claimed it was her reminding Abby of what she could do with that amount of cash that had caused her to give the offer a second thought. Jonah knew it was the thought that she would be helping them have the baby they'd dreamed of for so long.

"We have the number and type of volunteers we need for the Bash." Rachel took a sip of water. She glanced down at the paper she'd pulled from her purse. "These include Pre-Event Volunteers and Day-of-Event Volunteers. The report I sent you shows the wide variety of volunteers required for an event of this magnitude."

Jonah pulled the report up on his phone. He widened his eyes at the number. "That's a lot of manpower."

"It is." Rachel smiled. "They include everyone from those assisting the police directing traffic to our roving social media promoters who will be charged with pumping the event's online visibility."

"Thank you, Rachel." Abby took control of the discussion and reported on several other committees.

She'd grown up. When she'd left Springfield, she'd been in her mid-twenties and still finding her way. Oh, she'd always been mature for her years, but today Jonah was seeing a different side to the woman he'd known since childhood.

Did having a kid change you, he wondered? Or was it the fact that she'd been running her own business for the past two years? Whatever it was, power looked good on her.

"Sustainability? What all does that include?" Jonah interjected when she paused for breath. He'd asked the question not only because he wanted her to know he was paying attention, despite devouring some amazing Squash soup, but because he was interested.

"Think of it as anything related to reducing the event's 'carbon footprint.'" Abby's tone remained pleasant, but cool. "The committee's goal is to reduce, reuse and recycle wherever we can.

We really want to use paper wisely and save energy wherever we can."

"I'd say we're in good shape. You're doing a fabulous job keeping all of us on track, Abby." Rachel pushed back her chair and stood. "I wish I could stay longer, but the Food Bank calls."

"I'll walk out with you."

Jonah saw the startled look that flashed across Abby's face when Nell pushed to her feet.

"Ah, Nell." Abby hurriedly rose, placing a hand on the sleeve of the woman's dark suit. "Do you have to rush off so soon? There were several more things I wanted to discuss with you."

"Can we talk tonight? I really can't linger." A look of regret crossed the blonde's face. "I have court in twenty."

The three women must be close, Jonah surmised, as the other two each gave Abby a hug before they left. Or they might just be the hugging type. Some women were, he knew. Veronica had considered the behavior unprofessional.

Abby remained by the open door even after the two women's voices faded.

Jonah stood and began to gather the plates and dishes from the table.

"I can take care of that."

"I don't mind."

"I do." She started to say something more, then lifted a hand and took a moment to steady herself. "I'd like you to leave."

Jonah heard her sharp intake of breath when he strode across the room and picked up one of the photos. It was of Eva Grace as a toddler. The cake in the picture held three candles.

Unlike the child he'd seen in the classroom, this child wasn't smiling. She wore a frilly dress but there were no shiny shoes on her feet, only metal braces. "The braces had to be uncomfortable."

Crossing the room, Abby took the picture from his hands and placed it back on the table. "They had to be on twenty-three out of twenty-four hours. She'd just get used to them and then the doctor would order them tightened."

Abby closed her eyes and appeared to fight for control.

"I'm sorry you had to go through that alone." Jonah remembered what a soft heart she'd had and knew those times had hurt her as much as they'd hurt her child. Her child.

Though Eva Grace wasn't Abby's biological daughter, she was her mother in every other sense of the word. He needed to be respectful of that fact.

That didn't mean he wasn't going to stop pushing for contact with Eva Grace. Jonah firmly believed a child benefited from both a mother and a father.

He might be late to the table, but he was here. And, he wasn't going anywhere. Not now. Not ever again.

CHAPTER EIGHT

Abby considered the man in front of her. He had five inches and fifty pounds on her. She wouldn't be able to force him out of her apartment. She could threaten to call the police, but they both knew she wouldn't. If he bothered Eva Grace, yes. But not because he was determined to have a conversation about their daughter.

A conversation that was unnecessary because nothing he said would change her mind. She hadn't been able to count on Jonah when she needed him. How could she trust this man with her daughter's heart?

"Okay. We'll talk. But I need some air." She reached down and grabbed her bag. "Have you seen the covered bridge up close?"

Hope flooded his blue eyes. Eyes the same shape and vivid blue as Eva Grace's.

Abby's heart gave a ping but she ruthlessly tamped down the emotion. Never forget had become her motto.

"Are you referring to the one linking the business district with the Victorian Home district?" Jonah's voice remained conversational as he reached over and opened the door.

"It's called Crossover Bridge," Abby told him, breathing a sigh of relief when he followed her outside of her apartment. "The area where the homes are located are known as Victorian Village."

Jonah's lips quirked in that lopsided smile that had won many a girl's heart in high school. "There's much to learn when you move to a new town."

Abby turned to Nev as they strolled past. "I won't be gone long."

Nev's eyes sparked with interest at the sight of the man at Abby's side. "I've got everything under control."

"Thanks." Abby offered the girl a smile before returning her attention to Jonah.

"You look nice. Vintage." Jonah held the door open as she stepped out into the sunshine.

She'd gone with a 1940's look today, coupling the popular walking shoes of that era with a red-and-white striped shirtwaist dress, complete with shoulder pads. Because of time constraints she'd gone simple with her hair. Instead of going crazy with Victory rolls, she'd settled for a center part with the hair pinned back past the temples.

Since he appeared to expect a response, she nodded. "Thank you."

His gaze dropped to her feet. "Will you be okay walking in those?"

Abby glanced down at her stacked heel, lace-up Oxfords. "These are the most common walking shoes of the 1940's."

"Do you like dressing up in clothes of different eras?"

Either Jonah was simply making conversation, or he was truly interested. It didn't matter. Each step away from the hotel was a step in the right direction. Besides, it wasn't as if she hadn't been asked this question numerous times before.

It was the number one question she got from tourists and she had her answer at the ready. "I enjoy it. While it takes a little planning to make sure you have the dress, hair and shoes consistent, it's like playing dress up every day."

"I remember you and Jackie playing dress up." His lips curved. "You'd put on my mom's heels and clunk around the house."

For a second, Abby's mouth wanted to smile. She and his twin sister had been good buddies. But when push came to shove, his entire family had stood with Jonah.

Abby was spared the need to respond when the covered bridge came into view. "This was built in 1884. It's needed some structural work over the years but has held up remarkably well. Though originally built as a roadway for carriages, then cars, that changed when they expanded the park in the 1940's. Now, it's open only for bike and foot traffic."

She couldn't do this anymore, Abby realized, as she found herself falling into the rhythm of easy compatibility that had been the hallmark of her and Jonah's friendship.

"I need to get back to the hotel."

When she turned, he grabbed her arm, but quickly released it when she shot him a warning glance.

"You said we'd talk." He gestured to an ornate wrought iron bench under a large oak. "Your word used to mean something."

"Cheap shot, Rollins." Her voice dipped into the deep freeze. "Especially coming from someone with your history."

A muscle in his jaw jumped but he didn't snipe back. "Give me ten minutes."

She sashayed over to the bench and sat, arranging her skirt. "I'll give you five."

"Walking away from you and my baby was the most difficult decision I ever made." He dropped onto the bench but left a good amount of space between them. "Since time is limited, I won't go into all my reasons for choosing to stand with my wife. I will only say, that I look back at that decision, I realize it was wrong."

When the misery on his face began to tug at her heartstrings,

Abby bore down and remembered how scared she'd been and how alone. "It *was* wrong."

Jonah rubbed the bridge of his nose as if to ward off a headache. His gaze pinned hers. "Has there ever been a time that you've found yourself looking back and saying, I'd do anything to change what I said or how I behaved?"

She only stared, not about to get drawn into sharing regret stories with this man.

"I hope you don't have any, because they tear at your insides." He expelled a ragged breath. "The only thing I can do is move forward. Apologize to those I wronged--you, my parents, my siblings…and my daughter—and try to make it up to all of you."

"It's too late."

Abby caught the curious gazes of a group of tourists following a guide who was explaining the history behind the covered bridge. She supposed she and Jonah did make an attractive couple. Her, dressed in 1940's garb and him in his navy suit with a tie the color of her dress.

Instead of adversaries, they probably looked like a couple taking a late lunch and enjoying the beautiful late summer day.

"I don't believe it's too late." Jonah's tone turned persuasive. "Eva Grace is only five. You didn't have a father in your life and I remember how much you wanted one. You couldn't do anything about that. But I'm here and I want to be her dad. Do you really want to deny her that opportunity?"

She hated they had such a shared history. That fact had only made his betrayal even more painful. "This is different."

"How is it?"

She glanced at the Bulova with the thin black corded band that graced her wrist, and realized his time was up.

Instead of letting her speak, he rushed forward. "All I'm asking is you give me and Eva Grace a chance to know each other. You don't have to tell her I'm her father. Introduce me as a friend. If you shut the door without giving this matter adequate thought, I believe this will be one of those decisions you look back on and regret."

"I had a lot of time to consider how I'd respond if you ever showed up." Abby stood. "I need to get back to the hotel."

"Think about it, Abby."

He said something else, but she'd quit listening.

Jonah had made his decision five years ago. Sometimes, you just had to live with the consequences.

A day passed. Then, a week. Leaves crunched under Abby's feet on the sidewalk and the weather dipped leading her to dig out a jacket purchased for Eva Grace last year.

Jonah hadn't contacted her but she knew he was out there… waiting. When Iris mentioned something her and the "good-looking new Police Chief" a few too many times, Abby snapped then immediately apologized.

She knew she needed to give her close circle of friends the inside scoop but wasn't ready to go down that rabbit hole. Not yet. They knew she'd been a surrogate for a couple who changed their minds. They didn't know the man—Eva Grace's father—was Jonah.

Thankfully, there was only one more committee meeting scheduled before the Birthday Bash. Once that was done, there would be no reason for any interaction.

If Jonah chose to stay in Hazel Green, she would do her best to ensure their paths never crossed.

Abby reached the Ingram Club, a golf and tennis facility at the edge of town, just after one on Thursday. For the past five years the club had hosted a popular golf tournament prior to the Birthday Bash. The money raised each year went into a fund for a new Performing Arts Center. This year, a woman's tennis tournament had been added.

Prior to the day of golf and tennis, there would be exhibition games of ladies' tennis in the 1890's.

Abby's four friends were signed on to play. She was listed as a substitute and hoped her limited skills wouldn't be needed.

Iris, Rachel, Nell and Liz were standing courtside. The two courts they'd reserved still held players.

"What's the deal?" Abby gestured to the two men on one court and foursome of women on the other. "I thought we had the courts reserved?"

"There was a problem this morning and it affected everyone. When we got here the director asked if it was okay if we pushed our start time back fifteen minutes."

"Is that okay with you?" Abby's gaze landed on Liz.

"My mom is having a good day." The reporter's eyes were weary. "And Sawyer promised to be good for Grandma."

"I don't know how you do it." Iris shook her blonde head.

"Do what?"

The history teacher swished her racquet in a backhand motion. "Work in Chicago, help out your mom and be a single parent."

"I tell myself things will settle down." Liz shrugged. "One of these days I'll have some 'me' time."

Iris's gaze shifted to Rachel. "In the meantime, we'll all can live vicariously through Rachel."

A startled look crossed Rachel's face. "Me?"

"Last I knew the siblings were all out of the house." Iris cocked her head. "Unless a few of them have moved back."

"No." Rachel smiled, her brown eyes warming. "They're all doing well. Although I wouldn't mind if one of them wanted to come home."

"This is your time." Iris placed a hand on Rachel's arm, her gaze firm and direct. "Just like it's mine to explore and see what I want out of life."

"I don't see all that much exploring." Nell's tone might be

matter-of-fact, but it wasn't unkind. "You both latched onto the first man who showed you any attention."

"I haven't latched on to anyone." Iris's eyes flashed. "Chuck and I have been friends for years."

Rachel frowned. "I don't appreciate the insinuation."

"Hey, don't go ballistic on me." Nell pointed a well-manicured finger. "I'm just keeping it real."

Abby took a slight step back from the fray. While she understood—and, in many ways—agreed with Nell's observation, how Iris and Rachel lived their lives was their business. Just as how she chose to deal with Jonah was hers.

"I was merely pointing out that, after many years of marriage, Iris chose to reconnect with someone safe. A man she'd known since she was a child."

"What's wrong with that?" Iris lifted her chin.

Nell shrugged. "Nothing is wrong, if you really like him—"

"We're *friends*," Iris put exaggerated emphasis on the word. "How many times do I have to—"

"Hey, hey, hey." If Abby had a referee's whistle on her, she'd have blown it. "We're all friends here."

Abby wondered what her friends would think of her old *friend* Jonah waltzing back into her life. Pulling her thoughts back to the present, Abby found Nell's sharp-eyed gaze fixed on her.

"What are you thinking?" Nell asked.

"I agree with Iris," Abby told her. "We need to have each other's backs, no matter what."

Some unreadable emotion flickered in Nell's eyes.

"Friends support each other." Iris slanted a pointed glance at Nell. "Even if we don't always agree."

"All yours." An athletic, grey-haired man gestured to the court as he and his opponent headed to the locker rooms.

On an adjacent court, the women picked up their gear and strolled off.

Rachel raised a brow. "How do you want to divide up?"

It didn't surprise Abby that Rachel left the decision up to the others. Though she'd done an admirable job of raising her siblings, since the youngest left the house, she'd floundered.

"You decide, Rach." Nell took the words right out of Abby's mouth.

"Whatever you guys prefer is fine with me," Rachel protested.

Abby wondered why Rachel couldn't see that deferring to everyone else's wishes wasn't going to fly with Nell.

"Tick tock." Nell pointed to the large clock on the wall. "We're wasting valuable court time."

Rachel gave an exasperated huff and pointed to Nell. "Okay. You and I, far court."

"You're going to slam the ball in my face, aren't you?" Nell offered a cheeky grin.

"The thought does have appeal." Rachel turned to Iris. "You'll play against Abby and Liz. Because there are two of them, they'll play the ball into the singles court, but you can play the ball into the doubles alley."

Rachel shifted her focus to Abby and Liz. "As the side with two players, you'll do the serving. You'll rotate after every game."

Abby resisted the urge to glance at Nell and give her the thumbs up. Nell might come across sometimes as cool and uncaring, but she genuinely wanted the best for her friends.

Rachel had spent so many years catering to her siblings' needs that it was difficult for her to take the lead and express her preferences.

When Rachel had first started dating Marc, Abby had been pleased when she'd seen him asking Rachel for input on what they should do on their dates. But lately, everything seemed to revolve around what he wanted.

Abby stepped onto the court in her short white skirt and top. She was a passable tennis player at best. She could only imagine how she'd play in a long white skirt and blouse.

She hoped she wouldn't have to fill-in, but if she did, she

would do so cheerfully, showing Eva Grace that you didn't have to be the best to have fun.

There was so much she hadn't considered when Jonah had ignored the court summons and she'd been awarded joint custody. But that day she'd made a promise to herself and to Eva Grace. She would do everything in her power to keep her daughter safe and happy.

So far, she'd kept that promise.

The state highway north of Hazel Green that led to the Ingram Club was referred to by locals as "High Road." Abby wasn't sure if the moniker came from the fact that the two-lane highway was north of the town, making it "higher" or was if High was simply short for highway.

Regardless, she wasn't a fan of the roadway known for its hills. From what she'd observed those traveling it tended to drive too fast and pass too frequently, ignoring the solid yellow line.

But, it was the quickest way to Eva Grace's school and the tennis court snafu had absorbed the wiggle room she'd built into the schedule.

Traffic was surprisingly heavy for a Wednesday afternoon but moving, as expected, at a brisk pace. Though she heard her phone buzz, she kept her eyes on the roadway. The way she looked at it, there was nothing so important it couldn't wait until she stopped.

When Abby saw the truck, it took a second for her to realize the pick-up was headed directly for her. A stand of trees on her right precluded going off the road. She glanced left. The traffic going in the opposite direction was too heavy to allow her to cut over, even for an instant. Which meant there was no room for the driver of the truck to get back in his own lane.

Like a bad case of "Chicken," the truck kept coming.

Shooting her gaze to the right again, Abby saw trees give way to cornfields. The truck was close now, too close.

Jerking the wheel to the right, she sent her SUV off the road. She went down then found herself airborne. In those seconds, Abby thought of Eva Grace.

Please don't let me die was her last thought before the vehicle crashed back to earth and everything went black.

CHAPTER NINE

The call about a multi-car accident on High Road came shortly after Jonah's meeting with the mayor. Already in the car, he headed straight to the area.

The State Police had secured the scene, closing off the road in both directions. Jonah parked his vehicle off to the side and strode up to the barricades, hooking his badge in his suit pocket.

"What do we have here?" Jonah asked one of the officers.

The man's gaze dropped briefly to his badge.

"According to witnesses, pick-up was passing in a no-passing lane, one vehicle went off the road to avoid a head-on." The officer gestured to the field. "The truck hit the car behind that vehicle, pushing them into the other lane. Six vehicles involved, including the one in the cornfield."

"Lucky it wasn't more."

Relief skittered across the officer's face at the sound of sirens. "Finally."

Because of the traffic congestion, the ambulances had to make their way along the edge of a roadway that now held a line of cars as far as the eye could see.

While the officer directed the ambulances, Jonah moved closer to see if there was anything he could do to help.

His heart gave a solid thump when he saw the cherry red KIA in the field. Abby had a Sportage that color.

He started down the ditch, waving his badge without breaking stride when another officer called for him to halt.

One of his police officers, had the door to the vehicle open. He looked up at the sound of Jonah pushing through the corn stalks, but returned his gaze almost immediately to the vehicle's occupant. "Ma'am. I'd like you to stay where you are until the EMTs look you over."

"I'm fine."

Jonah's heart stopped. *Abby.*

"You don't understand. I need to pick up my daughter at school." Abby's voice quivered but held a stubborn edge.

"I'll call the principal." Jonah stepped forward, relief flooding him when he saw that, other than an abrasion on her face from the airbag deployment, she appeared unharmed. "Who do you want to pick her up?"

He would have gone there himself, but knew the offer would have had her jumping out of the vehicle and walking to the school, if necessary.

"Matilda." Abby took a breath, let it out then rattled off a number. "Tell her I'll be home as quickly as I can and not to say anything to Eva Grace about the accident. I want to tell her myself."

Jonah nodded and stepped away as an EMT made his way to the car.

Pulling out his cell phone, Jonah called Gage, grateful he and the principal were already acquainted, then called Matilda. It took several rings before the woman answered.

"Ms. Lovejoy, this is Jonah Rollins."

There was the briefest of pauses. "Why, Chief Rollins, how nice to hear from you."

"Abby needs a favor." Without waiting for a response, he laid out the situation quickly and efficiently, then reiterated, "Abby is fine. But she will be delayed. If you could pick up Eva Grace at school, I know that will take a load off her mind."

"I'm leaving now." Fear slithered through Matilda's calm tone. "Please tell me you're being honest and Abby is really okay."

"She's perfectly fine, other than a couple of scrapes. Again, she doesn't want you to say anything to Eva Grace about the accident."

"I won't."

Jonah heard the sound of a car door slamming shut and an engine roaring to life.

"Tell her I'll take care of dinner. When she's able have her call me."

"I'll do that."

"Jonah."

It startled him to hear her use his first name. "Yes?"

"Thank you for taking care of her." Matilda cleared her throat. "She means a lot to me."

"To me as well," he said before he could stop himself.

Thankfully, the call ended, so he didn't think she'd heard.

"If you tow my car, how will I get home?" Abby heard the whine in her voice but was powerless to stop it. Her nerves were raw and jittery and she couldn't keep her hands from shaking.

"One of the officers will give you a ride." Officer Wray's calm voice never wavered. "It may be a few minutes. We need to get this situation under control first."

"I can take her home, Officer."

Relief filled Abby when she saw Jonah had returned.

"Did you reach someone at the school? Was Matilda able to

pick her up?" Abby pushed to her feet, swayed slightly then steadied herself against the doorframe.

"Yes, to both questions." Jonah's gaze was steady and his tone, reassuring. "Matilda is probably already at the school."

"She won't tell Eva Grace about the accident." There was a question in the statement as Abby's gaze searched his face. "I don't want her to worry. I'm fine."

"Matilda promised not to say anything."

Abby expelled a shaky breath. "Good. Thank you."

Jonah flashed a smile. "What are old friends for?"

She caught Officer Wray casting her a speculative glance but Abby ignored him. She had more important things on her mind, like getting to her daughter as soon as possible.

"I appreciate you taking me home." Abby thought about pulling away when Jonah took her arm to steady her, but her legs felt like jelly and she didn't have the strength.

Concern filled his blue eyes. "Are you sure you shouldn't go to the hospital and be checked out?"

"I really am okay." She swallowed against the dryness in her throat and tried a smile. "Just a bit stressed."

"Can you tell me what happened?" He tightened his hold as they picked their way through downed cornstalks and an abundance of mud from last night's rain.

"A truck attempted to pass where he shouldn't. There were cars in his lane and he couldn't get back over." She'd given a clear, dispassionate account already to Office Wray. But somehow saying it again had fear rising up. "He was coming right at me. I kept thinking he'd go off the road, but he didn't. It was as if we were playing this horrible game of Chicken."

"It's okay." Jonah's voice remained low and soothing, his hand firm and supportive on her arm as they climbed up to the road.

"I jerked the wheel to the right, went into the ditch then up. Then I was airborne." She let out a shuddering breath. "It happened fast. Yet, for a second--and that's all it could have been-

-it was like slow motion. I thought I might die. I hoped once I hit the ground the airbags would deploy and protect me."

She stopped at the edge of the roadway and fought to catch her breath. Abby felt as if she'd finished a marathon instead of simply crossing a field and climbing a five-foot incline.

"Take a minute."

"I used the eye drops in my purse." She blinked rapidly and realized the gritty sensation was gone. "My ears are ringing."

"Give it time." Jonah gave her a reassuring smile. "Those airbags are loud when deploy."

Her teeth sought her upper lip as she rubbed her aching wrists, which were reddened.

His gaze sharpened. "Do your wrists hurt?"

"They're a little sore." Abby grimaced. "I think the airbag pushed my hands back from the steering wheel. But I can move them okay."

Seeing the concern in his eyes, Abby flexed and extended her hands to forestall any questions about x-rays.

She glanced around the scene filled with ambulances, firetrucks and police. Several firefighters were attempting to get a person out of a crumpled economy car.

The Silverado that had been coming at her was upright and though both sides were bashed in, it had come through the experience better than the other vehicles.

An ambulance left with its sirens blaring. Abby turned to Jonah. "Was anyone killed?"

She'd been so concerned with her own situation, she hadn't thought of the other people who'd been impacted.

"I haven't gotten a full report, but right now, no fatalities." Jonah tracked the progress of a second ambulance as the driver maneuvered it through the wrecked cars, police cruisers and fire engines. "Several people are badly injured."

"That silver car." Abby gestured with her head toward the crushed one with people still trapped inside and guilt washed through her. "I didn't even think of the vehicles behind me when I went off the road."

"You had no choice."

"Neither did they. It was my fault the truck smashed into them." Tears filled her eyes. "I'm why they're injured."

"No." Jonah spoke sharply. "The truck driver is the one at fault. There's a reason this stretch of roadway is a no passing zone. You reacted appropriately."

Abby nodded and resisted looking in the direction of the silver car. "You don't need to take me home. I'm sure you have a lot to do here."

"Though it might not appear like it, these responders have the situation under control. Besides, if I didn't take you home, I'd need to pull one of them off the scene to do it."

Abby supposed she could wait. But for how long? The adrenaline that had coursed through her body immediately after the accident had vanished, leaving her weak and unsteady. All she wanted was to get home to her daughter.

Jonah gestured with one hand. "My car is over there."

Over there was the other side of the barricades.

Abby nodded and began walking in that direction, trying to ignore the devastation around her. "Jonah."

He glanced over at her.

"Thanks."

"I'm here for you, Abby."

∼

I'm here for you...

Though Jonah's words kept circling, Abby didn't let herself think too hard. She focused on reassuring Matilda and Eva Grace that she was perfectly fine. Only once Matilda left and her child was in bed and sleeping peacefully did she let the tears come.

Thankfully, other than the scrape on her cheek, that was

beginning to bruise and her sore wrists, she was okay. The smartest thing she'd done was to text Matilda on the way home, and ask if there was a way she could have a few minutes alone in the apartment when she got home.

Abby had taken those minutes to clean up and steady herself before facing her daughter. To lighten the story, she'd made a big deal about Bebe-their name for the KIA—mowing down corn stalks when forced to leave the highway because of a truck driver who got his directions mixed up.

It had been the right approach. Even with fresh make-up and a steady smile, Eva Grace had gotten teary-eyed, crawling into her lap and begging her not to get hurt again.

It was then Abby realized she'd been a neglectful mother. Oh, she'd made sure her daughter had food on the table and a roof over her head. More than that, Eva Grace knew she was loved and cherished.

But today had brought up something she'd never considered. What would happen to Eva Grace if she died before her daughter was grown?

Abby knew all too well you didn't have to be old to die. With an illness there was usually time to plan, to make arrangements. But an accident on a bright September day could end things without time to prepare.

She didn't have a will. Tomorrow, she would speak with Nell and remedy that situation. That would take care of her business interests and ensure Eva Grace would have money for college.

But it wouldn't address Eva Grace's custody. Though technically Jonah retained joint custody—it was extremely difficult for a parent to relinquish parental rights in Illinois—he'd never been a part of Eva Grace's life.

That left the question of who was the best person to raise her daughter. Abby needed someone who would shower the child with love and help her grow into a happy, functioning adult.

She took a sip of wine. As she had no real family to speak of, that left her close circle of friends. A list. She needed to make a list. Abby pushed herself up from the sofa and groaned.

Every muscle in her body ached. Feeling at least a hundred years old, Abby hobbled across the room to retrieve a pencil and pad of paper from a drawer. Once she was finally back on the sofa, she made a list.

She trusted all these women. Loved each and every one of them. But were they in a position to raise a child? Were they the right one for her daughter?

As the names were in no particular order, Abby began at the top.

Matilda Lovejoy.

During the past two years, Matilda had become her mentor, and in many ways, her surrogate mother. At forty-three, the woman possessed the wisdom and insight that had helped guide Abby in many business and personal decisions.

There wasn't a single doubt in her mind that Matilda loved Eva Grace as if she were her own. Her only concern was, in the last year Matilda had mentioned several times the possibility of relocating to Oregon to open a restaurant there.

Though Abby didn't begrudge her this dream, the thought of Eva Grace perhaps being uprooted from her school, her friends, left Abby uneasy. She knew how difficult losing her own mother had been. She couldn't imagine if she'd had to move to a new state and start over.

Putting an X through Matilda's name, Abby moved on to the next on her list.

Cornelia Ambrose.

Nell was firmly entrenched in Hazel Green. She couldn't imagine her friend relocating. But with a busy law practice and her Hazel Green gig, Nell often joked she caught herself coming and going.

While she loved Eva Grace, Abby had heard Nell mention on

more than one occasion that she wasn't sure she ever wanted children. Of course, Abby had felt that way herself once upon a time so she couldn't hold that against Nell. Still, would it be fair to ask a woman who wasn't sure she wanted children to raise hers?

Crossing off Nell's name, Abby moved to the next one on the list.

Rachel Grabinski.

Rachel adored children and was definitely family-oriented. When her parents had died, her friend had stepped up to the plate and--at the tender age of eighteen--had obtained guardianship of her five siblings.

Only recently, now that the youngest was out of the house, had Rachel began to live her own life. Her friend would willingly, happily, take Eva Grace. But at what cost to Rachel? Then, there was Marc Koenig.

Abby didn't like the man. Didn't trust the man.

The way things were looking, if Rachel didn't come to her senses, she could end up marrying the guy. There was no way Abby could take the chance of Marc becoming Eva Grace's "father."

With a sigh, Abby drew a firm line through Rachel's name.

Before moving down to the next name on her list, Abby rolled her shoulders, trying to unknot some of the stiffness. She put down her pencil and did the same with her wrists.

Her wince made her think of the concern in Jonah's eyes. If the police chief had his way, she'd have ended up being checked out at the ER.

Pushing thoughts of Jonah aside, Abby took another long drink of wine and studied the next name on the list.

Liz Canfield.

Divorced mother of one, Liz had showed an amazing ability to balance a career with the needs of her nine-year-old son. If Eva Grace went to live with Liz, she would have a brother.

Because of the proximity to family, Abby didn't see Liz leaving Hazel Green anytime soon.

The only problem was, because of her mother's recent cancer diagnosis, Liz was stretched thin. Between her son, her job and doing what she could to help her mom, Liz had little free time. Would adding another child to the mix be too much?

Putting a question mark next to Liz's name, Abby reached the last one on her list.

Iris Endicott.

Iris was a high school teacher with a passion for teaching. She adored kids of any age. Abby knew she'd once longed for a child of her own and that she and her husband had been looking into adoption when he was murdered in a robbery gone bad. She was a definite possibility, other than she was still working through all the emotions that came with an unexpected and tragic death.

Also, there was the issue of a boyfriend. Whether that be the current or future one. How would that man feel about raising another person's child? Still, Iris was a possibility.

Abby placed a question mark next to her name before setting the pad on her lap and resting her head back against the sofa cushion.

An image of Jonah rose up. She opened her eyes to banish it but the sense of unease remained. If something happened to her, he would likely step forward and assert his rights.

I want to get to know my daughter.

Abby expelled a ragged breath and grabbed the bottle of wine, splashing more into the glass.

In her heart she knew that, even if she had a will with Eva Grace's guardianship designated, Jonah would never let his daughter go to Iris or Liz.

She'd be gone and Eva Grace would find herself in the care of a man who was a stranger.

Veronica hadn't wanted Eva Grace in her life, which in Abby's mind meant she had no worries about Jonah.

She should have considered they might not stick.

Abby set the wine glass down and pushed to her feet.

Today's near miss was a fluke.

She wasn't going to die, not for a long, long time so she didn't need to worry about who would care for Eva Grace.

She would be the one to raise her daughter.

The image of a truck headed straight toward her, flashed.

A fluke, she reassured herself.

She'd been on this earth thirty years and today had been her first near miss with disaster.

The knowledge didn't console or reassure Abby the way she hoped.

The idea of Eva Grace in the care of a stranger, a man who'd already shown he couldn't be counted on, formed an icy fist around her heart.

You could let her get to know him.

Abby rebelled against the thought. She tried to push it aside but it kept circling.

Over the years, she'd been faced with many difficult decisions, all centered around doing what was best for Eva Grace.

Always, the deciding factor hadn't been what *she* wanted, but what would lead to the optimum outcome for her child.

Expelling a harsh breath, Abby cursed Jonah for putting her in a position with only one option.

CHAPTER TEN

"Amazing turnout." Jonah slanted a glance at Leo, who stood beside him surveying the busy scene.

The mayor smiled in satisfaction. "Having a good mix of events for the locals, as well as pulling in tourist dollars, keeps everyone happy."

The "Green" was a park-like area in the center of town with a bandstand, numerous gazebos and walking trails as well as a huge pond. This weekend, a "Taste of Hazel Green" had taken over the sumptuous oasis. A Craft Beer Festival had commandeered the open-air pavilion and its parking lot on the southern edge of the park.

Adults who purchased tickets for the Beer Festival were treated to live music from a band out of Chicago and a sampling of local Illinois beers, national and regional craft beers and ciders.

Jonah recalled the Oyster and Beer Festival in Springfield and the Taste of Springfield, usually held at a local country club.

Neither event could match this one, either in scope or attendance.

"This," Jonah swept out a hand, gesturing to the sea of tents spread out before them, "is an unbelievable turnout for such a small community."

"It helps that we invite restaurants and caterers from surrounding communities to participate. The bigger the event, the more people we draw, which is good for everyone." Leo's gaze sharpened. "I love these events. It's like one big party where you get to see people you don't run nearly often enough."

Jonah turned and his system went on high alert.

Abby, one hand resting on Eva Grace's shoulder, stood chatting with Nell. Today, her dark hair was board straight and pulled her hair back from her face in a stretchy headband. Her very short dress, a bright hot pink swirl, showed off miles of tanned, toned legs.

Nell wore an equally short dress in an eye-popping psychedelic print with bright orange boots. The attorney had done something different with her hair, but Jonah barely noticed as his gaze dropped to his daughter.

As it had been in the classroom, Eva Grace's hair was pulled back into a curly tail but today it was tied with a bright blue ribbon that matched her dress. Her dress stopped mid-thigh. High-tops, covered in unicorns and rainbows, didn't fit the outfit but made him smile.

"Let's go say hello." Without waiting for Leo's consent, Jonah wove his way through the crowd. Once he reached the trio an awkwardness he hadn't felt since he was sixteen, stole over him.

Thankfully, Leo picked up the conversational slack. He rubbed his chin and studied the threesome. "I'm sensing a 1960's vibe."

"What gave it away?" Nell cocked her head, studying him from beneath heavily mascaraed lashes. "The bold colors or the paisley patterns?"

"Both," Leo admitted. "The mini-skirt clenched the era."

Jonah glanced down at his cargo shorts and polo shirt. "I

wouldn't even know where to start if I had to dress in a certain decade."

"Other than for specific events, it's totally your choice." Nell looped her arm through Abby's. "Abby and I enjoy slipping in and out of the different eras."

"Me, too." Eva Grace piped up. "I like playing dress up."

"You look lovely today." Jonah kept his tone light. When he'd moved to Hazel Green last month, he'd hoped by this time he and his daughter would be pals.

He should have known better.

"Mommy was in a car accident." Eva Grace told him. "She said you drove her home because Bebe wouldn't run."

"Bebe?" he ventured.

"The car," Abby clarified.

When he still looked puzzled, Nell let out a robust laugh. "Don't tell me you never named a car or a truck."

Jonah lifted his hands. "Not a one."

"If you want I'll help you name yours." Eva Grace's blue eyes, with their flecks of gold, met his. "I'm really good at picking out names."

Touched by the offer, he smiled. "I'd like that."

"Where are you ladies headed?" Leo's tone remained off-hand, but something in the way he looked at Nell told Jonah the mayor was hoping for an invitation to join them.

Jonah held the same hopes. On the day of the Abby's accident, for a brief moment, he'd felt a connection between them. Nowhere near as strong as the one they'd shared years ago. Just enough to have him hoping the door she'd shut would one day open wide enough to let him inside.

"We're going to every tent." Eva Grace giggled. "Mommy says we have to just take a bite or two or we'll explode."

"Thanks for that visual." Nell elbowed Abby.

Abby flashed a smile at her friend. An open, friendly smile.

The kind of smile that years ago she'd often sent his way. "Just keeping it real, girlfriend."

Jonah started to speak then noticed one of his detectives, in plain clothes for the event, speaking with a man. Not a simple conversation with a friend. Not from the look in the detective's eye.

"Is Kevin working this evening?" Nell asked in a low voice.

Jonah nodded, keeping his gaze on Detective Countryman.

"There's always a number of police, both in uniform and not, at these events," Leo explained. "People who are drinking and enjoying themselves with friends often aren't as careful as they should be."

"Why do you think the detective detained him?" Abby took Eva Grace's hand in a tight grip.

"Hard to say." Jonah narrowed his gaze as the man sauntered off, a smirk on his lips. "I would guess the detective noticed him acting suspiciously. Perhaps checking out potential marks."

"Though he sensed something was off, he must not have seen anything. Merely let the guy know he was watching him." Nell's eyes were cool. "That's standard."

Abby cocked her head. "I wonder why he didn't check to see if the guy had anything stolen in his pockets?"

Once again, Nell spoke before Jonah had a chance. "In this situation, where the detective didn't observe a crime being committed, a pat-down can only be conducted if there's reason to suspect the man is armed and dangerous."

"Spoken like an attorney." Jonah kept a smile on his lips and his tone off-hand.

"Fourth Amendment rights." Nell waved a hand. "This is boring talk."

"How can I resist that lead-in?" Leo offered her a winning smile. "I've something even more boring to discuss with you."

Nell arched a brow.

"It has to do with Hazel Green," Leo said.

"The town?" Nell probed. "Or the woman?"

"Both."

"Now," Nell spoke in a throaty whisper, "I'm intrigued."

"Take a walk with me to the sushi tent." Leo held out his arm. "I'll tell you everything."

Before responding, Nell turned to Abby, a question in her eyes. "Catch up with you later?"

Jonah expected Abby to at least hesitate. Instead, she offered a careless wave.

"Of course." Abby glanced at Leo then back at Nell. "Have fun."

Leo and Nell strolled off, leaving him with Abby and Eva Grace.

"Endless choices." Jonah kept his tone offhand as he gestured wide to the tents that stretched as far as he could see. "Mind if I join you?"

Abby hesitated for an imperceptible second, but it was enough time for Jonah's stomach muscles to clench.

"We should go this way." Abby pointed in the opposite direction, which told him she didn't anticipate reconnecting with Nell. "While we walk, I think it might be fun to tell Eva Grace how we first met."

Though Abby's smile didn't quite reach her eyes, her voice remained warm.

"H-how we met?" Jonah stammered.

Eva Grace's eyes lit up. "How?"

"My mommy and I lived down the street from Jonah and his family." Abby swung her daughter's hand between them. "We became friends. Like you and Sawyer."

"Sawyer?" Jonah asked, not certain where this was going but liking the direction.

"Liz Canfield's son."

"He's nine," Eva Grace told him. "He's a boy but he's nice. He lets me play with his race cars."

"When I was your age, Jonah let me play with his race cars," Abby told her daughter.

Eva Grace's eyes went wide. "Really?"

"Yep." Abby pulled her daughter close to her side when the crowd thickened.

Perhaps he shouldn't ask but…

"Would you like to ride on my shoulders, Eva Grace?" Jonah slanted a glance at Abby. "If it's okay with your mom, that is."

For just a second, Abby's mouth formed a thin hard line. Then, it relaxed. "It's okay with me, if that's what Eva Grace wants."

In answer, Eva Grace held up her arms.

Jonah wasn't ashamed to admit—at least to himself—that his heart melted. Simply dissolved into a puddle of love at his feet.

"Up you go." With one motion, he had her on his shoulders and shrieking with delight.

"I can see everything." The child's voice rang with delight.

Jonah kept his hands on her ankles as they made their way through the crowd. How many times had he envisioned such a scene? It was the kind of thing his father had done with each of his children.

"Thanks." He kept his voice low.

Abby gave a little nod then shifted her gaze. "That tent has little fried chicken legs."

Without warning, Eva Grace leaned over, her cheek brushing his. "I want a chicken leg."

It was the start of an afternoon that had Jonah blinking several times to see if he was dreaming.

Not wanting to waste a second of this precious time, Jonah embraced the day.

He ate chicken legs and porcupine meatballs, peach cobbler and tiramisu. By the time they'd made it to the far end of the Green, Jonah felt exploding was a distinct possibility.

"I want to go across the bridge and toss a penny in the

stream." Eva Grace, who now stood between them, glanced from her mother to Jonah. "Can we, please?"

The covered bridge was in sight. He was certainly up for continuing the adventure but, once again, deferred to Abby's wishes.

She leaned over and retied Eva Grace's ponytail ribbon. "Sounds like fun to me."

"Yay." The child did a happy dance, then surprised Jonah by grabbing his hand. "C'mon."

Jonah couldn't keep from smiling as he let himself be pulled along. While there were plenty of people on this side of the bridge, once they made it to the other side, the crowd thinned to a few strolling couples.

Eva Grace let go of his hand and galloped like a pony to a wooden rail overlooking the water. Her mane of gold glistened in the sunlight. She reminded him of a little angel.

"Hurry." The child motioned to him and Abby with her hand. "The fish want to say hello."

Abby moved to one side of the girl while Jonah flanked Eva Grace's other side. At the child's insistence he stared into the surprisingly clear water. Coins, mostly pennies, dotted the bottom while a school of goldfish swam lazily, basking in the late afternoon sunshine.

"I want to make a wish." Eva Grace glanced from him to her mother.

Abby opened her small bag then grimaced. "I used all my pennies at the store yesterday."

Eva Grace's smile turned upside down.

Jonah stuck his hand into his pocket and jingled. "I may have a coin or two."

"I only need one penny." Eva Grace told him, her expression serious. "I already know what I'm going to wish for."

Reaching deep into his pocket, Jonah pulled out the coins then held out his palm.

Eva Grace pursed her lips and studied the mix of pennies, nickels, dimes. She pushed a couple of coins aside, appearing to consider between a dull copper penny and one as bright and shiny as the sun overhead.

"I like this one." She plucked the shiny one from his hand, held it up and closed her eyes.

"What are you doing?" Jonah asked.

Her lids popped open and she grinned. "Making a wish. You have to close your eyes or it won't come true."

Leaning over the rail, Eva Grace dropped the coin into the water. "All done."

Jonah couldn't help but smile. He recalled his sister insisting if he told anyone his wish, it wouldn't come true. He wondered if that held true for wishes made on pennies as well as candles.

Eva Grace began skipping and twirling down the walkway in the direction of the Victorian homes. Jonah didn't mind.

The further they went in this direction, the longer it would take to get back, prolonging the adventure even more. But he reminded himself that Abby had been recently injured and might not be up to the exertion.

"How are you holding up?" He touched her arm but when she jerked back, he let his hand drop.

"I'm okay." She gestured with her head toward Eva Grace, currently twirling with her arms outstretched. "We've spent too much time indoors since the accident. I'm done being a slug on the couch. It's good for her to get out."

For one rash moment, Jonah considered asking why she was being so nice to him today. He kept his mouth shut. His desire to know the why wasn't strong enough to take the chance of ruining a very pleasurable afternoon.

"Look. An umbrella of trees." Eva Grace pointed when they caught up to her.

If they continued straight ahead, they would walk under that tree umbrella.

"Take my hand when we cross the street," Abby instructed. "Be sure and look both ways."

Eva Grace didn't simply take her mother's hand, she took his as well.

A lump rose to fill Jonah's throat as the little fingers rested trustingly in his. When thoughts of all the years he'd wasted away from his daughter intruded, he shoved them aside.

They continued down the street admiring the unique colors of the large Victorian homes.

"I like that one." Eva Grace pointed to a large two-story painted a pale yellow with swaths of stained glass above each window. The child's eyes narrowed at the sign in the yard. "For Sale."

She sounded out the words, then smiled triumphantly.

Jonah shot a glance at Abby. "She can read?"

"Eva Grace is very bright." Abby's gaze lingered on her daughter.

"What does it mean?" Eva Grace demanded.

"Being bright?" Jonah asked.

"No." The child pointed to the sign.

"It means the owner is selling the house." Jonah explained in a matter-of-fact tone. "He or she is moving somewhere else."

"I want to live there." Eva Grace turned pleading eyes to her mother. "Can we live there?"

"I thought you liked living at the hotel." Abby gaze slid to the house with the wraparound porch.

Jonah had a sudden memory of the afternoon drives he and Abby had taken when he'd first gotten his license, looking at the historic homes in Springfield. Like Eva Grace, Abby had loved the vibrant colors and styles of such homes.

"I bet that house has a back yard." The little girl's tone had a wistful edge. "And a dog."

"Do you like dogs?" How little he knew about this child who'd sprung from his seed.

She nodded vigorously, sending her curly tail swinging. "We can't have one because our 'partment is only big enough for Mommy and me."

Jonah knew many people who had pets in places smaller than the space where Abby and Eva Grace lived. But he also knew that pets were a commitment. Not only of time and energy, but of money. "Remember Ranger?"

The question popped out before he could stop it. He doubted reminding Abby of the past was a good idea.

When Abby didn't immediately respond, Eva Grace's head swiveled from him to her mother. "Who's Ranger?"

Despite clearing her throat, Abby's voice sounded rusty, as if she hadn't used it in a century or two. "It—he was a dog Jonah had growing up."

"Did you get to play with him sometimes?" Eva Grace smiled at the thought.

"Ranger adored your mother. He'd sit and hold out his paw for her to shake whenever she came over." Jonah pulled out his phone and scrolled to a picture of the black Lab. "This is Ranger."

Eva Grace stepped close and studied the picture of a black dog with glossy hair and a red ball in his mouth. She looked up. "Can I come to your house and play with him?"

Jonah hesitated. Should he tell the child that Ranger had died years ago? He looked at Abby. *Need some help here.*

"Ranger belonged to Jonah's parents. They live in Springfield." Abby kept her tone light.

"Could Ranger some for a visit sometime?" Eva Grace pressed. "I could throw the ball to him."

"Ranger lived a long life." Abby spoke matter-of-factly. "When he was very, very old, he went to live in heaven with your grandmother. I'm sure she's throwing the ball to him right now."

"I don't want him to be in heaven." Tears filled the little girl's eyes as her gaze settled on her mother. "I don't want you to go to heaven."

Abby swallowed convulsively. "I'm not going anywhere."

"If you did, I'd be all by myself." Like a dog with a bone, the child persisted. "You'd be with grandma and Ranger but I'd be alone."

How had a simple conversation about a dog gotten so out-of-control, Jonah wondered?

"I'm young," Abby reassured her daughter. "I'd never leave you alone. A mommy's job is to take care of her children."

Her gaze flicked to Jonah.

It seemed she was passing the relay baton to him. Though he hadn't a clue how to handle, he could punt with the best of them.

He gestured with his head to another home across the street. "What do you think of the purple house?"

CHAPTER ELEVEN

Abby's head pounded by the time they turned back toward The Green. She felt like a conversational slug as she remained silent, letting Jonah and Eva Grace talk.

Once they'd gotten off the subject of death and her leaving Eva Grace alone, the walk had proceeded smoothly. Especially when they stopped at a small park enclosed in an ornate black wrought iron fence with a gilded gate.

She'd expected Eva Grace to head toward the swings but had been startled when Jonah had claimed one of the u-shaped swings as his own. Exhausted, Abby took a seat on one of the benches beside a bush carved like a fawn.

She watched Jonah and Eva Grace fly high into the air. She smiled at her daughter who emitted a shriek of laughter and loosened one hand enough to wave.

Seeing them side-by-side, blonde hair catching the rays of the sun, blue eyes sparkling, made the resemblance between father and daughter even more obvious.

How easy it would be to simply forget the past and fall under the spell of that charming smile. Her past was filled with so many wonderful memories. Memories that included Jonah, Ranger, his parents and Sunday afternoon drives.

Before that day in the doctor's office, she was convinced she knew Jonah Rollins, knew how he'd respond in any situation. But that day, when it really mattered, she learned she didn't know him at all.

When someone shows you what they're like, believe them.

That day Jonah had showed his true colors. In the process, he'd broken her heart.

"You can't go down the slide." Laughter filled Eva Grace's voice. "You're too big."

"Watch me."

Abby turned in time to see Jonah slide down the vintage metal slide.

Eva Grace shrieked and clapped her hands.

Abby's heart clenched when he picked up her child and spun her around until they were both laughing and no doubt, dizzy.

"Do it again," Eva Grace ordered when he set her down.

He reached for the child, as if prepared to do just that, when Abby rose. "It's time to head back."

Two disappointed faces turned in her direction.

Jonah wisely said nothing.

"Awww, Mommy, can't we please stay longer? Me and Jonah are having fun."

"Another time, perhaps." Abby forced a smile. "I'm feeling tired."

Abby knew that look in Eva Grace's eyes and braced herself but Jonah placed a hand on the girl's shoulder. "How 'bout you ride on my shoulders until we reach the bridge? You can count the number of dogs we see on the way."

Jonah spoke as if the matter was already settled.

To Abby's surprise, Eva Grace didn't protest but giggled when he hoisted her to his neck.

He shot Abby a wink then gave Eva Grace's foot a tug. "How high can you count?"

"Fifty." Eve Grace's blonde brows furrowed. "Maybe higher."

"I doubt we'll see that many dogs before we reach the bridge." Jonah spoke in a conversational tone as he held the gate open for Abby. "If we do, either I or your mother will take over the counting."

"I can do it." Eva Grace asserted. "Even if I see a hundred zillion dogs."

Jonah's lips twitched. They were back on the sidewalk now and headed toward the bridge. "While you look for dogs, I'm going to talk with your mom."

Eva Grace chewed on her lip and thought for a moment. "You talk. I'll find the dogs."

Beside him, Abby stiffened. She hoped Jonah had more sense than to bring up anything heavy while Eva Grace was within hearing.

He smiled. "Since I'm new to Hazel Green, why don't you tell me what you like about the community?"

Jonah's voice turned conversational. Almost as if she was an interesting young woman he'd recently met and wanted to get to know better.

Abby would prefer to spend the rest of their time together in silence. Simply being with him had been more difficult than she'd expected. And the walk had left her exhausted.

Yet, even though Eva Grace's gaze continued to scan both sides of the street, Abby sensed the child was listening.

"I like the size. Twenty thousand isn't all that big but being a Chicago suburb gives us big city amenities with the charm of a small town." Abby didn't wait for him to ask questions. If they were going to have a conversation, she preferred to control it. That way she could be assured they wouldn't venture into any uncomfortable areas. "The medical care available in the community is excellent and the--"

"I used to go to doctors all the time."

It wasn't Jonah interrupting, but Eva Grace.

"I had braces." Eva Grace lifted a leg that had been resting against Jonah's chest. "My foot turned in funny and they had to get it to go the right way."

"Is that right?" Jonah spoke as if sensing the girl expected a response. But his gaze turned wary as he slanted a glance in Abby's direction.

She realized he was as eager as she to avoid certain topics.

"Yes," Eva Grace nodded for extra emphasis. "The braces hurt. I used to cry and cry and beg Mommy to take them off."

A look of pain, too potent to be faked, filled Jonah's eyes. "You had to wear the braces for a long time."

"Since I was a baby. But not anymore." Eva Grace lifted both legs at the same time and would have tumbled back if Jonah hadn't grabbed her ankles. She giggled. "Mommy took me for ice cream when we got them off."

"Sounds like that was a happy day." Jonah kept his gaze focused ahead, seeming to avoid glancing in Abby's direction.

"Mommy cried." Eva Grace's tone was matter-of-fact. "Now, I wear pretty shoes and dance and spin anytime I want."

Jonah cleared his throat. "That's good."

"That's five," Eva Grace announced.

"Five?" Abby asked.

"Dogs." Eva Grace pointed. "See him by the water."

A bull dog, short and squatty, walked beside a tall red-headed woman at the edge of the pond.

"Someday, I'll have a dog," Eva Grace spoke with the certainty of youth. "Maybe with a smushed face like that one. Or shiny black fur like Ranger."

They'd reached the bridge. Jonah glanced up at her. "Time to walk, munchkin."

Her arms went around his neck. "I want to ride."

Abby opened her mouth but before she could speak, Jonah

chuckled and swung her down, making her fly through the air first.

Eva Grace was laughing by the time her feet hit the pavement.

Jonah cocked he head. "Can you hop like a frog?"

Without answering, Eva Grace crouched down and hopped her way across the bridge.

Jonah smiled. "If we could bottle that energy, we'd be millionaires."

Abby sighed. "I could use a gallon or two of it right about now."

After slanting a glance in her direction, Jonah's brows pulled together. "You're pale as a ghost."

"Thanks."

"We walked too far."

Abby shook her head. "Eva Grace needed to get out."

"Do her needs supersede yours?"

Abby shot him a sharp glance. "Her welfare comes first."

"You won't do her any good if you get rundown." His lips curved as his gaze lingered on Eva Grace twirling in the sunshine at the end of bridge. "She's such a happy child."

Abby's heart swelled with love. "Eva Grace has the biggest heart."

"Seeing her in pain had to be difficult."

Abby did not want to go down that path. Today's conversation had solidified her belief that she must make sure Eva Grace would be cared for if anything would happen to her.

While she still wasn't convinced that Jonah was that person, she believed that giving Eva Grace an opportunity to get to know him had been the best course of action.

Tonight, she would ask Jonah if he was interested. Based on his supposed purpose in coming to Hazel Green, she didn't doubt he'd be all for it.

It would be awkward, but Abby meant what she'd told Jonah.

Eva Grace's welfare came first.

Jonah expected Abby to go her separate way once they returned to the park. Eva Grace's eyes had started to droop and Abby looked dead on her feet.

"I guess it's time to call it a day," Jonah offered reluctantly.

A scowl blanketed Eva Grace's face. "I don't want to go—"

"Jonah didn't get a chance to see your new curtains when he was over." Abby's tone remained easy. "Would you like to show them to him?"

Eva Grace's blue eyes brightened. She took his hand and began to pull. "They're Princess curtains."

"Really?" Jonah let himself be pulled along.

Abby had done a one-eighty since the day of the committee meeting. There had to be a reason, but right now he was just happy for extra time together.

When they reached the hotel, Matilda stepped out of the restaurant, her gaze settling on his hand, the one Eva Grace still held.

"Hi, Matilda." Eva Grace sang the greeting. "I'm showing Jonah my Princess curtains."

"Is that right?" Matilda shifted her gaze to Abby.

"That's right." Abby offered her friend a reassuring smile.

Something in Matilda's eyes told him the woman knew all about his tie to Abby and Eva Grace.

Her other friends didn't possess that knowledge. Not as far as he could tell, anyway. Other than Nell, none of them seemed to be good enough actresses to hide it.

"Have a nice night." Matilda leaned over and hugged Eva Grace. "Sweet dreams, little one."

Matilda's eyes filled with concern when they landed on Abby. "You need to rest."

"I won't be staying late," Jonah told her.

"You don't have to answer to me." Matilda winked. "Abby is more than capable of telling you when to head home."

Once inside the apartment, Eva Grace tugged him to her room.

An explosion of pink was Jonah's first impression. The curtains, which he dutifully admired, were pink with white polka dots and bows. They matched the polka dot bedspread, where six or seven stuffed animals rested against the pillows.

The room had been decorated with love.

Jonah cleared his throat. "You have a beautiful room, Eva Grace."

"Thank you," she said almost primly. "I like it very much."

"Eva Grace needs to take her shower, then we read a story," Abby announced, her expression inscrutable. "Perhaps, you'd like to read to her tonight?"

Gratitude flooded Jonah. He didn't know what had caused Abby's change of heart, but he was profoundly grateful. "I-I'd like that very much."

"There's beer and soda in the refrigerator." Abby spoke matter-of-factly. "Feel free to grab whatever you want and relax while I get her ready for bed. I'll let you know when it's story time."

The two chatted, the woman and the child, as they headed down the hall. Seconds later, he heard the sound of running water.

After retrieving a beer from the refrigerator, Jonah moved to the table of pictures. Because he had the time, he took it, picking up a picture and studying it intently before moving on to the next.

The pictures afforded him a snapshot of Eva Grace's childhood; from infancy to her fifth birthday party. There was even one of her holding the dreaded braces, obviously taken the day she'd gotten them off, a broad smile on her face.

Several of the pictures were of her and her mother. The one

of Abby, leaning over an isolette holding an infant Eva Grace was like a knife to the heart.

Abby looked so young. Fear mixed with love on her pale face. Thanks to some contacts at Arborview Hospital, Jonah was aware Eva Grace had undergone surgery soon after she'd been born, spending a day or two in the NICU after the meningocele repair.

He'd wanted so much to go to Abby and the baby, but believed his wife would have carried through with her threat to make life for Abby a living hell legally if he did. Those last months of Abby's pregnancy had been difficult ones for his wife emotionally.

Veronica's mother had told him many times how worried she was about her daughter. For an entire year he and Carole had been united when Veronica had pushed for contracting with another surrogate.

Veronica had seemed to settle down. Then, she'd once again broached the subject of trying again with a different surrogate. Again, he'd put her off.

"We're ready," Abby called from down the hall.

Jonah placed the beer he'd barely touched on a coaster and headed to his daughter's room.

Eva Grace was sitting up in bed, her face clean and shiny, her hair twisted on top of her head. Her eyes lit up like Christmas tree lights when she saw him. "Are you really going to read to me tonight?"

Jonah glanced at Abby.

She inclined her head.

"I am." He glanced at the stack of books beside her on the bed. "Are we reading all of those?"

Laughter bubbled from Eva Grace's lips.

"I read two each night." Abby smiled at her daughter. "Eva Grace picks the books. I thought I'd read one and you'd read the other."

"Sounds good." Jonah shoved his hands into his pockets and rocked back on his heels. He kept his tone even, though his insides quivered like a race horse at a starting gate.

This morning, when he'd rolled out of bed, he never imagined that tonight he'd be in Abby's apartment reading a book to his daughter.

Abby's hand was gentle as it pushed a strand of hair back from Eva Grace's face. "Which books will it be tonight?"

"Best Friends for Frances." Eva Grace reached over and pulled the book from the middle of the stack with amazing accuracy. She shoved it into her mother's hands.

Something about the book cover with its two badgers, at least he thought they were badgers, rang a distant bell in his memory. Had his mom once read this story to him and Jackie?

He took a seat in a white wicker chair near the wall as Abby read the story about Frances, who didn't think her little sister, Gloria, could be her best friend.

When Abby reached the end, Eva Grace's smile turned beguiling. "Someday, maybe, can I have a sister?"

Jonah expected Abby to shut that down. Instead, she smiled and shrugged. "Maybe. Some day."

Satisfied, Eva Grace searched through the pile and pulled out another book, her gaze now focused on Jonah. "I want you to read me this one."

"Sit here." Abby rose and exchanged places with him.

Jonah sat on the bed and read the title- *"Mercy Watson: Princess in Disguise."* He studied the cover. "Looks like Mercy has a pet pig."

Eva Grace fell back on her pillow and roared with laughter.

Jonah glanced at Abby. "What?"

Abby's lips twitched. "Mercy Watson *is* the pig."

Jonah flipped open the book. It appeared he had a lot to learn.

CHAPTER TWELVE

"And they lived happily ever after." Jonah closed the book.

Eva Grace giggled, wrinkling her nose. "It doesn't say that."

Jonah grinned. "My mother used to add that to every story."

"Your mommy sounds nice."

"She is." Jonah cleared his throat. "You'd like her."

Abby thought of his mom, a woman she'd once adored. She pressed her lips together. Not being a part of her or Eva Grace's life had been Nancy's choice.

"Give me a kiss and a hug, Evie Walnut and then it's lights out."

Eva Grace flung her arms around Abby's neck and gave her a smacking kiss on the lips. Then she shifted her gaze to Jonah. "Now, you give Mommy a kiss and a hug."

Before Abby could even react to the ridiculous command, Jonah leaned over. He brushed his lips across Abby's and gave her a quick hug.

Eva Grace gave a nod and smiled in satisfaction. "Good night."

Though Abby's heart raced and her lips tingled from the brief contact, she calmly rose and blew her daughter a kiss. She waited until the door was closed and they were at the end of the hall to stop, ready to round on Jonah.

"Evie Walnut?" He lifted a brow.

The question stopped the anger bubbling up.

"I craved walnuts when I was pregnant. It's a pet name, something just between the two of us." Abby fought to bring her thoughts back to the kiss.

"I remember when Mom used to call my little sister, Hannah Banana."

Hannah had been the youngest in his family. Sometimes, Eva Grace's giggle brought Hannah to mind. Abby started to smile, then realized what she was doing and pulled her lips into a stern line. "What were you thinking?"

His brows pulled together in confusion. "Bringing up Hannah?"

"No." She expelled an irritated breath. "Kissing me."

He waved a distracted hand. "That wasn't a kiss."

It had sure felt like a kiss. She resisted the urge to bring her fingers to her lips. "Why did you do it?"

"I didn't want to make a big deal out of her request." Jonah shrugged, his face expressionless. "If I would have asked—"

"I'd have said no and—"

"Eva Grace would have gotten upset, wondering why it was such a big deal. Then you'd have had to come up with some long explanation that would have left her confused and wondering what was the big deal."

"I'd have simply told her that we just don't kiss someone we barely know."

"You told her we were old friends," he reminded her. "Besides, we'd still be in her bedroom talking about it. This way she's likely already asleep."

All true, but it didn't negate the fact that he was wrong and seemed determined not to admit his error. This time she'd let it go. They had a lot to discuss and kissing wasn't on the agenda. "Don't do it ever again."

He offered her a lopsided smile. "Seriously? It was so bad you have to ban my lips for life?"

His humor and gentle teasing had always been part of his appeal. Once upon a time, in another life, she loved their playful sparring.

Then, she'd discovered what he was really like beneath all that charm. An ache gripped her chest. She wanted him out of her apartment, wanted to make it clear she didn't want to see or hear from him again.

She took a deep breath--not easy with her chest so tight-- and told herself to be rational and not respond based on emotion.

Taking a deep breath, Abby wiped sweaty palms against her skirt and calmed herself. The books were read. Eva Grace was asleep.

Over the years, Abby had faced many difficult conversations. The first was when her father just up and left. She remembered her mother sitting her down and telling her he wasn't coming back.

There had been the police officer, she couldn't even recall his name, who'd informed her that her mother had passed away. Then, the conversation in the doctor's office and the Spina bifada diagnosis. Now, this…

Abby never shied away from the difficult, though she wished to God she could start now. Or, at least put the discussion off until she could wrap her head around the fact that Jonah was back in her life.

But she couldn't allow herself to shirk her responsibility in this area any longer. The near miss on High Road had showed that her life could end with little warning.

As a parent, it was her duty to do the responsible thing. That meant not putting off a difficult, but necessary, conversation.

Jonah shoved his hands into his pockets and rocked back. "I'd better get going. Your little girl isn't the only one in this household who needs to sleep."

Abby opened her mouth but Jonah rushed forward. "I enjoyed today very much. Getting acquainted with Eva Grace, well, it meant the world to me."

"Did you mean what you said?" This wasn't how Abby had meant to start the conversation but jangled nerves and fatigue meant she wasn't at her best.

Confusion furrowed his brow. "I've meant everything I said to you."

"Sit down." She gestured toward the sofa. "We need to talk."

The bald hope in his eyes irritated her. As did the knowledge that she would likely be giving him everything he wanted.

Jonah waited for her to take a seat on the sofa before settling himself at the other end. He shifted his body to face her. He didn't say a word, just studied her with warm blue eyes so much like his daughter's she wanted to weep or throw something at him.

Instead, she clasped her hands together and plunged ahead. "Seeing that truck coming straight at me was a wake-up call. Although my life didn't flash before my eyes, sitting in that cornfield I realized I was lucky. I could easily have been seriously injured or killed."

Even now, just recalling that moment, had Abby closing her eyes and breathing a prayer of thanks.

When she opened her eyes, she sensed Jonah staring. She avoided his eyes, focusing instead on a spot over his shoulder. Abby let her gaze settle on a Felix the Cat wall clock that once belonged to her great-aunt. While it didn't really fit with the décor, Eva Grace loved the swinging tail. Having it with them was like having a bit of family.

Jonah cleared his throat when the silence lengthened. "What are you saying, Abby?"

"I've reconsidered my earlier refusal. You and Eva Grace need to become better acquainted." She held up a hand when joy flashed in Jonah's eyes. "If something should happen to me, I want to be assured Eva Grace will be cared for and loved. I have good friends in this community but none are in the position to raise a child, should that become necessary."

"I promise you, Abs, you won't regret giving me another chance."

He reached for her hands, might have taken one of hers in his if she hadn't sat back, crossing her arms across her chest.

"Let me be clear." The flat tone to her voice had his smile disappearing. "I don't want you back in my life, although I will play nice, for Eva Grace's sake. What I'm suggesting is a trial period where you and my daughter get to know each other. If things go well, then I'll look at the next step."

Jonah's gaze searched hers. "Will you tell her I'm her father?"

Abby shook her head. "Not now."

"When?"

"I don't know." She shrugged. "Maybe never."

His brows slammed together and she could practically see the protest rising to his lips. It was clear he wanted to argue the point. Yet, he'd always possessed a great deal of self-control so she wasn't surprised when he took a second to speak. "Won't she wonder why I'm hanging around?"

"She's aware we knew each other growing up. She'll accept the fact that we're…friends." Abby forced herself to choke out the word. "You'll spend time with us. We'll go on outings."

The plan sounded stupid when spoken aloud. Or maybe it was simply her way of explaining it that made it sound that way. "You're right. I am tired and probably not making much sense. The bottom line is I'd like you and Eva Grace to become acquainted. That will help me decide the next step."

He nodded slowly, his expression unreadable. "What about us?"

Abby watched Felix's tail go back and forth. It reminded her of this conversation. Back and forth and going nowhere.

"I trusted you once, Jonah. Way back when, I considered you my best friend." A lump rose to Abby's throat and that tight squeezing returned, stealing her breath. She absolutely did not want to go down this road again. But she couldn't seem to stop herself. "You let me down. Big time. Not only that day in the office but you weren't there when I delivered. I was so scared. And all alone."

"I came to your apartment after that office visit. I tried to discuss the situation with you." Jonah leaned forward, resting his forearms on his thighs, his gaze riveted to her. "You wouldn't listen to anything I had to say. You screamed at me to leave you alone and made it clear you wanted nothing more to do with me."

"Do you blame me?" She cursed the fact that her voice was thick with emotion. "You wanted me to kill the baby growing inside me."

He flinched and his cheeks reddened as if she'd slapped him. But he couldn't argue the point. No, he couldn't argue because everything she'd said was true.

"Veronica was—"

"Screw Veronica. Stop using her as an excuse." Abby's tone sliced the air like a whip. "We're talking about *you*, Jonah, not her. We're talking about you abandoning the child—your child—who was growing inside me. We're talking about you leaving one of your oldest friends--who'd only wanted to help you and your wife--swinging alone in the wind."

"You still hold that decision against me." He voice was heavy with resignation.

She didn't feel an ounce of sympathy.

"Damn right I still hold that against you. And I will until the day I die." Though blood ran hot through her veins, her tone could have frozen ice. Abby's heart hammered against her chest and her entire body trembled with rage. She was glad she was seated because she wasn't sure she'd be able to stand.

She lifted her hands, palms down and concentrated on calming herself. "This is about Eva Grace and what's best for her."

From the moment Abby first felt the baby first move inside her, everything had become about what was best for this child growing inside her. The hope of one day owning and running a successful business, the reason that had led her to accept Jonah and Veronica's offer, had fallen to a distant second place.

Jonah leaned back against the sofa and expelled a heavy breath, suddenly looking much older than thirty. "Let's see if I've got this straight. You're willing to let me become better acquainted with Eva Grace so you can assess if I'll make a proper guardian for her in the event you're unexpectedly killed."

"In a nutshell, yes."

"You realize she's my biological daughter. I've paid child support since she was born. While I may not have asserted my legal rights before, that doesn't mean I couldn't take you to court now."

Abby quit breathing. The blood in her veins stopped flowing and she went cold all over. She'd been a fool to let him get close to Eva Grace, to even consider for one moment that she could trust—

"I won't pursue legal action." He spoke quickly as if realizing a second too late he might not have been clear. "I sent the money because Eva Grace is my daughter. You are her mother. You're the one who has cared for her and loved her even before she was born."

"Why did you bring up taking me to court?" Abby clasped her hands together to still their trembling. Her entire body quivered, not with fear, but rage.

Like a snake, anger slithered and coiled around her.

"I want to get to know my daughter." His eyes were fierce and determined. "But this isn't a game. I won't have Eva Grace used as a pawn."

"I would never make her a pawn in—"

"You said you'd decide the next step after she and I become acquainted." Jonah inclined his head. "Were you thinking of simply tossing me aside if you decide Matilda or Nell would be a better choice?"

"I'm still figuring this out." Abby lifted her chin. She would not let him make her feel inadequate simply because she didn't have all the steps plotted out.

"Let me tell you how I see it." The stubborn tilt to his jaw, the same one she'd seen many times growing up, returned. "Eva Grace and I will get better acquainted. But I will not, I repeat, I will not step out of her life. I will not become her friend and then abandon her."

"I wasn't suggesting—"

"It sure sounded that way to me." Blue eyes glinted with warning. "I abandoned my daughter once. I won't make that mistake again."

"I imagine bringing Jonah back into Eva Grace's life was a difficult decision." Nell slanted Abby a sideways look as the two women jogged at a steady pace down one of the many hiking/biking trails that ran through town.

After dropping Eva Grace off at school, Abby met Nell at The Green. Over the course of a three-mile run, she told Nell everything. All about the surrogacy contract, about Jonah and Veronica and about her decision to let Jonah get to know acquainted with Eva Grace.

Nell let her talk uninterrupted until she finished. Though her friend hadn't commented as Abby relayed the facts, her attentiveness told her Nell's attorney brain was busy processing everything she said.

"I'm still not certain it was the right decision." Abby slowed her pace as the end of the course came into view.

"You could have asked one of us." Nell's ice blue eyes searched Abby's. "I can't speak for anyone else, but I'd happily take in the munchkin."

"I know you would." Abby stopped at a bench and bent over to stretch.

"You made yourself believe he was your only option." Nell paused and stretched beside her, her body long and lean.

"I did."

"Even though you had other options."

Trust Nell to cut to point.

"I never knew my father."

If Nell found the abrupt comment confusing, it didn't show. She gestured to Starbucks coffee kiosk, located in the center of the Green. "Let's fuel up. My treat."

Once they had the steaming cups of their favorite dark roast in hand, they took a seat on one of the benches scattered throughout the area.

Nell studied Abby over the top of her cup. "What happened with your dad?"

"He left when I was six. I remember only bits and pieces of him." Abby sighed. "But I missed him. As I got older and watched my friends with their dads, in one breath I desperately wished he'd come back. In the next breath, I hated him for leaving me."

Nell took a long drink of coffee and sat back, cradling the cup between her fingers.

At that moment Abby understood why she was so effective in the courtroom. When Cornelia Ambrose looked at you in that way, you wanted to tell her everything without her even asking.

She met Nell's gaze. "I didn't ask for Jonah to come here. But now that he is…"

Abby's voice trailed off. When she'd spoken with Jonah she'd been certain involving him in Eva Grace's life was the right decision. Now, she wasn't so sure.

"Do you think he'd harm Eva Grace?"

"Harm her?" Abby's voice rose.

"Physically? Emotionally? Psychologically?"

"No." Abby answered immediately.

"He ran out on you. Left you with total care of *his* baby. You had to give up your dreams." Though the words were harsh, Nell's voice remained conversational. "All you were trying to do was help give two friends their dream."

Abby expelled a ragged breath. She couldn't argue with facts. "That's why I'm not telling Eva Grace that he's her father."

"To punish him?"

"What? No." Then again, for more emphasis. "No."

"Frankly, I don't see the purpose in not telling her." Nell tilted her head. "C'mon, Abs. You decide to let him in—"

"Just a little."

"You decided to let him in," Nell repeated. "The odds are, during these next few weeks or months, he's not going to do anything so heinous that you'll kick him out of her life. With that being the case, why not tell the munchkin the truth upfront?"

"I don't want Eva Grace hurt." Abby lifted her chin, but the movement reminded her of Jonah. She immediately lowered her jaw. "We'll take this slow and we'll do it my way."

CHAPTER THIRTEEN

Jonah wondered if it was deliberate that his first outing with Abby and Eva Grace involved a whole herd of people. Though he would have preferred some one-on-one time, he had to admit Liz Canfield's backyard barbecue was a good opportunity to get better acquainted with the citizens of Hazel Green.

Abby had been matter-of-fact when she'd texted about the Friday event. She'd given him the date and time and told him to meet her and Eva Grace there…if it worked for him.

He'd met Liz at Leo's party but wasn't sure she would remember him. Still, Abby would hardly invite him without checking with her friend first.

Liz lived in a neighborhood of what he recognized as Craftsman-style homes. Her single-story home, painted dark blue with ivory trim, boasted a large porch that ran the entire length of the front. The door, a vivid burgundy, drew the eye.

Jonah started up the front steps but paused at a burst of raucous laughter coming from the back of the house. With a six pack of beer dangling from one hand, he backtracked and followed a walkway around to the terrace.

A monster grill, manned by Leo, held burgers and brats. A quick scan of the crowd told Jonah all of Abby's friends—at least the ones he'd met--were here. He located Abby, surrounded by three of them.

Safety in numbers.

The second the thought flashed, he dismissed it. If she truly felt that way about spending time with him, it was going to be a long and arduous getting re-acquainted period.

The only child in attendance, other than Eva Grace, was a boy several years older. The two of them were in the far back of the yard, playing tether ball.

Jonah wondered if Abby noticed the boy was a full head taller than Eva Grace. While at the moment he appeared to be taking her younger age into account, if he let loose with the ball it could do damage.

It would be good to remind the boy to be gentle with—

"Jonah." Matilda stepped in front of him. "Abby mentioned you were going to try to stop by."

He glanced around her, keeping Eva Grace and the boy in sight. Thankfully, his daughter was getting ready to serve. That wasn't to say the boy couldn't do damage if he blocked and smacked the ball back in her face.

Matilda's hand settled on his arm. "Sawyer is a kind boy."

Jonah inclined his head.

"Sawyer, Liz's son." Matilda smiled. "He's the child playing with Eva Grace. He won't hurt her."

It was crazy the way the woman had read his mind.

"He's bigger, stronger."

"Sawyer understands she's a little one."

"If he forgets…" The thought of that hard ball hitting Eva Grace in the face made him shudder.

"He won't." Matilda patted his arm.

Though Jonah doubted the woman was much past forty, there was something mom-like in her manner.

"Have you met our hostess?" Matilda shifted, effectively blocking his view of Eva Grace and Sawyer.

"Briefly at Leo's party." He brought the picture of her into his head. Brown and brown. Five five. One hundred twenty pounds. Early thirties. "She's a reporter."

"She was."

Jonah pulled his brows together. "She was interviewing Nell, er Hazel Green, for the local paper."

"Freelance work, though it'd be nice if it became permanent." Matilda slipped an arm through his. "Liz had been a reporter for one of the Chicago dailies but was cut in the big layoffs last year. She found a job at a rival paper, but in circulation. She's a reporter at heart."

Jonah nodded. He understood. Liz obviously felt the same way about reporting as he felt about law enforcement. His passion for justice was something Veronica had never understood.

"Let's say hello to the hostess, then I'll take you to Abby." Matilda slanted a glance at him. "She'll be happy to see you."

Jonah wasn't sure about that, but he was here. And he wasn't going anywhere.

Abby's breath caught in her throat when she spotted Jonah. She kept her gaze focused on Nell and pretended to be engrossed in the story her friend was telling. But her gaze kept slipping back to the police chief who didn't look much like a cop in his jeans and long-sleeved t-shirt. Especially with a six pack of beer dangling from one hand.

When Abby had seen the barbecue on her calendar, she decided it would be a way to observe Jonah's interactions with Eva Grace. Best of all, she wouldn't be alone with him.

Which seemed ridiculous considering all the years she'd

known him. Until she reminded herself the man had proved unpredictable.

Abby sensed him behind her, even before there was a lull in the conversation and he spoke her name.

She turned and offered a polite smile, the kind you give a person you're trying to remember. "Jonah. Glad you could make it."

"It was kind of Liz to invite me." Jonah nodded to everyone in the circle, noting Rachel was there with the salesman.

"Marc, this is Chief Rollins." Rachel offered him a warm smile. "He took Harold's place on the Birthday Bash committee. He's done an amazing job with event security."

"Harold and his team did the amazing job." Jonah spoke easily, then extended his hand. "Jonah Rollins. I don't believe we had a chance to meet at the party."

"Marc Koenig." The man clasped Jonah's hand in a shake that could easily have turned into a wrestling match.

Five seven. Receding dark hair with pale blue eyes. Too much wining and dining of clients had left Marc soft and paunchy.

"You're a salesman?" Jonah asked politely.

"I'm a Financial Advisor for Lawton Wealth Management."

At Jonah's blank look, Marc continued. "Lawton is one of the top wealth and investment management firms in the Midwest."

"Sounds interesting." Jonah shifted his gaze to Rachel. "You're both in service professions."

Marc scoffed. "You can hardly compare herding a bunch of volunteers at a local Foodbank to handling millions of dollars in assets for some of the wealthiest families in the Chicago area."

The smile that had blossomed on Rachel's lips disappeared.

Beside Jonah, Abby began to vibrate.

Abby opened her mouth but Rachel's hand on her arm stilled whatever she'd been about to say.

"Marc, I know I said I wasn't hungry, but the smell of those brats have convinced me to give one a try." Rachel smiled up at him. "Would you mind getting me one?"

He hesitated for only a second, then glanced around the circle. "If you'll excuse me."

"Gladly," Nell muttered.

Jonah fought the urge to smile.

"Why do you let him say those things?" Abby's soft voice radiated concern as did the look she offered her friend.

"Marc isn't a bad guy," Rachel spoke slowly, as if carefully choosing her words. "He's a bit insecure. That insecurity sometimes comes out as jerkiness."

Nell, Abby and Matilda didn't say anything for several heartbeats. Then Matilda cast a pointed glance at Abby.

"I don't mean to get into your business." Abby lowered her voice when she saw Marc headed back in their direction. "I just want the best for you."

"We all do," Nell said.

"Rachel is a strong woman." Matilda gave Rachel's shoulder a pat. "She makes good decisions."

Jonah wasn't sure what to think when Abby slipped her arm through his. "Let me show you Liz's flowerbed. It's incredible. She even has hollyhocks."

He barely had a chance to lift his hand in farewell, when Abby pulled him from the group.

"I've had enough of that man to last me a lifetime," Abby muttered once they were out of earshot. "That last comment of his nearly pushed me over the edge. If I stayed any longer, I'd have punched him."

"Don't hold back." Jonah chuckled. "Tell me how you really feel about the guy."

"He's not good enough for her."

"On that, we're in complete and total agreement."

Surprise flashed in Abby's dark eyes. "You barely know him."

"Trained observer, remember?" He grinned, then sobered. "How did she get hooked up with someone like him?"

"You mean a man whose 'jerkiness' comes out when he feels insecure? Which, based on his behavior, is all the time?"

"Yeah." Jonah nodded. "That's what I'm asking."

They stopped in front of a large, well-tended flower bed which held a stand of hollyhocks in rich shades of purple, red, orange and yellow. Jonah knew Abby had likely mentioned the old-fashioned flower as a diversion, but wondered if she remembered they were his mother's favorite flower. Her garden back home held all these colors and more.

Abby absently rubbed a petal between her fingers. "Once Brandon--he's Rachel's youngest sibling—graduated from high school, she started dipping her toe into the dating pool."

The imagery had Jonah smiling.

"For the first six months or so, she dated a variety of guys. Then, Marc asked her out." Abby's lips thinned. "At first, he was very charming. He'd ask her where she wanted to go, what she'd like to do. He was attentive and sweet."

Jonah frowned. "What changed?"

"He did." Abby's tone was matter-of-fact. "Or rather his true self came out. Now they do what he wants to do. He picks where they eat He even orders for her."

Abby sounded so appalled at the notion, he had to grin. "The nerve of the man."

Jonah expected a swift comeback but the lines between Abby's brows only deepened. "It's creepy when he does it."

She was genuinely worried about her friend. Jonah dropped the teasing tone.

"Have you tried speaking with her privately about your concerns?" He swiveled, just enough to keep Sawyer and Eva Grace in sight.

Abby sighed. "I mentioned it might be good to see what other guys were out there before settling down to one."

She looked so unhappy Jonah had to resist the urge to pull her into his arms and assure her everything would be okay. But, she likely wouldn't appreciate him touching her and the truth was, he didn't know if Rachel's relationship with Marc would end well.

During his law enforcement career, he'd seen his share of controlling men. Sometimes the women stayed with them, even when it was clear they should leave. "Rachel is a smart woman."

Abby glanced at him in surprise. "How do you know that? You've barely exchanged ten words."

"We had a nice conversation on the walk to your hotel the other day." Jonah informed her. "She's sharp."

"She's also nice. And kind."

Jonah forgot all about Marc and Rachel when he saw Eva Grace and the boy had abandoned the tether ball and were now playing tag. He returned his attention to Abby and discovered her attention was also on Eva Grace.

"I worried about them playing with the tether ball." Abby kept her voice low. "Sawyer is a nice boy, but he's bigger and stronger than Eva Grace. If he hit that ball hard—"

"It could smack her in the face and do some serious damage."

"Exactly." Her gaze grew thoughtful. "I was super protective of her those first years. I'm trying to loosen the reins and give her some freedom, but it's difficult."

"With her in braces, you had to watch out for her."

Surprise skittered across her face. "I'm surprised you're not on Nell's 'let the kid be a kid for goodness sake' bandwagon."

"Nell doesn't have children."

"Neither do you." Abby caught herself. "I'm sorry, I—"

"No. You're right." Jonah tried not to take offense. He hadn't spent the last five years raising a child. This *was* new to him. "But remember, I have siblings. I hit the tetherball into Jackie's face one summer so hard I knocked out her front tooth. Luckily it was a baby tooth and already loose, but still—"

"You do understand."

Something in Abby's tone told him she was uncomfortable with them being on the same parenting wavelength.

"Marc brought her a beer." Jonah narrowed his gaze. "She's not taking it."

Even from where they stood, Jonah heard the anger in Marc's voice.

"He knows better." Abby motioned for him to follow her as she headed toward Rachel.

"She doesn't like beer?"

"Her parents were killed by a drunk driver." Abby's words rushed out only moments before they reached the couple.

"I've had one beer," Marc's eyes flashed. "Big deal."

"You've had two." Rachel didn't raise her voice to his level.

Jonah wondered if that was a trick she'd learned when raising her siblings. His mom always spoke even more softly when involved in a 'discussion' with one of her children.

"I'm the designated driver this evening, so I'm sticking to iced tea."

"You really think one beer will put you over the legal limit?" Marc taunted.

"I will not drive after drinking. Period. I don't care if my blood alcohol level is under the legal limit." Rachel's chin jutted out. "We agreed I would drive tonight."

Her tone brooked no argument. It was clear, at least to Jonah that no matter what Marc said, he wasn't going to change her mind.

The fact that the rising tension between the couple was threatening to derail Liz's party, had Jonah clapping a hand on Marc's shoulder. He forced a friendly tone. "You've got a smart woman there. I wish every citizen of Hazel Green showed such restraint and good sense."

When the tense set to Marc's jaw didn't ease, Jonah added, "I don't know if you heard, but the guy who nearly hit Abby head-on had been drinking."

"His blood alcohol was twice the legal limit." Nell simply shrugged when Jonah glanced at her. "I have friends in the district attorney's office."

"The man who killed Rachel's parents was drunk." Liz placed a supportive hand on her friend's shoulder. Though she spoke to Rachel, she shot a pointed glance in the salesman's direction. "You're making the right decision. Everyone here should support you."

It was a dig. From the hot flush creeping up Marc's neck he got the message loud and clear.

Jonah waited, knowing this would play out in one of two ways. Either Marc would say to hell with everyone and become even more belligerent, or he'd back down.

"If you don't want a beer, that's okay." Marc popped the top. "I'll just enjoy it myself."

Rachel didn't say anything and neither did anyone around her when Marc slung an arm around her shoulder.

Other than that incident, the evening was pleasant with lots of laughter and conversation.

When Abby announced it was time to head for home, Jonah and Eva Grace had just finished slaughtering Liz and Sawyer in lawn darts. Who knew a childhood talent for tossing oversized darts into rings could come in handy?

"We won every game," Eva Grace told her mother as Jonah walked them to their car. The child shot him a blinding smile. "It was fun."

"I enjoyed it," Jonah agreed. "Perhaps we can do it again sometime."

He kept his tone off-hand, hoping Abby didn't feel as if he was pressuring her. Still, he wanted her to know he was interested in continuing to get better acquainted with his daughter. And her.

"Do you like school carnivals?" Eva Grace asked.

Jonah smiled. "I haven't been to one in long time, but yeah, I used to love them."

Eva Grace turned pleading eyes in her mother's direction.

After an instant's hesitation, Abby turned to Jonah. "Eva Grace's school is holding a carnival on Sunday. Would you like to go with us?"

"I'd love to go."

"Yay." Eva Grace twirled.

Jonah understood. Right now, he felt like twirling, too.

CHAPTER FOURTEEN

Abby instructed Jonah to meet her and Eva Grace in the school gymnasium at one. Since it was a beautiful fall day, she and Eva Grace set out for the school on foot.

Being behind the wheel still caused her stomach to jitter. She could drive. Had driven herself a few blocks. But it didn't give her the pleasure it once had.

Baby steps, she told herself.

Given time, the fear would fade completely. Or so she hoped.

"Jonah." Eva Grace called out then sprinted down the sidewalk.

When Eva Grace reached him, he swung the child high in the air. Then, he turned to her, his grin infectious. "Hi, Abby. Beautiful day for a walk."

For the first time Abby realized she didn't know where Jonah lived. Had he secured a place near downtown? Hers was the only hotel in the historic district and he wasn't staying under her roof. No, siree, that would be *way* too close for comfort.

Setting Eva Grace down, but keeping her small hand in his, he fell into step beside Abby. "This is a nice coincidence."

For a second, Abby said nothing. She knew as surely as she

knew her own name that him showing up on the street in front of her hotel was anything but random.

She lifted a brow. "I don't believe I asked where you're living."

"I was lucky enough to get a short-term lease on a condo in Greenbriar Place."

"Those are nice units." In this instance, nice fell under the category of extreme understatement. The 20-unit brick and stone condominium building had been erected late last year. With ten-foot ceilings, a rooftop garden and underground parking, the high-end units sold for astronomically high prices. "I didn't think rentals were allowed."

"Short-term leases only," Jonah confirmed. "This one was available for three months while the owner is out of the country. That suited me fine, since it gives me a chance to get to know the community better and decide where I want to live."

"Your condo is just down the street from Eva Grace's school."

He nodded absently, his gaze drawn in the direction of a black squirrel Eva Grace was pointing at.

"Both of those buildings are on the other side of The Green."

The blue eyes that fixed on her looked like pools of azure in the sunshine. "Are you trying to make a point?"

Busted, she wanted to say, but refrained. Instead, she pointed out the obvious. "We live in the opposite direction of the school."

He chuckled. "I got ready early and decided to take a walk before heading to the school."

"That's when you saw me and Mommy," Eva Grace's loud voice had the squirrel scampering up the nearest tree.

"I did." He gave the child's hand a swing. "Now, we can walk to the school together."

Was he telling the truth? Impossible to say. That worried her. She needed to keep control of the situation and right now things felt out of control.

"Watch me skip." Eva Grace let go of Jonah's hand and took off down the walkway.

"I didn't deliberately run into you." Jonah's gaze met Abby's. "I'm grateful to you for letting me spend time with you and Eva Grace."

Those blue eyes were strong and steady on hers.

She gave a curt nod, ignoring the pressure inside her chest. They'd once been friends, good friends, and seeing him again brought old memories flooding back.

But she couldn't forget what he'd done. If she pushed those hurts to the back of her mind, he could hurt her again. And, if he hurt her, Eva Grace could be caught in the crossfire.

Abby expelled a breath when the school came into view. The new, one-story brick building took up an entire block. Today, a banner over the front door announced the "Helen Potter Elementary Fall Carnival" in brightly colored letters.

Jonah held the door open for them.

When Abby stepped inside the shiny hall, signs lined the hallway advertising the booths they could expect to see once they followed the arrows to the gym.

"Twenty ways to—" Eva Grace paused in front of a sign featuring pumpkins covered in everything from candy corn to googly eyes. "de-co-"

The child looked to Jonah for assistance.

Abby gave a subtle shake of her head.

"You're doing great. Keep sounding it out." Jonah offered the girl an encouraging smile. "You'll get it."

Eva Grace's brows pulled together and her face held a look of intense concentration. Abby recalled seeing that same look a time or two on Jonah's face when he was stumped by something.

"Rate?" The little girl cast imploring eyes in Abby's direction.

Abby could see the frustration starting to build. She reminded herself that though Eva Grace was a whiz at reading, she was still five years old.

Putting a hand on her daughter's shoulder, Abby kept her voice calm. "Let's you and I put it together. De-co-rate."

She saw the second the word registered. "Tell me what it is."

Eva Grace smiled triumphantly. "Decorate."

Jonah held out a hand for a fist bump. "Twenty ways to decorate pumpkins."

"Without carving," Abby added, reading the small print.

"Can we do that?" Eva Grace's gaze shifted from Jonah to Abby then back to Jonah.

Jonah grinned. "I believe that's why we're here."

Jonah stood beside Abby and watched Eva Grace round the squares in the cake walk. A bright bouncy tune that reminded him of a carnival played, then abruptly stopped.

He recognized the volunteer running the game as Frank Partridge. The white-haired man with a full beard, was the postal carrier assigned to the downtown district. In a deep voice, capable of carrying to the back row of any theater, Frank called out the next number.

Eva Grace glanced down, then shrugged good-naturedly while the boy in front of her jumped high in the air and uttered a loud whoop.

This was Eva Grace's second time around the circle and he had the feeling she was going to go round and round until she won something. Of course, it wasn't like there were other games left to play.

They'd already visited the ring toss, the balloon pop and the tic-tac-throw. But Jonah's favorite was the picture Abby held in her hands, the one taken of him and Eva Grace at the photo booth. Eva Grace had stuck her head through the lion's face and his had gone through the opening for the Circus Ringmaster.

Abby glanced down. "She looks just like you."

Jonah studied the picture. "You can see the resemblance."

She pushed the photo into his hands. "Keep it."

"You don't want it?" he asked even as his fingers closed around the precious photo. It was the first—and only—photo he had of him with his daughter.

"I have lots of pictures." Her gaze didn't meet his.

She was being generous, but didn't want to appear so.

He gave a short nod and slipped the picture carefully into his jacket pocket just as Liz hurried up.

"Abby." Her friend's eyes widened just a little at the sight of Jonah. "Chief."

"I think we know each other well enough that you can call me Jonah."

Liz smiled. Then, catching Eva Grace's eye, she waved at the child.

Abby glanced around. "Where's Sawyer?"

"It's his weekend with his dad."

"Did you tell him the school carnival was this weekend?"

"Yes." Liz lifted her hands, let them drop, then changed the subject. "Can I get a picture of the two of you?"

A startled look crossed Abby's face. "Why?"

"I'm doing a small article on the carnival for the Chronicle. Even though Hank didn't ask for photos, I thought I'd take a bunch and see if any of them work."

"Fine with me," Jonah said. "If it's okay with Abby."

"I suppose."

If Liz noticed Abby's reluctance, it didn't show. "Just turn back like you were and watch the cake walk. Pretend I'm not here."

Just then the music stopped and Frank bellowed out another number.

The smile on Eva Grace's face when she realized she was standing on the winning square had Jonah forgetting all about Liz.

He gave Eva Grace thumbs up then turned to Abby. "She won."

"She did." Abby's smile was as big as Eva Grace's.

For a second Jonah basked in the warmth of it.

"I'll catch up with you guys, later." Liz patted Abby on the shoulder, shot Jonah a speculative glance followed by a smile and hurried off.

Jonah lifted a hand in farewell then turned back to Abby. God, she was beautiful. While the mustard-colored shirt matched the plaid pants that hugged her slender legs like a glove, and her hair, pulled back from her face with a stretchy band, shone like polished mahogany under the fluorescent lights, it was her full lips that captured his attention.

Slick with gloss, he couldn't identify the color except to say it was some shade of red. Whatever it was it looked amazing on her.

Jonah had gotten a brief taste of her mouth the other day. That had been a mistake. The problem was, it hadn't felt like a mistake. It had felt real. And right.

A platter containing a chocolate cake covered in plastic wrap shoved into his midsection, pulled his thoughts back from the fantasy of him and Abby. After what he'd done, he was lucky she was even talking to him.

"Look what I won." Eva Grace hopped from one foot to the other.

"I can't believe you carried this big cake all the way over here by yourself," he told her, lifting the platter from her hands.

"You were looking at Mommy." She smiled, not seeming bothered by that fact. "She was looking at you."

Jonah's gaze shot to Abby. Could it be he wasn't the only one interested?

The cool look in her eyes dashed that second of wishful thinking.

"Well," Abby's smile didn't reach her eyes, "as fun as this has been, it's time to head home."

"Please, can't we--" Eva Grace stopped when Abby shot her a glance.

"You have school tomorrow. We still need to eat dinner then get your bath—"

"I've an idea." Jonah tightened his fingers around the cake platter. "My refrigerator is fully stocked. Why don't you stop at my place? It's a block away. We can whip up something then eat on the rooftop garden?"

"Eat on a roof?" Eva Grace's eyes went wide. "Like the kind on top of a house?"

Jonah smiled. "This roof is flat with lots of flowers. And it overlooks The Green."

"I want to eat on a roof." Eva Grace spun around. "That would be awesome."

"If we did, we wouldn't be able to stay long." Abby chewed on her bottom lip, her desire to end the day with him clearly at odds with a desire to get an up close and personal look at Greenbriar Place.

Still, she hesitated. Likely calculating how much extra time this would add to their day. As much as he'd envisioned them cooking together, he'd save that for another time.

"There's an organic grocery store just around the corner that has take-out. We could grab something and take it up to the roof."

"Please, Mommy." Eva Grace put her hands together as if praying. "I've never eaten on a roof before."

Abby's gaze slid from her daughter to Jonah. When she gave a little laugh, he realized this 'awesome' day wasn't over yet.

Abby finished off the last bite of her caramel sea salt macaroon and realized how much better she felt ten days post-accident. Her wrists no longer ached and the scratches and facial bruising weren't anything a little make-up couldn't conceal.

It wasn't only the physical, Abby realized. Making the decision to let Eva Grace get better acquainted with Jonah had eased some mental strain. She still wasn't certain she could fully trust him, but was reminded of what Nell had once said; people are incapable of hiding their true self.

When Nell had tossed out the comment last year, after a breakup with an attorney from Chicago, Abby remembered nodding her head in complete and total agreement.

She'd been thinking of Jonah at the time, recalling how he'd disappointed her. What did it say about her that she was now giving a man who'd shown her his true colors a second chance? She glanced across the table where he and Eva Grace were making up a story. From the way they were laughing it must be a funny one.

Abby reminded herself that she wasn't really giving him a second chance. That would mean opening up her heart and letting him back in. That, was definitely out of the question.

What she was doing, was making the best of a bad—and awkward—situation. She was merely seeing how Jonah interacted with Eva Grace so she could assess whether he would be the best choice to care for her daughter if anything should happen to her.

So far, he hadn't done anything to make her eliminate the possibility.

"Then the big bear growled and said, "Give me your bike." Eva Grace offered up a monster growl then fell into a fit of giggling.

With a grin a mile wide, Jonah shifted his gaze and met Abby's eyes.

The look of pure joy on his face was so engaging, she couldn't help but smile back. By the time Abby realized what she was doing and squelched the smile, his attention was back on Eva Grace.

"But the girl jumped on her bike and rode away, the sound of the bear's roar following her down the path."

Abby resisted the urge to roll her eyes. While she'd give them two points for creativity, this was no Caldecott award winner they were plotting.

With the macaroon now history, she took a sip of wine and leaned back in her chair. The rooftop garden was nicer than she'd imagined. Strategically placed heat lamps warmed the air just enough to take away any chill. Humongous urns filled with flowers added bright splashes of color.

There were even trees, actual trees, planted in huge containers, their leaves beginning to turn red, yellow and orange. When they'd first stepped out of the elevator, most of the tables had been filled with residents and their guests enjoying wine and conversation.

Eva Grace had been the only child in view and they'd been the only table eating. Over the last hour, the rooftop had cleared and right now, for the first time since they arrived, they were alone.

That was one of the reasons, she didn't make any attempt to shush Eva Grace when her daughter squealed with glee. From what Abby could gather, the bear fell into a deep hole while chasing the girl.

"I want to make up another story." Eva Grace leaned forward, resting her arms on the table. "This one will have fairies."

Jonah slanted a glance in Abby's direction. "We've been ignoring your mother."

"Mommy can make up stories with us."

"That's one solution." Jonah appeared to be giving Eva Grace's suggestion a lot of thought. "Or, we could go back to my apartment and pick out a game we could all play? Maybe have a cookie?"

"We just had macaroons for dessert," Abby reminded him.

Eva Grace wrinkled her nose. She'd only taken a tiny bit of hers forcing Abby to finish it for her.

"Do you have chocolate chip?" Eva Grace asked.

"Of course." Jonah grinned. "They're the best."

They reached Jonah's floor and Eva Grace ran ahead, his key card clutched tightly between her fingers. On the way down to his floor, Eva Grace had asked politely if she could open the door to the apartment with 'the card.' She'd been fascinated ever since she'd watched him open the door to his unit without a key.

"I don't know what kind of games you have," Abby kept her voice low. "But with her being only five, there's not many games she can play."

"I think I've got one or two that we can all agree upon."

Abby started to open her mouth again, but decided to wait and see if any of the ones he had were appropriate.

Once inside, Jonah headed to the spacious, state-of-the-art kitchen and retrieved a white cookie jar in the shape of a clown.

It had a big red nose and a creepy grin.

Abby recognized the jar instantly. "That used to be your mother's."

He pulled out several cookies and set them on a blue ceramic plate. These chocolate chip cookies were too perfect to have come from anywhere but the bakery down the street. "Mom gave the jar to me after Veronica and I split."

Abby understood why Nancy Rollins had waited. She couldn't imagine Veronica ever allowing the clown in her kitchen. Where would she put it? Certainly not next to the stylish Radio Eight coffeemaker with its black walnut wood and hand-blown glass that had been Veronica's pride and joy.

Not that Abby blamed the woman for not wanting the clown. There was something about the grin that made her shiver. But she knew Jonah loved it.

"Do you want to take the cookies and the games back up to the roof or play here?"

Abby wondered if Jonah would be willing to give Marc a few lessons on give and take. The thought made her smile.

"Let's play here." As much as Abby had enjoyed the rooftop, the setting had a romantic feel that made her uneasy. "We can't stay long. Eva Grace has school tomorrow. What games do you have?"

Ignoring the question, Jonah held up a glass milk bottle and raised a brow. Abby recognized the brand. Hormone and antibiotic free.

She inclined her head and watched Jonah fill a glass half-full.

"Would you like a glass as well?"

Abby shook her head. "I'm not sure it goes all that well with wine."

Eva Grace sat at the counter with her cookies and milk while Jonah opened a cabinet under the large flat-screened television. He glanced back at Abby. "I'll tell you what games I have and you and Eva Grace can pick."

"I want to play Hisss."

Abby turned to her daughter. "I'm sure Jonah doesn't have—"

"As a matter of fact, it's right here." Beneath several games Abby recognized, Jonah pulled out a bright blue box with a multi-colored snake on the front.

"Yay." Eva Grace set down her glass of milk and clapped. "I'm going to get the most snakes."

"We'll see about that," Jonah teased.

"How do you have all these kid's games?" Abby was genuinely perplexed. She'd counted at least five in the drawer, four that she had in her home.

"I wanted to be prepared if Eva Grace ever came over." A sheepish look crossed his face. "I did some online research and these games are top-rated by both parents and children in her age range."

It was, Abby thought, incredibly sweet. It also had a knot forming in her gut. She couldn't forget that his arrival in Hazel Green hadn't been simply happenstance.

They'd just finished setting up the game on the glossy black dining room table when the buzzer sounded from the lobby. Requiring the residents to release the door leading to the elevators added an extra layer of security.

Jonah moved to the intercom. "Yes?"

"Jonah." Though it had been over five years, Abby recognized Nancy Rollin's voice immediately. "Your dad and I are in the lobby. Can you buzz us up?"

"Sure."

When he turned away from the intercom, Abby had to resist the overwhelming urge to bolt. Her gaze narrowed on him. "Did you know they were coming? Is that why you invited us here?"

"What? No." Then he repeated, as if wanting to make sure there was no misunderstanding. "No. I had no idea they were coming. I'm not sure why they're here."

The puzzled look in his eyes told Abby this hadn't been a set-up. Still, seeing his parents again was bound to be awkward. While she wasn't about to race out the door like a scared rabbit, neither did she plan to hang around a second longer than necessary.

"Eva Grace. We need to get going."

Her daughter looked up, cookie in hand, her face dusted with crumbs. The same puzzled look that had been in Jonah's eyes now filled hers. Only for a different reason. "But we were going to play Hisss."

"Another time." Abby flashed a bright smile. "Jonah has company."

"You could stay." He offered her a hopeful look. "I know they'd love to see you both."

"No." Abby stood, knowing any minute his parents would be at the door.

Good manners dictated a pleasant hello, but that's all Michael and Nancy would get out of her.

They hadn't had time for her five years ago.

She didn't have time for them, now.

CHAPTER FIFTEEN

Jonah wasn't sure who was most startled to see Abby and Eva Grace. His mom, who gave him a quick hug, or his dad, who greeted him with a slap on the shoulder. Both came to an abrupt stop just inside his doorway when they spotted Abby.

His mother's gaze fell on Eva Grace and she sucked in breath. He knew what she was thinking. The child was the spitting image of his twin sister, Jackie.

Because he was watching, Jonah saw the muscle jump in Abby's jaw when his mother's gaze dropped to Eva Grace's feet, to the stylish high-tops decorated with unicorns and rainbows.

Not that Jonah blamed his mother. They'd learned through a friend who worked at the hospital, that Eva Grace had been born with a meningocele and had undergone surgery after birth and spent time in the NICU.

That was all Jonah knew until he'd seen her bounce out of her chair with those cherry red lips for Show and Share.

"Abby." Nancy Rollins's voice was thick with emotion. "This is a wonderful surprise."

Nancy glanced at Jonah as if requesting information. He gave his head a barely perceptible shake. Now was not the time or place for that discussion.

"Hello, Nancy. Michael." Abby reached down and took her daughter's hand. "We were just leaving."

Before she could make her exit, Eva Grace spoke.

"Hi. I'm Eva Grace Fine. What's your name?"

Nancy crouched down so that she was at eye level with the child. "My name is Nancy. I'm Jonah's mother."

Eva Grace's face brightened. "You gave him the clown."

Nancy glanced at her son for clarification.

"Abby recognized the clown cookie jar." Jonah rested a hand on his daughter's shoulder in a gesture that had Abby shooting him a sharp look. "I mentioned my mother had given it to me."

"When Jonah was a little boy, I always kept that jar filled with cookies." Nancy offered a stony-faced Abby a smile before refocusing on Eva Grace. "Your mommy used to help me bake when she was not much older than you are now."

The child's eyes brightened as she looked to her mother for confirmation.

"That was a long time ago." Abby squeezed her daughter's hand. "Well, it's been—"

"I'm Michael Rollins." Jonah's dad stepped forward and extended his hand to the child. "I'm Jonah's dad."

Eva Grace released her mother's hand and put her small one in his. "Pleased to meet you, Mr. Rollins."

Jonah knew Abby had been working with her daughter on manners and the girl's flash of a smile nearly undid his father's control. His Adam's apple worked convulsively in his throat.

"It's a pleasure." Michael's voice sounded rusty as if it hadn't been used in ages. He cleared his throat. "You can call me—"

Though Jonah truly hoped his dad hadn't planned to ask the child to call him 'grandpa,' just to be sure he shot him a warning glance.

"Michael," his father said after a tense second.

"There's a Michael in my class at school." Eva Grace lowered her voice. "He can be mean, sometimes."

Michael blinked. Then the experience of raising four kids kicked in. "I'm not mean, but I can be silly."

Eva Grace giggled. "I like you."

The remark had his father clearing his throat once again. "I like you, too."

"We really must be going." Abby's tone remained polite but distant.

She held out her hand to Eva Grace, but before the child could reach over and take it, Nancy wrapped her arms around Abby for a long second, then stepped back. "It's so good to see you."

Jonah held his breath, not sure how Abby would respond.

Her face remained carefully blank as she took her daughter's hand then turned to Jonah. "Don't worry about taking us home. I can get an Uber."

"I'm driving you. It will just take a few minutes." Jonah spoke quickly when her eyes flashed dark fire. "Mom, Dad, make yourself at home. Abby and Eva Grace live close. I won't be long."

Without waiting for his parents to answer, he ushered Abby and Eva Grace out the door. They were nearly to the elevator before Abby spoke through gritted teeth.

"This is absolutely unnecessary. You have guests."

"Who are perfectly happy relaxing for a few minutes while I take you home." When the elevator door opened, Jonah shifted his attention to Eva Grace. "You have good manners."

Eva Grace nodded, her expression thoughtful. "You have a mommy and a daddy. I just have a mommy."

Over the child's head, Jonah exchanged a look with Abby. How the heck did he respond to that?

"I remember when the clown was in Nancy's kitchen." Abby's tone was off-hand as if the thought had just popped into her head. "Do you know what kind of cookies she put in it?"

Eva Grace's eyes brightened. "What kind?"

"Name your favorites." Abby kept her tone light and a half smile on her face as they made their way to Jonah's truck. "I'll tell you if she made them."

As they rode the elevator to the parking garage, Eva Grace listed a plethora of cookies, though Jonah didn't think for one minute that chocolate chip potato chip cookies existed.

When he lifted a skeptical brow, the child only giggled.

Abby stopped short when they reached the truck. She smacked her hand against the side of her head. "Eva Grace needs a booster seat."

Jonah opened a door and pointed to a high-backed booster in the back seat. "When I moved here, I hoped we'd be spending time together so I picked up one, just in case."

"It's red." Eva Grace squealed at the red-and-black seat. The girl shifted her gaze to her mother. "It's my favorite color."

"It's top-rated," Jonah assured Abby as he opened the back door and with quick, efficient movements latched the seat into place. He'd done his research.

"It's the same brand I had in my KIA."

Taking that as consent, Jonah stepped aside to let Eva Grace jump in. He turned to help her buckle in and realized she didn't need his help.

"Thank you," Abby said grudgingly. "That's nice of you."

He shot her a wink. "I'm a nice guy."

Before Abby could respond, Eva Grace piped up from the back seat. "What kind of cookies is Jonah going to keep in *his* cookie jar?"

Jonah smiled, knowing this conversation could take them all the way home.

By the time he opened the door to his unit, barely fifteen minutes had passed. He found his mother and dad on the sofa, enjoying a glass of wine.

"I hope you don't mind." His father lifted a glass. "Your mom and I felt we needed it after the jolt."

Jonah ambled to a nearby chair and dropped down. "I understand a little of what you're going through. The first time I laid eyes on Eva Grace and then on Abby, well, I felt as if I'd been sucker-punched."

"She looks so much like you." Nancy blinked back a sheen of tears and took a sip of wine. "She appears perfectly healthy."

Why did that comment grate? Jonah wondered. Was it knowing that Eva Grace was the type of child Veronica had always wanted; pretty and smart with *no physical defects*. Was it that he knew if Veronica saw her now, she'd want her, when she hadn't wanted her before?

"It's only within the past six months that she got the braces off her legs." Jonah lifted his father's glass of wine from the table and gulped down half of it. "It's been a long, hard haul for Abby."

"Abbey looks wonderful," his mother said into the awkward silence that followed. "And Eva Grace's outfit reminded me of something I wore when I was a little girl in the sixties."

"Hazel Green bills itself as a place where history comes alive. The merchants all try to dress in the clothes of various decades to make it more fun for the tourists." Jonah's lips lifted into a smile. "Abby says it's like playing dress up every day."

"I love that." The tension seemed to leave his mother's shoulders. "I remember well how much she and Jackie loved to play dress up."

"We talked about those days." Jonah admitted.

"And apparently about the clown cookie jar," his mother said.

"Does this mean that the two of you—?" His father paused, as if waiting for Jonah to finish the sentence.

"We're taking things slow." Jonah expelled a heavy breath. "She feels I let her down and "

"Did she really expect you to go against your wife?" his mother asked.

"Yes," Jonah said. "She expected me to stand by the child I helped make. In Abby's mind it wasn't about me making a choice between her and Veronica, as much as it was making a choice between killing my baby or standing by my wife."

Nancy inhaled sharply. "You never advocated killing your baby."

"Didn't I?" Jonah stared down into the glass of wine he realized he still held in his hands. "Oh, I tried to talk Veronica into holding to our agreement. I knew I could handle whatever we had to face. But, as we continued to discuss the matter it was clear to me Veronica couldn't. That incident with her cousin's baby dying when she was in the room nearly pushed her over the edge."

"You seem to forget, based on information at the time, there was also a quality of life issue." His father spoke in a low tone, his gaze steady on Jonah. "You made what you thought was the responsible choice."

"The responsible choice in regard to Veronica." Jonah surged to his feet, the emotions swirling inside him too violent to let him sit. "But what about my baby? What about Eva Grace? Didn't she have rights?"

He began to pace the area in front of the fireplace. "If it wasn't for Abby, that smart, funny little girl wouldn't even be alive. It makes me sick to think of my actions."

Jonah collapsed onto the chair. He raked a hand through his hair. "I'm not certain Abby will ever fully forgive me. I sure as hell will never forgive myself."

The three of them sat without speaking for nearly a minute while the grandfather's clock in the corner loudly ticked off each second. It felt like an eternity. Still, Jonah was grateful his parents didn't fill the silence with platitudes.

Finally, his father spoke. "I know about regret. At least when it comes to battle."

His dad had served two tours in Afghanistan as part of the

Illinois National Guard. He rarely spoke of those months away from his family.

Nancy reached over and took her husband's hand. Their fingers locked together.

"You look at all the intel and make your decision. Sometimes it works out. Sometimes it doesn't." His father expelled a ragged breath. "When you look back, you think why did I do that, why didn't I—"

"Hindsight is always twenty-twenty." His mother spoke in a soft, soothing tone.

Jonah knew his father had commanded men. He could tell by the look on his face that some of the decisions he'd made had resulted in loss of life. Loss of men and women he knew. Men and women with spouses and families waiting for them to come back home.

"How do you live with it?" Jonah could hear the anguish in the words. He took a breath and tried to bring his rioting emotions under control. Emotions that had been stirred up ever since he'd come to Hazel Green and first set eyes on Eva Grace and Abby.

"You get up in the morning and put one foot in front of the other." His dad's gaze met his. "What I'm trying to say is often there is no easy answer. Life forces you to move forward. If you live long enough, and are brave enough to live fully, at one time or another you'll disappoint someone you love, or you'll disappoint yourself. Sometimes, both."

His mother's slender fingers tightened around father's broad ones. They were a working man's hands. Despite owning a successful construction company, in addition to his management duties, Michael still worked alongside his crew every day.

He'd taught his sons and daughters the value of working hard for what you want and the value of doing an honest day's labor.

"I want to make things right with Abby."

"You will," his mother assured him. "You'll show her she can trust you not only with her emotions, but with Eva Grace's as well."

Jonah nodded. The thought of what would happen if he couldn't convince her had his insides jittering. He'd had enough of this conversation.

He did what had worked so well for Abby and changed the subject. "I didn't realize you were coming to Hazel Green."

"It was a last second decision." His mother smiled at her husband. "Michael is attending a two-day conference specifically geared to owners of small to mid-sized construction companies. At the last minute, I convinced him to let me come along."

His father brought their joined hands to his lips for a kiss. "It didn't take any convincing. Having you along makes this more of a pleasure trip than business."

"That's so sweet." Nancy's face glowed with undisguised pleasure before she focused on Jonah. "I thought since we'd made the three-hour trek from Springfield, it would be extra special to pop in on you and check out your new surroundings."

"I'm glad you did."

"I knew you'd relocated here in the hopes of getting to know your daughter. Well, when I saw Abby and…" Nancy's voice trembled, "our granddaughter, it was a dream come true."

They'd talked enough about Abby and Eva Grace for one evening. "Let's talk about the next few days. I'd like you to stay here."

His mom and dad exchanged glances.

"We have reservations at the Palmer House," his father said, sounding unsure. "That's where the conference is being held."

"Why don't you see if you can cancel the room?" Jonah's voice turned persuasive. "It's a short train ride into the city. One of the stops is within easy walking distance of your meetings. If mom wants to do some shopping, she can go into the city with you then hop on the train and come back whenever she wants."

"That's fine with me, if it's okay with you, Michael." Nancy shifted her gaze to her son. "I'd also love the chance to explore your new town."

"I have to work but—" Jonah began.

His mother waved an airy hand. "I'm quite capable of finding my way."

When Jonah turned to his father, he realized his dad was on the phone with the hotel. After a second Michael clicked off and dropped the phone into his pocket. "The room is cancelled."

"I'm so excited my hands are shaking." His mother's laugh reminded him of Eva Grace's. "I've got the feeling this visit is going to be something special."

CHAPTER SIXTEEN

"Do you have a table for me?" Abby paused at the hostess stand and surveyed the dining area.

Only a couple of tables were occupied. Because it was Tuesday and after one, most of the lunch crowd that visited Matilda's had already been and gone.

"I always have a place for you." Matilda straightened from behind the stand and smiled. "How did the volunteering go this morning?"

"It was fun. Eva Grace seemed to really enjoy having her mom helping out in her classroom." Abby studied her friend in an informal "guess the decade" game they often played with each other.

Matilda's foundation was a shade lighter than normal while her red lips were darker than usual. Her auburn hair was piled up with side slicked bangs.

She wore a faux fur skirt with a crimson belt and a stretchy gold top.

Abby pointed. "1990's."

Her friend grinned. "What gave it away?"

"What didn't?" Abby laughed. "The hair, the make-up and that fur skirt that makes me want to pet you, screams the dot-com decade."

She followed her friend to a table in the dining room. Though Matilda insisted the intimate space worked for her, Abby knew if there had been room, she'd have expanded.

Unfortunately, that wasn't a possibility. The hotel had been granted historic status which meant Abby couldn't simply tear down an exterior wall. Even if she could have gotten a building permit, there was no space between her hotel and the buildings on either side.

That's why it didn't surprise Abby when Matilda occasionally brought up moving back to Oregon and opening a restaurant there.

"You decided not to dress up today." Matilda made the observation as she laid the menu on the table.

Abby glanced down at her green floral midi wrap dress with ankle boots topped by an over-sized cardigan. "Since I was just volunteering at the school, I decided to stick to this decade for a change."

"Well, you look quite lovely."

The scrape on Abby's cheek was nearly healed and a little well-placed foundation this morning covered it completely. Despite the stress of seeing Jonah's parents last night, she'd slept well and had felt 'awesome' when she'd hopped out of bed.

Her plans were to enjoy a quick lunch, then take over front desk duties until it was time to pick Eva Grace up from school.

"Why, this is a nice surprise."

Abby froze, recognizing the familiar voice. She turned to face the woman who'd walked up behind her. Abby had thought last night would be the only time she'd see Nancy Rollins during her visit to Hazel Green. Apparently, she was wrong.

"Nancy, I didn't expect to see you today." Cognizant of Matilda's curious gaze on her, Abby quickly performed introductions.

"So, you're Jonah's mother." Matilda's smile was warm and friendly.

Surprise flickered in Nancy's eyes. "You know my son?"

"Everyone knows our handsome new Chief of Police." Matilda patted Abby's shoulders. "I'll let you two catch up. Angeline will be right over to take your order."

Abby had hoped to entice Matilda to join her but by the time the words made it to her lips, her friend was halfway across the dining area.

"Would you…" Nancy hesitated, "care to join me?"

"I wouldn't want to interrupt your lunch."

"Actually, I just ordered, then went to the restroom to wash my hands." Nancy gestured with one of those recently cleaned hands toward a table for two by the window.

A two-top. A sense of relief flooded Abby. It didn't appear Jonah was joining his mother for lunch.

Still, Abby hesitated. Making conversation last night had been brutal. She really didn't want to do it again so soon.

"Will you be changing tables?" Angeline, a mother of three who worked during the day while her children were in school, held a glass of ice water.

"Yes, thank you, Angeline." Abby smiled. "I'll be joining Mrs. Rollins."

Abby recited her order before she'd even taken a seat. She didn't want to extend this luncheon a second longer than necessary.

The woman returned a moment later with a tall glass of iced tea for Abby, then left them alone.

Abby took a long sip and for a second avoided meeting Nancy's gaze. But when she set the cut crystal tumbler down, she looked up.

It was hard to decipher the expression on the woman's face, but the warmth and concern in her eyes had Abby's heart slamming hard against her chest wall. Unexpected tears pushed against the backs of her lids.

Darn it. Darn it. Darn it.

This was someone she'd once thought of as a second mother. Which only made her betrayal that much more bitter.

"You have a beautiful daughter." Nancy's lips curved upward. "Funny, smart and so precocious."

"And to think if you and your son had had your way, she wouldn't be here." Abby lifted the glass, intending to take another sip but set it down when her hand trembled. She folded her hands in her lap.

Nancy's gaze didn't waver. "Is that what you think, Abigail?"

"It's what I—"

Abby stopped when Angeline returned with the daily special she'd ordered, which apparently had been what Nancy had chosen too.

The farmer's market pasta salad with a thick slice of apple bread looked wonderful, though Abby's appetite had vanished. "Thanks, Angeline."

When the waitress was out of earshot, Abby carefully unfolded the linen napkin and placed it in her lap. She took a breath and let it out slowly, regaining her composure. "We both know that's what you wanted me to do."

"Eva Grace is my granddaughter."

"You have no claim on her."

"Eva Grace is my granddaughter," Nancy repeated in a low tone, her gaze firmly fixed on Abby's face. She stabbed a piece of pasta but didn't lift it to her mouth. "The second I heard you were pregnant, I was ecstatic. We had to celebrate."

Abby remembered vividly when Nancy had called her up and insisted on taking her shopping for maternity clothes. "We went shopping and had lunch at Charlie Parker's Diner."

The popular eatery, once featured on Diners Drive-Ins and Dives, was a Springfield institution.

"You were hooked on their cherry shakes."

Abby felt sick inside, the memory of everything she and this woman had shared, forever tainted. "If you wanted her so much, why did you side with Veronica and Jonah when they wanted to kill her?"

Nancy flinched but Abby didn't regret the harsh words. This had been a life or death decision.

"I didn't have a vote." Nancy brought a bite of pasta to her lips in a semblance of eating. "Any decisions that needed to be made were between you and Jonah and Veronica."

"What about afterwards, when the decision was made and I was on my own?" Abby's voice shook and several tears slipped down her cheeks. She hurriedly brushed them back. "When I was growing up, you said more than once that you loved me like a daughter. Then, when I protect the life of your grandchild, you cut me off. You didn't call to see if I needed anything. All of a sudden, I meant nothing to you."

Tears filled Nancy's eyes. "I couldn't contact you."

Abby waved a hand and fought to bring her emotions under control. "Forget it. It doesn't matter—"

"Veronica said if any of us had anything to do with you, she would take you to court for breach of contract."

Not sure what kind of game Nancy was playing, Abby considered the words carefully. "The contract was considered breached when I refused to have an abortion. Why would she take me to court?"

"To make your life a living hell." Disgust sounded in Nancy's voice. "Those were her exact words. She didn't care if she had a legal leg to stand on or not."

"I knew she was angry but I was the one who was going to have to raise this child." This was a puzzle where the pieces didn't quite fit.

"It was a side of my daughter-in-law I had never seen before." Nancy took another bite of salad and chewed automatically. Abby doubted she could even describe the taste. "Vindictive and filled with rage. I really think she went insane for a few months."

Nancy's blue eyes, not quite as vivid as her son's and Eva Grace's filled with sorrow. "I truly believe she'd have followed through with the threat. I couldn't add any more to your plate. But please know, it cost me dearly to step out of your life."

The soft, silly girl who had once loved this woman and her family wanted to believe her. The cynic, who had weathered too many storms to count in the past five years, found holes in the story.

"Veronica was off the hook, free to find another surrogate and move on with her life." Abby broke off a piece of apple bread, idly crumbling it between her fingers.

It was hard for Abby to get past her hurt and anger of the last five years. Yet, she'd known Nancy Rollins since she was a little girl. She knew the other woman well enough to know she was telling the truth.

At the next table she watched a moth flutter near a candle, the speckled creature with the soft wings drawn to something that could destroy it.

It was that way for her with Jonah, Abby thought with sudden clarity. Though she'd tried to ignore it, the pull was still there.

"Veronica was filled with rage." Nancy sighed. "She couldn't move on. Not at first. Not for a long time."

Abby lifted a brow at the same time she lifted her fork. "If she was so vindictive, why did she agree to send me money?"

For a moment, the older woman's expression was blank. "Pardon me."

"The money from her and Jonah. It came every month."

Understanding filled Nancy's eyes. "She didn't know."

The moth drew closer to the heat.

"Didn't know what?"

"Jonah sent the money from a private account." Nancy lifted

her hands, let them drop. "That's all I'll say on that. If you want to know more, you'll need to speak with my son."

Abby watched the moth, so drawn to the flame that it forgot to protect itself. Then, it was too late.

"You understand, don't you?"

Abby thought of the moth and nodded. She understood perfectly the need to keep a distance between her and Jonah.

While she needed to assess his interactions with Eva Grace, she must take care not to get drawn in by his charm.

She'd been burned by him once.

She couldn't let him destroy her and the life she'd worked so hard to build.

Jonah realized he didn't know Abby as well as he thought he did. When she accepted an invitation to go with him and his parents to Fingel's Pumpkin Patch on Wednesday, he was caught completely off guard.

His father's meetings in Chicago were over and his parents planned to head back to Springfield tomorrow morning. His mother had mentioned how nice it would be to spend some time with Abby and Eva Grace before they left. His father heartily seconded the idea.

Jonah had hesitated to text Abby, certain she would turn him down without a second thought. Instead, after a long thirty minutes with no reply, she'd agreed to meet him and his parents in the parking lot of Fingel's.

"I'm so happy this worked out." His mother's voice shook with eagerness.

"It would have been a shame to come this far and only see Abby and Eva Grace that one night," his father agreed.

"I wonder if we can get some pictures of all of us," Nancy mused.

"Don't push it, Mom." Jonah and his parents stood near the entrance. He resisted the urge to pace.

Part of the nervous tension was due to the excitement of sharing this experience with Abby and Eva Grace, but the other was the fear that something would go wrong and Abby would cut him out of her life. And, his daughter's life.

Though he knew he could push for visitation, he wouldn't do that to Abby. Not after everything she'd been through.

"There they are." Relief filled his mother's voice. "Oh, she looks adorable."

Jonah's gaze settled on Abby. He had to admit that his mom was right. While he liked seeing her dressed up in vintage clothes, she looked, well, sexy, in her jeans, sneakers and a red hoodie.

He lifted his hand in greeting and she nodded acknowledgement. Beside her, Eva Grace jumped up and down and waved wildly.

The little girl wore an orange dress with a smiling jack o'lantern across the chest and a tulle skirt with black spots. Instead of pulling the child's hair up into a bouncy tail, Abby had let the curls hang loose.

Jonah felt sure Eva Grace would have taken off running, if Abby had released her hand.

It seemed to take forever for them to make their way through the crowd.

Abby glanced at the line in front of the Admissions Barn. "I didn't expect such a crowd on a Wednesday. But Fingel's draws from a wide area."

"Are the kids out of school for the day?" When he'd texted Abby, he hadn't given a thought to the fact that Eva Grace might be in school.

"No." Abby spoke matter-of-factly. "But your parents are leaving. They won't be around this weekend. I had the teacher send me what they're going over today. I'll work with Eva Grace tonight on the lesson."

Jonah cleared the lump that had risen to clog his throat. "Thank you."

"We better get in line." Abby started in that direction but Jonah touched her arm.

She didn't jerk away but he felt her muscles tense beneath his fingers. "What?"

"Dad already purchased tickets for everyone."

Abby turned toward his father.

Michael held up a hand, the tickets fanned out in his fingers like a deck of cards. "My pleasure."

"Thank you, Michael." Abby turned to Eva Grace. "Mr. Rollins is treating us to a day at the Pumpkin Patch. Can you tell him thank you?"

Eva Grace shot the older man a blinding smile. "Thank you very much."

"This is awesome." The child let go of her mother's hand and twirled. "I'm so happy."

Out of the corner of his eyes, Jonah saw his mother take his dad's hand and give it a squeeze.

"I'm happy, too." His mother cast a glance at Abby and mouthed, 'thank you.'

Abby merely nodded then focused on her daughter. "Eva Grace, there's going to be a lot of people here today, so when we're making our way to each of the attractions, you need to hold an adult's hand."

Taking a breath, Abby continued, "It doesn't have to be my hand. You can hold Jonah's hand or…"

She paused as if trying to consider what to have her daughter call Nancy and Steve.

"If you wouldn't mind, she could call me Nana." Nancy spoke quickly, the words tumbling out as if she wanted to get them all out before Abby stopped her. "And 'Papa' works for Michael."

The bald hope in his parents' eyes was like a dagger to Jonah's heart. He'd told them not to push. What has his mother done?

She'd pushed. He prayed they wouldn't be too disappointed when—

"That works." Abby turned to Eva Grace and pointed to Nancy then to Michael. "You can hold Nana or Papa's hands. Or Jonah's."

What would she say, Jonah wondered, if he asked if Eva Grace could call him daddy? But he kept his mouth shut.

He and Abby had an agreement. His presence wasn't guaranteed in Eva Grace's life. And, after what he'd done, he wasn't sure he deserved being called 'daddy.'

CHAPTER SEVENTEEN

"Mommy. I want to go on the slide next." Eva Grace held Nana and Papa's hands, the brightness of her smile only surpassed by those of the adults standing beside her.

Ignoring the gratitude in their eyes, Abby tipped her head back and glanced at the monster slide. Simply looking at all the steps leading up to the top made her dizzy.

As if recalling the time Abby had to be led down from the top of a slide at Knight's Action Park in Springfield, Nancy smiled understandingly. "Michael and I can take her."

"You expect me to believe you and dad are going to ride down on a piece of burlap?" Jonah's obvious disbelief had his father's eyes firing.

"I know it might be hard for you to believe but your mother and I are capable of having fun." Michael shifted his gaze to Abby. "If it's okay with you, that is."

"Please, Mommy, please." Eva Grace clasped her hands together.

"Have fun." Abby chuckled when the threesome headed toward the steps. "Glad it's them and not me."

"Since we're alone, there's something I want to say."

Abby turned, the smile slipping from her face. "Can't you just let things be?"

Puzzlement crossed his face and for a few blessed seconds there was silence.

"I only wanted to say thanks." Jonah spoke stiffly, haltingly. He gestured with his head toward where his parents and Eva Grace climbed the steps. "This has probably been one of the best days of their life."

Abby lifted her lips in a sardonic smile. "I hardly think making their way through a corn maze, dressing-a-Scarecrow and now, going on a big slide, qualifies."

"No, but spending time with you and Eva Grace does." He shifted from one foot to the other. "Letting her call them Nana and Papa—"

"Don't make a big deal out of something that isn't." Abby set her jaw. "It was easiest to let her call them that. That's all."

Her tone dared him to disagree.

Putting his hand over his eyes, Jonah glanced up. "It looks like they're going to be in line for a while."

"They don't appear to mind the wait." Even from this distance, Abby could see by her daughter's expansive hand gestures that Eva Grace was entertaining them with one of her stories.

"Do you still like pumpkin donuts?"

Abby blinked at the question that seemed to come out of nowhere. "Who doesn't?"

"Let's get one." Jonah's gaze searched hers.

He was asking something that didn't have a thing to do with pumpkin donuts, but darn if she could figure out his hidden agenda. And now that he'd mentioned the treat, her mouth began to water. "Okay."

As the day had turned into mid-afternoon, the after-school crowd had flooded into the Pumpkin Patch. When Jonah took her elbow as they wove their way through kids with sno-cones and adults with cups of sweet-smelling Apple cider, Abby didn't protest.

She didn't like him touching her, even in the most impersonal way, but she had to be practical. If they got separated, finding him quickly might prove difficult.

As they reached the Food Barn, he shot her a quick grin. He ordered a donut for each of them, as well as cups of warm apple cider. A wave of longing rose up inside her.

Abby missed the boy she'd grown up with, the one she'd trusted with her hopes and dreams. But she told herself that boy was gone. Unless she wanted to be like the moth and the flame, she needed to keep her distance, at least emotionally.

His parents were another story. At the end of her lunch with his mother, Nancy had asked for forgiveness. Abby had looked into the woman's eyes and had seen the regret, the pain and the sincerity.

Abby was convinced that Veronica's threats were the reason Nancy and Michael had kept their distance at first. But she still wondered why they'd stayed away this last year. Had they really worried Veronica would follow through with her threat once she and their son had divorced?

Regardless, they were Eva Grace's grandparents. The only ones her daughter would ever have.

She was beginning to realize that keeping Jonah away from Eva Grace would only be punishing her daughter.

Fact: Jonah was Eva Grace's father.

Fact: he wanted to be part of Eva Grace's life.

Fact: all the reading she'd done lately indicated having a positive father-daughter relationship had a huge impact on a girl's self-esteem and confidence.

All Abby had ever wanted was the best for her little girl. Which meant, letting Jonah Rollins—and his family--be a part of Eva Grace's life.

"That was an awesome donut." Jonah popped the last bite into his mouth and washed it down with the last of the cider. "The glaze kept it from being too dry."

"I feel bad we didn't get anything for your parents, but I don't like Eva Grace loading up on sweets." Abby's dark hair shone like polished walnut in the afternoon sun.

In her jeans and hoodie, she looked comfortable and approachable. This outing had been the stuff of dreams. It was as if the past five years had never happened. But Jonah wasn't foolish enough to believe all was good between him and Abby.

While it wasn't as bad as walking on eggshells, he was well aware that trust, once lost, didn't easily return.

"You're a good mom, Abby."

To his surprise, she frowned. "You sound surprised."

"I'm not." He kept his voice off-hand, even though his heart tripped at the edge in her tone. "It was a simple compliment."

He tossed his cup in a recycle bin for paper then shoved his hands into his pockets. *Don't go there*, the rational part of his brain urged. But the thought that had been circling all day had him blurting out, "I don't think Veronica would have been a good one."

Abby dumped her cup, then turned, a look of puzzlement on her face. "A good what?"

"Mother." Jonah rocked back on his heels, blew out a breath. "It somehow feels disloyal to say, but watching you—and knowing her as I did—I don't think she'd have been a good mother."

Though he certainly didn't expect her to stand up for Veronica, Jonah knew that at one time, Abby and his ex-wife had been friendly. Abby had agreed to carry a baby for him and Veronica. Which meant, she must have thought Veronica would be a good mother.

Abby remained silent for a long moment.

"I thought I knew Veronica. I didn't." Abby shrugged. "Since I was so utterly wrong about what her heart was like, anything I say now will be pure speculation."

Jonah wished he'd kept his mouth shut. Why had he brought up the past? Right now, Abby was probably thinking how wrong she'd been about *him*.

The phone in his pocket vibrated. "It's a text from my father. They want to know if it's okay if they take Eva Grace on the Pumpkin Wheel."

Their gazes lifted as one to the giant Ferris Wheel. Painted a vivid orange with green spokes, it rose high over the pumpkin patch.

"Eva Grace has never been on a Ferris wheel before." Two lines of worry furrowed Abby's brow. "Find out where they're at and tell them we'll be right there. I want to speak with my daughter before saying yes or no."

Jonah quickly texted his dad, then received a response back with the location. He took Abby's arm as they wove their way toward the Ferris Wheel.

He wasn't sure if it was her concern about Eva Grace that had her not pulling away, or the knowledge that it would be easy for them to become separated in the mass of people.

They found his parents enthralled by some story Eva Grace was spinning.

Abby gave Eva Grace's hair a tug to get her attention.

A brilliant smile flashed across the child's face. She pointed to the gigantic Ferris Wheel. "Mama. Can I go on the Pumpkin Wheel with Nana and Papa, puh-leeze?"

Abby tilted her head back and winced. "It's very tall."

Something in the way Abby said the words had Eva Grace going still, a flicker of uncertainty entering her eyes. She turned to Michael. "I don't want to do it, anymore. I'm scared."

"That's okay, sweetheart." Michael patted her shoulder. "There are lots of other attractions."

The little girl had picked up on her mother's fears. Jonah thought about saying something about the ride being safe, but kept silent.

Abby swallowed hard. Then, stunned him by smiling brightly. "It looks like a lot of fun."

Eva Grace blinked. "It does?"

"I've always wanted to ride on it." The lie, at least Jonah thought it was a lie, slipped easily from Abby's lips.

"Me, too." Eva Grace offered a tentative smile. "But it's…high."

"That's part of the fun." Abby cleared her throat. "In fact, I think we should all enjoy the ride."

"I went crazy for a second," Abby muttered as the attendant made sure she was secured behind the metal bar.

"Pardon?" The ride operator's bald head glittered like a highly polished cue-ball and his gold canine glittered in the sunlight.

"Sorry." Abby waved an airy hand. "Just talking to myself."

The man shot Jonah a glance. "Everything okay here?"

Jonah gave him thumbs up. "We're good."

A second later the enclosed cart lurched upward, swinging back and forth. Abby gasped and squeezed her eyes shut.

Jonah reached out and she gripped his hand tight.

"In case you were wondering," Abby kept her eyes closed, "this is the reason I didn't want to ride with Eva Grace."

"You'll be fine, but I think you'll do better with your eyes open." His deep voice was low and reassuring. "There is something about swaying when you have them closed that makes everything worse."

"I don't want to look out and see how high we are."

"You don't have to look out. Just fix your gaze on me."

He was right. The swaying with her eyes shut was making her nauseated.

She shifted in her seat, as much as the bar across her front would allow and slowly opened her eyes.

His gaze was steady, as comforting as the clasp of his hand. "You're doing this for Eva Grace. You don't want her to be afraid."

She blinked in surprise. "How did you—"

He gave a little chuckle. "You don't like heights. I can't think of another reason that would get you on one of these things."

The car lurched upward and swung back and forth wildly, as if someone had given it a good strong shove.

She tightened her fingers around Jonah's. "I don't want her to be afraid, like me. I've been uneasy around heights my entire life. I don't even like being on tall ladders. The last thing I want is to pass that irrational fear on to my daughter."

Before he could say a word, Abby took a breath and continued on. She didn't care if she was rambling. When she was talking she didn't have to think about where she was or the confusing knowledge that simply being with Jonah steadied her. "I put that flicker of fear in her eyes with my thoughtless comment and I couldn't let it stay. But I wasn't sure I could hide it from her if we were in the same cart."

Overhead, she could hear Eva Grace's laughter.

"My parents are thrilled you let her ride with them."

"She likes them. I can tell." The cart jerked upward again then stopped. Abby's breath froze. "Why is it taking so long to load?"

The one thing Abby knew was the ride couldn't end until it began.

"I believe there was a large group with mobility issues in line behind us."

"There were?" She might not be a trained observer but Abby prided herself on noticing her surroundings.

"You were too busy keeping that brave smile on your face to notice." Jonah's tone was gentle with understanding.

Abby nodded, the queasiness in her stomach rising with each movement of the cart. By the lurching upward she knew they were higher, higher than she'd ever been in her life. But she wasn't about to look out the metal grating to see just how high.

"Remember our Junior prom."

Abby pulled her thoughts from her stomach, not an easy task, and focused on Jonah. "What about it?"

"You'd gone with Kevin Murphy and I was there with—"

He paused as if searching for a name.

"Lucy Brogan," she offered

He nodded. "It was hot in the gym."

"I slipped outside for some air when Kevin went to the restroom…and there you were." Abby remembered her delight when she'd spotted Jonah.

"Lucy was out doing some synchronized something with other members of the dance team." Jonah gave a laugh. "A good boyfriend probably should have stayed and watched."

"The cool air outside felt wonderful." As had his jacket when he'd wrapped it around her when she shivered. The clean scent of his soap and shampoo had lingered on the jacket and she'd felt surrounded by him.

The moon had been full and cast a golden glow. For those few moments, it had felt as if no one else in the world existed.

"You kissed me." She nearly sighed the words, then shook her head. "It was wrong."

"Because I had a girlfriend." It was a statement, not a question.

"And, because I had a boyfriend."

"It felt like my only chance to show you how I felt." There was a sadness in Jonah's eyes. "I'd started to feel as if the fates had conspired against us. Each time I was free, you were in a relationship. When you were available, I wasn't."

"Then, you went off to college and I stayed in Springfield." Abby kept her tone light even when her heart began to ache. "You found Veronica and the rest is history."

"You were the most intelligent, focused girl I'd ever known." The soft words wrapped around her like a lover's caress. "You knew the tough fight you would have to build a business of your own but you didn't let that dissuade you. You were determined to make it happen."

Abby smiled. "I wanted that coffee shop so bad I could taste it."

"I never understood why a coffee shop."

Abby felt the ride picking up speed and knew they were high by the drop in the air temperature. When the cart began to drop, panic clawed at her throat.

For a second she feared she might lose it, but his fingers tightened around hers. "Tell me why a coffee shop."

She forced herself to stare into his intense blue gaze. Her skin prickled and an emotion she didn't want to examine too closely filled her. "Remember Sunrise Coffee?"

Jonah nodded. "The place on Plaza."

"That's the one. I used to go there all the time after school." Abby grabbed onto the memory. "Even now, I'll catch the scent of a rich Ethiopian blend and I'll be right back there. The place was nothing special but Joe and Sue--they were the owners—made me feel welcome. I wanted to give that feeling back to other kids and other adults."

"Now you welcome guests to your hotel."

"I do." She smiled. "It isn't quite the same but I enjoy it."

As if he'd sensed there was more, he probed. "Have you ever thought of opening a coffee shop in the historic district?"

"There aren't any open locations." She shrugged. "I think there's a need, but there isn't a space for a shop. People have to settle for the Starbucks kiosk in the Green."

"You're an amazing businesswoman. Heck, you're amazing period."

The warmth of his tone had her heart skittering. Abby took a deep breath and willed herself to relax.

When he released her hand, she stopped the protest rising to her lips. She wasn't a frightened child who needed to hold someone's hand.

Without warning, before she had a second to breathe, his lips were on hers, exquisitely gentle and achingly tender. Her heart squeezed tight in her chest.

This was a dangerous game. As much as Abby knew she should push Jonah away, another part of her yearned for this closeness. Even if it was just for the moment.

His fingers weren't quite steady as they touched the curve of her cheek and trailed along the side of her jaw.

He didn't say a word. Perhaps if he had, she'd have come to her senses. Instead, she leaned forward and planted a kiss at the base of his neck, his skin salty beneath her lips.

Then he was kissing her, long dreamy kisses that had her forgetting everything in the pleasure.

"I hope you enjoyed the ride." The door to their cabin opened abruptly.

Abby sprang back from Jonah. Well, as far back as the bar across her mid-section would allow.

The attendant flashed a knowing smile as he helped Abby out onto the platform leading to the exit steps.

She took a second to steady herself, then turned to Jonah. Though her quiet voice shook when she spoke, she met his gaze firmly. "This can't happen again."

CHAPTER EIGHTEEN

"I realize this may be asking too much. If it is, just tell me." Nancy gripped her husband's hand as her gaze darted a short distance away where Eva Grace stood exchanging 'Pumpkin Wheel' stories with a school friend. "Tomorrow morning, Michael and I will be heading back to Springfield. We thought it might be nice for you and Jonah to have some time alone. It's a beautiful night, so if you'd like to take a walk or something, we could play a game with Eva Grace or—"

Abby wasn't sure if Nancy stopped because she realized she was rambling. More likely, the woman had run out of breath.

The fact that Michael and Nancy had so easily slipped under her guard worried her. Jonah simply stood at her side, not saying a word. Once they'd gotten off the Ferris Wheel, he'd started to respond to her comment but was interrupted by Eva Grace racing to him.

Apparently, the ride had been 'awesome' made even better when 'Papa' made the cart swing wildly.

"Thank you for taking Eva Grace on the ride," Abby began. "I worry if she'd have gone with me, she might have picked up on my…fear…even if I'd tried to hide it."

"I loved showing her the clouds." Michael grinned, reminding Abby in that moment of his son. "Eva Grace was convinced if she could have gotten her hand through the cage, she'd have been able to grab a cloud."

"Thank heavens for closed gondolas." Abby knew they were waiting for her answer but she was having a difficult time deciding the best course of action.

It didn't help that Jonah stood close enough that she breathed in the tangy scent of his cologne with each inhale. Her body vibrated from his nearness and an aching filled her limbs.

Abby opened her mouth at the same time Eva Grace rushed back.

"Papa." The child tugged on his arm then pointed. "My friend Bristol has a black dog just like Ranger."

Surprise skittered across Michael's face. "How do you know about Ranger?"

"I told her," Jonah answered.

Abby took in her daughter's ease with the couple. If they lived in Hazel Green, all this togetherness might be too much, too fast. But Michael and Nancy lived three hours away, on the other side of the state. They'd be gone tomorrow. Who knew when Eva Grace would see them again?

Besides, she did need to have a private conversation with Jonah, away from little ears that could often be razor sharp.

"What do you think?" Abby settled her gaze on her daughter. "Would you like Papa and Nana to put you to bed tonight?"

A sly look filled the little girl's eyes. "Would we get to read lots and lots of books?"

"Good try." Abby smiled. "Two books, then sleep."

Eva Grace thought for a moment, then took Jonah's parents' hands. "I've got all the Mercy Watson books."

"Mercy Watson is a pig," Jonah clarified. "Not a girl."

He and Eva Grace exchanged a smile.

Abby had them come to the hotel. She helped her daughter

shower and get into her pajamas. Nancy had assured her she take care of the child's wet hair before settling her in for stories.

"There's absolutely no need to rush back," Michael assured her. "If we have any questions, or if anything comes up, we'll give you a call."

Abby thought about giving her daughter one last hug, but Eva Grace was chattering to Nancy, while Jonah's mother flipped over the child's thick curls, twisting the strands into a loose bun and securing with a scrunchie.

The leave-in conditioner was something Abby had already been using, but she'd not yet added the scrunch gel she'd recently purchased. Nancy had informed her that her daughter Jackie, who had hair as curly as Eva Grace's, swore by the product.

"Have fun," Abby called out.

Eva Grace looked up and waved. "We will."

Abby knew she should be happy that Eva Grace was so comfortable around the couple, but had to admit her little girl's easy acceptance of her mother's absence stung.

"What would you like to do?" Jonah asked when they stepped outside.

"Have you been to Goose Island Grog yet?" She needed quiet for her discussion with Jonah.

He shook his head.

"The place was inspired by 1800's Irish drinking dens. The main floor can get a little noisy, especially on the weekends. The upstairs is more--," Abby paused, searching for the right word, "--refined. We could get a glass of wine. It will be quiet enough for conversation."

"Sounds good to me." Jonah reached out as if to take her hand, but she turned slightly and he got the message.

Another good thing about Goose Island, Abby thought, was that it was only a few blocks from the hotel. Jonah held open the heavy wooden door with the frosted glass insert and stepped aside to let her enter.

The main floor catered to those looking for whiskey and beer. The floor underfoot might be rough and covered in sawdust but the long wooden bar was polished to a high gloss.

Most of the tables were filled as well as the stools at the bar. The far side of the room held two dart boards, both currently in use. "On a normal weekend night, this place is standing room only. I came here with a friend on a Saturday night and it was like sensory overload."

"A guy friend?" Jonah's expression gave nothing away. "Or girl?"

"Nell. She loves these kinds of places." Abby wondered what Jonah would have said if she'd told him she was on a date. She nearly chuckled. As if she'd had time to date the last five years. "I couldn't figure out why she brought me here. She knows I don't like a lot of noise."

"You never did." Jonah's gaze appeared to miss nothing as he scanned the room. "Hanging out at a coffee shop was always more your speed."

Abby gestured with her head toward the stairs. "Wait until you see what's up there. Trust me. There's nothing like this in Springfield."

She climbed the steps and paused, letting Jonah get the full feel of this level before looking for a table.

His eyes reflected his shock. "It's a different world."

While this floor also had a bar and tables scattered throughout the room, that's where any similarities to the main level ended. Here the wooden floor had been polished to a high gloss and there wasn't a peanut shell in sight.

The predominant wood was cherry with the tables strategically positioned over muted patterned Persian rugs. An ornately carved ceiling added to the elegance. A mural of two peacocks facing each other added vibrant color to the wall behind the bar.

Abby glanced down at her jeans and hoodie and winced. "I should have changed."

"You're the most beautiful woman in the room."

Abby rolled her eyes, but had to admit the compliment made her feel better.

"I think there's a table…" Abby stiffened, then cursed under her breath.

Jonah gaze swiftly searched the room to locate the threat.

"It's Rachel. She's with Marc." Abby kept her voice low. "I don't think she saw—"

Rachel's eyes brightened and Abby knew they'd been spotted. Her friend stood and motioned them over.

Abby kept a smile firmly fixed on her face as they crossed the room. "I'll try to get out of this."

Both Marc and Rachel were standing by the time she and Jonah reached their table.

"This is so cool." Rachel gave Abby a quick hug. "I didn't realize you were seeing each other socially."

Abby saw the assessment in Marc's cool blue eyes.

Jonah flashed an easy smile. "This is a nice place. Very unique."

"Please join us." Rachel pointed to the two empty seats at the table.

There was no easy way out of this, Abby thought. Rachel had a tender heart and would be hurt by a refusal.

"Thank you." Though her smile remained on her lips, Abby's mind searched for something that would offer a quick retreat.

If she mentioned needing to relieve Jonah's parents that would only bring up questions. Rachel knew Abby didn't leave her daughter with just anyone.

When nothing came immediately to mind, Abby took a seat. She would deflect until something came to her. Abby had always believed the best defense was a good offense. Which meant she had to set the direction of the conversation. Otherwise, she and Jonah would end up playing twenty questions.

She turned to Rachel. "Have you been to Fingel's yet? I took Eva Grace today and she had a ball."

The flicker of Jonah's eyelashes told her that he'd picked up on the fact she didn't want him mentioning they'd gone together. Not that Rachel wouldn't find out. But there was something about Marc's assessing gaze that had Abby not wanting him to know any more of her business than absolutely necessary.

"I wanted to go tonight but—" Rachel paused then shrugged.

"You love the Pumpkin Patch." Abby smiled, remembering Rachel talking about taking her brothers and sisters every year when they were small.

"A commercialized waste of money." Marc gestured with an imperious gesture to a server, who took their wine order then slipped away.

"I take it you've been there?" Jonah's tone remained friendly, but there was a watchful look in his eyes.

Marc made a dismissive sound. "You don't have to pay an exorbitant admission price to know it's not worth the money."

Rachel chewed on her lip and remained silent.

What had happened to her confident, feisty friend? Okay, so maybe Rachel had never been feisty. But she had been confident and had stood up for herself.

Something had happened since she'd hooked up with Marc. Abby wished she knew what it was, wished she knew what to do to counteract what he'd done and bring back her friend.

"Personally, I think it's well worth the price." Abby smiled her thanks as the server, a young woman dressed in traditional Irish attire set two wine glasses on the table.

Before she could reach into her bag, Jonah handed her a twenty and told her to keep the change. A gesture that had Marc and Rachel exchanging glances.

"One entry fee gives you access to everything on the Pumpkin Patch grounds." After making a mental note to pay Jonah back, Abby continued as if there had been no interruption. "You can even go on the Big Slide and the Pumpkin Wheel without paying extra. Eva Grace loved both."

Surprise widened Rachel's eyes. "You let her go on those alone?"

"Of course not." Abby waved a hand, deciding to ignore the Big Slide and focus on the attraction she had gone on. "Considering my aversion to heights, I never thought I'd say this, but the Pumpkin Wheel was amazing."

The tiny smile tugging at the corners of Jonah's mouth disappeared when he lifted the glass of wine to his lips.

"You went on the Pumpkin Wheel?" Rachel repeated, disbelieving.

"Pumpkin Wheel? What is that?" Marc asked before Abby could assure her friend she had indeed gone on the ride. Not that she remembered all that much about it. She'd been too focused on covering Jonah's mouth with hers.

"It's like a giant Ferris Wheel." Rachel's lips curved. "It's painted orange and green and—"

"I get the picture." Marc cut her off, obviously bored with the topic.

"What brings you to Goose Island tonight?" Abby asked, deciding she'd milked the topic of the Pumpkin Patch dry.

"It's the one-year anniversary of our first date." Rachel reached over and squeezed Marc's hand. "We had dinner at Matilda's then came here for a drink."

"Sounds like a special evening." A sense of unease wrapped around Abby's spine. Had the two really been together an *entire* year? She thought they hadn't gotten together until Christmas.

"Marc had roses delivered to the Food Bank." Rachel's dark eyes shone as bright as her smile.

"It's a special day." Marc's fingers curved around Rachel's. "You deserve only the best."

"Especially after spending most of the morning in Nell's office." Rachel lifted her glass of champagne and took a sip.

Abby stilled. "I hope nothing is wrong."

Rachel wave a dismissive hand. "Just some estate stuff."

"Your parents' estate?" As far as Abby knew there hadn't been any recent deaths in Rachel's family.

"Much of the money from my parents' estate has been held in trust for each of the children. Each child has to reach the grand old age of thirty to access their portion." Rachel smiled. "That milestone birthday is just around the corner for me."

"I've been counseling Rachel on where to invest the money." Marc's tone could have melted butter. "I don't know why she felt she had to consult an attorney."

"Nell is also my friend," Rachel reminded him.

Something told Abby it wasn't the first time, Rachel had reminded him of that fact. Which made her even more glad Nell was involved.

"Not to change the subject," Jonah spoke for the first time since sitting down, "but Abby told me she wanted to spend a few minutes getting an update on my committee's progress related to the Birthday Bash."

Rachel shook her head. "I can't believe that's getting so close."

"Neither can I." Abby took a sip of wine.

She realized what Jonah was doing and the plan was absolutely brilliant. Marc wouldn't want Rachel discussing business on their romantic night out, which gave Abby and Jonah their excuse to move to a different table. Preferably one far away from Marc.

"We don't want to ruin your evening with business talk." Jonah pushed back his chair. "It looks like a table just opened up along the far wall."

"I don't mind talking about—" Rachel stopped when she saw the darkening cloud settle over Marc's features. "Actually, Abby, I'll get an update to you tomorrow. Will that be soon enough?"

"That'll be fine." Abby stood, glass of wine in hand and gave Rachel a warm smile. "Enjoy your evening."

Then, out of obligation, smiled at Marc. "Great to see you again."

Once they were out of earshot, Jonah spoke in a low tone. "Great to see you again?"

"What was I supposed to say?" Abby whispered as they reached the just-cleared table. "Eat dirt and die?"

Jonah chuckled at the phrase straight out of their childhood. "It would have been appropriate."

They settled into their new table, with Abby making a concerted effort not to glance in Rachel and Marc's direction. When Jonah ordered an Antipasti platter, even though she'd eaten earlier she found herself popping a marinated olive into her mouth.

There was something relaxing about eating, Abby thought, taking a sip of wine. Then, she remembered there was something she needed to discuss with him. The olive became a hard lump in the pit of her stomach.

"We need to talk."

Jonah's hand stilled on the pepper that had made its way halfway to his mouth. He set it down on the small plate in front of him, then carefully wiped his hand on the napkin. "Don't tell me I was right."

She blinked, nearly losing track of the words she'd been putting together in her head. "Right about what?"

"About you wanting an update on the Security committee?" Though his tone remained light, his expression was serious. "I don't have my notes but I can give you an overview of the advances in the last few weeks. I can also assure you that we're on target to have everything ready by the Bash."

Did he really think she wanted to discuss that now?

"I thought that was simply a story you made up to get us away from Rachel and Marc." She smiled. "It was brilliant, by the way."

"So what you want to say to me has nothing to do with the Birthday Bash."

"No." Abby met his gaze. "It has to do with Eva Grace."

The second her daughter's name left her lips, Abby realized she couldn't do it. She'd *almost* decided it was best to tell Eva Grace that Jonah was her father and propose they come up with the best way to share the information. But now she worried she'd been rash in making that decision. His kisses seemed to have muddled her brain.

He was looking at her so expectantly, she knew she had to come up with something. If only she hadn't shot down the committee report.

She gestured with her head in the direction of Marc and Rachel. "What does she see in him?"

Jonah's brows drew together. "I suppose the flowers, the romantic evening, the charm he turns on and off at will. All surface stuff, but it's easy to get caught up."

Abby inclined her head. "Is that what happened with you and Veronica?"

He shrugged.

"I've heard you're doomed to make the same mistakes in future relationships if you don't deal with past issues."

Jonah leaned back and studied her.

Abby smiled in what she hoped was an encouraging manner.

"My problem was I settled," he said after what seemed forever. "The person I wanted seemed out of reach."

That gaze, fixed so steadily on her, gave Abby a jolt. Surely, he couldn't be talking about *her*?

Though she'd dated her share in high school and college, she'd never been in what she considered a serious relationship. Her only love, if there'd been one, had been her all-consuming ambition. "It just shows why settling is a bad idea."

How inane, but with those piercing blue eyes studying her, it was the best she could muster.

"I won't repeat that mistake." His gaze never wavered. "What about Eva Grace?"

She couldn't do it. Telling Eva Grace he was her birth father would mean letting him fully into her life. She'd already gone too far letting Eva Grace call his parents Nana and Papa.

What had she been thinking? If she'd been alone, she might have smacked herself up against the side of her head.

The only saving grace was that Eva Grace was unaware of the significance of those terms.

"Eva Grace," Jonah prompted, his fingers twirling the wine glass back and forth between his finger and thumb.

Back and forth.

Back and forth.

The man was like a dog with a bone. She'd bought as much time as possible. He wasn't going to let this go.

Abby thought quickly.

"It's really more of a question." Abby forced a little laugh. Jonah lifted a brow.

"Can you watch Eva Grace Saturday morning for me?"

CHAPTER NINETEEN

"This was as Eva Grace would say, an 'awesome' day." His mother glanced at Jonah. "You have an amazing daughter."

Jonah was still trying to figure out how to respond to that comment, when his father spoke.

"I thought Mercy Watson was a girl, too, but Eva Grace set me straight." Michael's lips quirked upward. "She's such a bright girl."

"And so funny," his mother added.

For the next minute all Jonah had to do was nod his head as his parents extolled Eva Grace's attributes.

"She doesn't call you Daddy." His father's comment had Jonah jerking his head up.

When they'd gotten home from Abby's apartment, no one had been ready to sleep. Jonah had suggested they relax on the rooftop, which was deserted on a Wednesday night. Though the night held a slight chill, a light jacket and the heat lamps were all that was needed to be comfortable.

"I don't deserve that title." Saying the words brought a sharp pain in the vicinity of Jonah's heart.

"Why, you most certainly—" his mother began, stopping when his father laid a hand on her arm.

"Have you and Abby spoken about that possibility?" The acceptance in his father's voice encouraged confidences.

These people didn't judge him. Not like Abby did. Not like he did.

Jonah took note of the stars winking overhead. There was something peaceful about sitting here in the near-dark with his parents.

"She told me I hadn't earned the title." He shrugged. "She's right."

"But she's letting you spend time with Eva Grace." Confusion furrowed his mother's brow. "It's apparent how much the child likes you."

"Abby had a near miss accident out on the High Road several weeks back." Jonah took a moment to explain what had happened that day.

"Oh, my." Nancy brought a hand to her mouth. "She could have been killed."

Jonah nodded. "It got her to thinking what would happen to Eva Grace if she'd have died. Knowing I am her biological father made me the most likely possibility."

"The only possibility." His father's blue eyes flashed. "If something happened to Abby, you would never allow your child to go to strangers."

"They wouldn't be strangers, they'd be friends of Abby's." When his father opened his mouth to protest, Jonah continued, "But no, I wouldn't let her go to anyone else. Abby knows that."

"Why is she refusing to tell Eva Grace who you are?" The hurt in his mother's voice sliced a hole in Jonah's gut.

By his choices, he'd brought this pain into his family's life. "She doesn't trust me."

"That's crazy," Michael shook his head. "What is Abby thinking?"

"I don't blame her. I don't want you blaming her, either."

Jonah knew his parents were firmly on his side, but he wouldn't have them dogging Abby.

"But—" his mother began.

"No." Jonah spoke firmly so there would be no misunderstanding. "I walked away from her. She never wanted a child. She agreed to be a surrogate to help me, to help Veronica."

"And for the fifty thousand dollars," his father reminded him.

"The reason she even considered doing it was because of our friendship," Jonah told them. "If you recall, she turned us—and the money--down at first. Until Veronica went to her and reminded her that having that amount of money would make getting a business loan a slam dunk."

His mother's hand shook as she reached for the cup of hot cocoa she'd brought up with her. "Abby didn't plan on raising a child."

"Thankfully, she's done well for herself." Michael's tone had turned somber.

"Only because of inheriting the hotel." Jonah expelled a harsh breath. He raked a hand through his hair. "But it's been a struggle."

Jonah told them what the last five years had been like for Abby. By the time he finished tears filled his mother's eyes and his father was clearing his throat.

Nancy bit her lower lip. "I can't imagine her going through that alone."

"It isn't only Eva Grace who's amazing." Emotion thickened Jonah's voice. "Abby is amazing."

"I always hoped the two of you would end up together."

Jonah turned to his mother, unable to hide his surprise. "You never said a word."

"Who you kids dated was up to you." His father glanced at his wife. "Who you married was up to you, not us."

His parents had been cordial and welcoming to Veronica, done everything possible to make her feel a part of the family.

"You never liked Veronica." The words spilled out. Why, Jonah wondered, had it taken him so long to realize the fact?

"I liked many things about Veronica. She had many good qualities," his mother said diplomatically.

"But—" Jonah prompted.

Nancy hesitated, then admitted, "She wasn't the most compassionate of women."

Michael gave a snort. "There's an understatement."

"Your son was married to her," Nancy reminded her husband, shooting him a warning glance.

"That's okay." Jonah sat back. "That ship has sailed. I see clearly the mistakes we made. Not just Veronica, but me as well."

"She was the one who didn't want the baby." His mother, loyal to the nth degree, pointed out.

Jonah remembered Abby's words. He would not foist the blame for his actions on anyone else. "The baby Abby was carrying was mine. Yet, she was the only one who stood up for the child. My child."

He pounded a fist against his heart. "She was my child. Yet, I would have allowed Abby to terminate the pregnancy if she'd been willing."

His father's attention appeared focused into the darkness, while his mother's gaze had dropped to the mug she cupped between her fingers.

"I don't deserve to have that sweet child call me 'daddy.'" Jonah swallowed against the lump in this throat. "Abby was my oldest and dearest friend. She's right. I left her hanging in the wind. I can't even look at myself in the mirror. What kind of man—"

"Enough." His father's voice boomed as his hand crashed down on the table. Michael's unflinching gaze met Jonah's. "You are a good man. You tried to do the right thing."

"But—"

"You let me finish." The older man's tone brooked no argument. "Hindsight, as we all know, is twenty-twenty. From what I understand when the doctor spoke to you that day, the prognosis for the baby appeared grim."

Jonah reluctantly nodded.

"There was genuine concern about the baby's quality of life. That's the issue Veronica raised. Am I correct?"

"Her cousin's baby had died, not even a year before of a severe birth defect. Veronica was in the room when he passed." Jonah could still see her shattered face when she'd arrived home that night. "It devastated her."

"The infertility treatments also took their toll." His mother sighed heavily. "Then, when the adoption fell through..."

It had been a punch in the gut when the birth mother had backed out at the last minute. "She'd had a few baby showers and the room was all decorated. It was a difficult time for both of us."

"Then, you found out just how expensive it was to hire a surrogate." His mother spoke in a low, soothing tone.

He thought she probably had a purpose in taking him down this road again, but darn if he could figure it out.

"I'd never seen Veronica so distraught. Out of the blue she mentioned asking Abby to carry the baby." Jonah rubbed the bridge of his nose. "I thought it was a crazy idea. Abby hadn't ever had a child. We didn't know for sure she could even carry a child to term. But on positive side, Abby didn't think she wanted children and we'd be using a donor egg, which cut down on the connection. And she needed the money."

Jonah scrubbed his hands over his face and met the concerned looks on his parents' gaze. "I'd say I wished we'd never approached Abby, but then there would be no Eva Grace. Now that I've met her, I can't imagine a world without her in it."

When neither of them spoke, Jonah gave a bitter laugh. "Of course, if it had been up to me she wouldn't be here."

"The time for self-flagellation is past." His father narrowed his gaze on his son. "You forget the doctor was the one who suggested terminating the pregnancy. From everything you told me, he pulled no punches regarding the baby's likely quality of life. You had a wife who wouldn't be able to handle a special needs child."

"That doesn't excuse—"

"Stop." The single word from his father cut the air like a knife. "This was an unfortunate situation with enough guilt to go around."

Jonah offered his father a quizzical look.

"You think your mother and I don't share your guilt?" Michael took a second as his voice had begun to shake. "Abby was like a daughter to us. She didn't have a father. And when she needed one the most, I wasn't there for her."

"I should have said to hell with what Veronica threatened and been with Abby during her pregnancy and after the baby came." A tear slipped down Nancy's cheek. She swiped it away.

Jonah wasn't sure what surprised him most. His mother using the word 'hell' or that he wasn't the only one flooded with regret.

"We believed Veronica would go after Abby," Michael reminded his wife, then turned to Jonah. "I really thought she would have followed through on her threat."

There was a question in his father's searching gaze.

"She absolutely would have followed through." Jonah pushed back his chair and rose, unable to sit with the emotions churning like storm-tossed seas in him. He rested his back against the wall overlooking the city and faced his parents. "That's why I made sure she didn't learn about the money I sent Abby every month."

Even in the dim light, Jonah saw the surprise skitter across his father's face.

"You never told us you sent Abby money." There was a hint of puzzlement in his tone.

"I didn't want to keep it from you." Jonah held his gaze steady. "I could say I considered sending the money to be between me and Abby. But it went beyond that...I couldn't take the chance that Veronica would find out and carry through with her threat."

"A marriage with that kind of secret is on a rocky path," his father said.

"I'm not proud of lying to my wife." Jonah expelled a ragged breath. "The alternative was to do nothing for Abby and the baby. My baby. I couldn't have lived with myself if I'd done that."

"It appears Abby is willing to give us a chance to be a part of her and Eva Grace's life." Nancy closed her eyes for a second. "When that little girl called me Nana..."

His mother pressed fingers to her lips to still their trembling, her eyes glistening in the lamplight. "I get choked up just remembering. You probably think I'm making too much—"

Michael took his wife's hand and clasped it tightly in his. "I feel the same way when she calls me Papa."

"That was incredibly generous of Abby." His mother said and his dad nodded.

"It was a good day."

What would have made it even better, was if Eva Grace had called him 'Daddy.'

Though he knew he didn't deserve the title, Jonah couldn't help wondering what it would feel like to be Eva Grace's daddy in every sense of the word.

Jonah said good-bye to his parents first thing Thursday morning. The rest of the day and all-day Friday Jonah spent on the budget, one of the least favorite parts of his new position.

The only highlight to his day was when Abby texted and asked him if he could be at her place the next morning at eight a.m. to watch Eva Grace.

By the time Friday evening rolled around, all he wanted to do was to go home and relax. Instead, Jonah headed to Chicago to have dinner with his friend, Noah Garrity. Noah, a former fraternity brother, had recently become engaged and wanted him to meet his fiancé.

The Italian restaurant on North Dearborn was a popular one which meant the place would be crazy busy on a Friday night. Noah assured him reservations were in place. When Jonah gave his name to the hostess, he was ushered through several archways to a white linen-clad table for four.

As three of the four seats were occupied, he concluded he was the last to arrive.

Noah rose, his dark hair razor cut in a style that suited his strong features. He must have come straight from the office as he still wore a dark suit. His fiancée, or at least the one with the blonde hair who fit Noah's description, wore pearls.

When Jonah had heard Italian, he'd assumed casual and had worn khakis and a light sweater. At least, he told himself, he hadn't showed up in jeans. Not that mattered. He didn't feel the need to impress.

Noah gave his hand a firm shake, his blue eyes twinkling mischievously. "I'm glad you could make it. I hope you don't mind that Stephanie brought along a friend."

When Noah had mentioned his girlfriend wanted to fix him up with one of her friends, he'd made it clear he wasn't interested. That discussion had taken place the week before he'd moved to Hazel Green. Since he'd reconnected with Abby, he was even less interested.

"Of course not." Jonah smiled while Noah made the introductions. Stephanie was indeed the blonde. She and her auburn-haired friend—whose name was Ryann—were both paralegals in the law firm where Noah practiced.

Knowing he had to drive home, Jonah turned down a glass of wine, but snagged an olive from the antipasto platter that Noah had ordered for the table.

After the server took their orders, Jonah found himself on the receiving end of an inquisition.

Stephanie sipped her Italian cocktail, her gaze sharp and assessing. "Noah tells me you're the Chief of Police in Hazel Green."

"I am." Jonah reached for a second olive.

She continued to study Jonah as if he was a witness ready to be deposed. Or maybe, it was more like a bug under a microscope.

Jonah had no doubt she and Ryann--who'd just ordered her second Negroni—had already done a thorough social media search on him. Heck, the intensity of their focus had him wondering if the two had also ran a background check.

Stephanie arched a brow. "You're divorced."

Was that a question? It sounded more like a statement. Jonah lifted his glass of water and redirected. "How long have you known Noah?"

Now, that was a question. He could only hope she'd take the conversational ball and run with it.

"We met at the law practice." Stephanie slanted Noah a playful glance. "He asked me out for weeks before I decided to give him a shot."

Noah took her hand and brought it to his lips. "When you see something—or in this case—someone, you want, you give it your best. I knew we'd be good together."

Jonah experienced a pang of envy.

"Do you have any children?" Ryann asked him, reopening the questioning phase.

It shouldn't be a difficult question. Yes, as much as Jonah wanted to claim Eva Grace, he wasn't sure he had the right. Not yet, anyway.

"Jonah."

He turned and pushed to his feet. Nell stood at the side of the table, her gaze clearly curious. He watched her eyes flick over the table. Noah and Stephanie were obviously together. Their fingers were intertwined with the large diamond on Stephanie's left hand catching the light. Then there was he and Ryann, who probably looked like a couple, but weren't in any sense of the word.

"This is quite a surprise." With her silvery blonde hair and ice blue silk suit with heels, Nell looked like a modern woman tonight, rather than one from a bygone era. "Noah, I wasn't aware you and Jonah were acquainted."

Noah glanced questioningly at Jonah, then the confusion cleared. "That's right. You both live in Hazel Green."

"How do you know this guy?" Jonah gestured with his head toward Noah.

"AAML," Noah and Nell said together, then laughed.

"American Academy of Matrimonial Lawyers," Nell explained. "We're both members."

"I keep forgetting you're an attorney." Jonah glanced around. "Are you here with someone?"

"I was stood up." Nell lifted a shoulder as if it was of no consequence. "I was going to say it happens all the time, but it really doesn't."

"I'd imagine not." Jonah smiled. "Would you like to join us?"

Nell's expression turned thoughtful. She tapped her lips with a finger, her gaze narrowing on Noah. "You wouldn't mind?"

"Absolutely not." His friend said heartily. "I'll have the hostess bring over another chair."

Jonah moved his chair, making space between him and Ryann. The paralegal was probably a very nice woman. He just wasn't interested.

Ryann moved her chair closer to Stephanie to make room for Nell, who offered her a conciliatory smile. "It's nice of you to be so welcoming."

Ryann's only response was a quick twist of her lips.

Once Nell was settled and her order taken, Noah gestured

with his glass of wine toward Jonah. "You and this guy know each other."

Nell smiled. "We've attended several functions that—"

"We?" Ryann lifted a brow. "Like on a date?"

Instead of answering, Nell studied the young woman for a moment then lifted her glass of San Pellegrino and shifted her attention to Stephanie. "What a lovely ring."

The conversation about the proposal, the engagement and wedding plans lasted through much of the meal. Nell, Jonah was beginning to realize, was a master at controlling conversations.

She revealed only what she chose to reveal and learned nearly everything there was to know about the other three at the table. Not through direct questions, the tactic employed by Ryann, but by comments designed to get the person talking.

The only person at the table she spared was Jonah. He wasn't certain why, but he appreciated the consideration. By virtue of keeping everyone else talking, she shared very little about herself. Only enough that the others thought she was participating in the sharing.

Only once did she appear to falter. That was when a dark-haired man passed by the table.

If Jonah hadn't been sitting where he was and been focused on her, he'd never have noticed the slight inhale when she spotted him. The guy was dark and lean, wearing a hand-tailored suit and Italian loafers. The two men with him with older and distinguished looking. If Jonah had to guess, it appeared to be a business meeting.

He wondered if Nell had dated the guy, was dating the guy, or perhaps this was the man who'd stood her up. Jonah didn't ask. That would be putting her on the spot, something she'd very graciously avoided doing to him all evening.

The three men were seated at a nearby table. While the conversation shifted to the Cubs chances this year, Nell excused herself to take a phone call.

"I didn't hear her phone ring." Stephanie punctuated the comment with a little giggle. She was now on her fourth Italian cocktail.

"It vibrated." Seconds earlier, Jonah had watched the dark-haired man at the other table rise and pull out his phone.

"Are you and Nell dating?" Ryann asked.

Was there an echo in the room? Hadn't he heard that question before? Heard, he realized, but never answered.

"No," he told Ryann. "We're simply friends."

When a look Jonah recognized all too well flared in Ryann's eyes, he knew he had to shut this down. If he didn't, he'd have to worry about Noah springing Ryann on him every time his buddy wanted to get together.

"I have a girlfriend." Jonah thought of Abby. His lips curved. Okay, so perhaps girlfriend was a stretch, but she was a girl and he hoped she considered him a friend.

"He didn't tell me." Noah lifted his hands at the piercing look Stephanie shot him. "I didn't know."

"It's a recent thing." Jonah assured Stephanie, not wanting to get Noah in hot water.

"What's recent?" Nell asked.

Before he could rise and pull out her chair, she was already seated.

"Jonah has a girlfriend." Suspicion lingered in Ryann's eyes.

"Yes, he does." Picking up her glass of Pellegrino, Nell nodded. "And, she just happens to be a good friend of mine."

CHAPTER TWENTY

"Let me get this straight." Nell leaned back in the chair and stared incredulously at Abby. "You wanted to meet me for breakfast to give Jonah a reason to watch Eva Grace?"

"I would have eaten by myself, but I knew it'd be more fun with you." Abby had chosen the Green Gateau, a bistro located just off the Green. The place, known for their eclectic Euro-American menu, served a cherry stuffed French toast that was positively orgasmic. "Besides, it's so much food and this way we can split."

Nell sipped her coffee, a rich Columbian blend. "Why did you want him to watch Eva Grace so badly?"

"I didn't." Abby couldn't resist pouring some table cream from the pretty cobalt blue pitcher into her coffee. "I'd told him I wanted to speak with him about something. Then, I changed my mind and instead, asked him to watch Eva Grace."

Nell leaned back in her seat, looking incredibly lovely in her form-fitting blue sweater and plaid skirt. Chains of stones hung in varying length around her neck. Her friend had gone for a late 60's look and it suited her short blonde hair.

"What was your--?" Nell paused when the waitress brought

out the French toast on mismatched china plates, then flashed a brilliant smile. "You divided the order for us."

"It can be kind of messy to separate on your own." The girl, who couldn't have been more than eighteen, flushed with pleasure at the delight in Nell's voice.

"That was nice of you." Nell glanced down at the china plate ringed by tiny rosebuds. "This will be worth the increased cardio."

"I agree." Abby shifted her attention back to the server. "Thank you so much."

"No problem." The girl smiled. "I have to take out another order then I'll bring you ladies more coffee."

"*Ladies.*" Abby grimaced when the girl was out of earshot. "We're not that old."

"When you're her age, women who are thirty qualify as ancient." Nell forked off a bite of the French toast and watched cream cheese and cherries ooze out.

"We're not ancient."

"In my early twenties, a hot weekend night would have been spent clubbing." Nell shook her head and heaved an exaggerated sigh. "Ah, the good old days."

"Speaking of hot weekend nights." Abby motioned in a give-me-the-deets gesture. "How was your date last night with the sexy stockbroker?"

"I'm not certain that sexy and stockbroker ever go together." Nell brought the French toast to her mouth and chewed, closing her eyes. A look of pleasure washed over her pretty face. "This is fantastic. Why haven't we come here before?"

Abby waved the question aside. "How was the guy? C'mon, spill."

Nell placed her fork on the table. Picking up the coffee cup, she peered at Abby over the rim. "Would you believe he stood me up?"

"No way." Abby couldn't imagine any man not showing up for

a date with Nell. Her friend had the trifecta: brains, class and a killer body. Oh, and a wicked sense of humor.

"It's true." Nell lifted a shoulder and let it fall. "He texted me this morning with some lame excuse. I deleted it. Bye, bye, Calvin."

"I'm so sorry." Abby reached across the table and squeezed Nell's hand. "You're better off without him."

"I agree." Nell kept her eyes on Abby, her gaze watchful. "At least the evening wasn't a total loss."

"Really?" Abby took a bite of the French toast and agreed with Nell. It really was—

"I ran into Jonah." Nell's tone was matter-a-fact. "We had dinner together."

The cream cheese, cherries and bread formed a hard lump in Abby's throat. She forced herself to swallow. On the verge of choking, Abby washed the rest down with the last of her coffee.

Jealousy spewed hot embers in her belly. Still, she told herself if Nell could play it cool, so could she.

"That's interesting." Abby could have cheered when her voice came out casual and offhand, just as she intended. "How did that come about?"

Jonah hadn't said word one to her this morning about spending last night with Nell. Beautiful, accomplished, Nell.

Of course, she hadn't given him much of a chance to tell her anything. Eva Grace had been eager to play the game of Hisss he'd brought with him. Still, she'd have thought he would have mentioned something as important as having dinner with one of her best friends.

"Calvin and I were supposed to meet at a Trattoria on Dearborn. I waited thirty, which was twenty more than I should have. On my way out of the restaurant, I ran into Jonah." Nell paused and smiled when the server stopped by to refill their cups.

"How is your breakfast?" The girl politely inquired.

"Fine." Abby had to force out the word. She didn't want to talk about food, she wanted to talk about Jonah. And, she wouldn't get anything out of Nell until the girl left.

But, she reminded herself, her personal situation heading toward the toilet wasn't this girl's fault. "Actually, it's excellent. Thanks so much."

"Let me know if you need anything else."

Once she'd slipped away, Abby refocused on Nell. "And?"

"He invited me to join him for dinner." This time, Nell didn't wait for questions but continued. "He was there with a guy and his fiancée and another woman."

"A date?" Abby heard the shock in her voice. But really, why did it matter? Jonah was certainly free to date whoever he wanted. Yet, after the kisses they'd shared, it felt like a betrayal.

Nell's eyes were steady and very blue. "Not a date."

"How do you know that?"

"He barely paid attention to her. He asked me to join them and seemed relieved when I agreed." Nell picked up her fork, her gaze shifting for a second to a Blue Jay chattering on a leafy limb nearby.

"Not conclusive." Abby shook her head. The knot that had been in her throat had taken up residence in the pit of her stomach.

"He told her he had a girlfriend."

Abby blinked. "What?"

"She asked if he had a girlfriend and he said yes."

Even as her blood began to hum, Abby brought her brows together and considered the comment. "Do you think he has a girlfriend back in Springfield?"

"I believe he was referring to you."

The thrill that traveled up Abby's spine made absolutely no sense. She took a gulp of the steaming coffee, relishing the burn against her throat that brought her back to reality. "He's mistaken."

"Why?"

"You know why."

"Humor me." Nell sat back in her chair. "Spell it out."

Though there was no one seated nearby, Abby lowered. "There can never be anything between Jonah and me. I know what kind of man he is deep down."

Something flickered in the depths of Nell's ice blue eyes. "One mistake. Made years ago."

"It speaks to character." Abby lifted her chin. "What's that saying? When someone shows you who they are, believe them."

"Let me make sure I understand." A tiny muscle in Nell's jaw jumped. "You're saying that a decision made years ago, a path chosen--even if regretted--makes up the sum of that person's character."

The bite underscoring Nell's words surprised Abby. She could count on one hand the times she'd seen her friend show such intense emotion.

Abby hesitated, feeling the ground shifting beneath her feet. But darn it, she was right about this. "He wanted to kill Eva Grace."

She'd never explained Jonah's action in such bold terms and the words held power.

Nell took another bite of French toast, then dabbed a bit of cherry from the corner of her mouth. "You told me the doctor had painted a bleak picture of what the fetus's life would look like."

"It wasn't a fetus." Abby balled her hands into fists. "She was a baby. I'd felt her move."

"To *you*, she was a baby." Nell agreed. "But Jonah and his wife hadn't had the experience of feeling her move. They had yet to bond with her in the way you already had. Doubtless, all they heard were the physician's dire warning about a baby that didn't yet seem real to them."

"Maybe," Abby grudgingly conceded.

"From what you describe, Jonah had a wife on the verge of a

nervous breakdown. No way would she be able to cope with a severely handicapped child."

"So you just kill it?"

"There are many people who believe terminating a pregnancy under these circumstances is the humane choice."

"Is that what you believe?"

"I don't have a horse in this race." Nell's gaze turned to the blue jay. But the faraway look in her eyes told Abby she didn't see the bird. "I can tell you that life is rarely as black and white as you're making it. There are events in my life that I would go back in a heartbeat and change if I could."

The pain in Nell's voice had Abby's brows winging upward. She didn't know a lot about her friend's background, but from what Nell had shared, it had sounded like a normal childhood and upbringing.

Abby wasn't sure how to respond. She didn't want to pry into Nell's past, especially if the events were painful. "If you ever want to talk about it, know that I would keep your confidence."

Nell's lips lifted in a humorless smile. "Are you sure you want to know? I'm afraid once you did, you might find my character lacking."

Jerking back, Abby simply stared, hurt welling up inside her. "I would never—"

"You've done it to Jonah." Nell blew out a harsh breath. "I'm not proud of some of the choices I've made. Like I said, if I could go back and choose differently, I would. I can't."

It suddenly struck Abby that this discussion may be hitting too close to home for Nell. Was her friend haunted by a pregnancy termination? Had she kept that information from her because of Abby's past situation?

Abby took a breath and let it out. "If you had an abortion, I want you to know that won't affect our friendship."

"Abortion?" Nell looked too startled to be faking. "No. No. Nothing like that."

"Then what?"

Nell studied her for a long moment. "Some things are better kept to oneself."

Abby's heart sank. "Because you think I'm judgmental."

Her friend's expression softened. "I think you're one of the nicest, most loving, people I've ever known. But I choose to believe a person's character is made up of a variety of behaviors and attitudes. A single decision, or perhaps multiple decisions over a certain span of time, doesn't make that person good or bad."

"Maybe," Abby grudgingly conceded. "But decisions made when it really counts, tell us a person's character."

"You were deep in the situation, so I know it's hard for you to step back and look at it objectively."

Abby could tell where Nell was going with this and it was the wrong direction. "We're going to have to agree to disagree on—"

"You're judging Jonah when you don't know everything that went into his decision."

"Why are you on his side?" Abby cried out in frustration. "I thought you were my friend."

She'd spoken so loudly several people at a table across the terrace, turned to stare. But Abby was too hurt to care.

As if sensing her distress, Nell spoke softly in a soothing tone. "You like him."

Reluctantly, Abby nodded. "But I refuse to make excuses just so things can be the way they once were."

"Things will never be the way they once were." A sad smile lifted Nell's lips. "Not for me. Not for you. Not for him. That doesn't mean it can't be different, perhaps even better."

Abby's doubt must have shown on her face because Nell smiled. "All I'm saying is perhaps it's time you and Jonah discuss everything that went into his decision back then. After you've talked it out, then you can decide how the two of you can move forward."

The knee-jerk response was to tell Nell that she already knew everything there was to know about that time. But that would be a lie.

Nancy Rollins's revelation about Veronica had taken Abby completely by surprise. She'd had no idea Jonah's ex-wife--a woman she'd known--could be so vicious and vindictive.

Perhaps she didn't know all that had gone into Jonah's decision. She thought she knew, but they hadn't ever revisited that time. Why? Because she was afraid what she'd find out would put even more of a wedge between them.

As far as she was concerned, there was no reason he couldn't have been there with her in the delivery room. She'd been so scared, so completely alone. The baby she'd carried had been his. After all they'd shared growing up, had it really been too much to ask him to be there for her?

He hadn't even bothered to respond. Though she thought she'd moved on from that, the knowledge he hadn't cared enough to do even that, still gnawed at her.

"You're right." Abby expelled a ragged breath. "I don't know the whole story. But, I'm afraid once I do, I might not be able to stand having him around."

"Don't worry about what's going to happen once you know it all. There will be plenty of time to decide how to proceed." Nell's eyes warmed. "I have faith you'll make the decision that's right for you."

"You mean, that I'll make the right decision."

Nell shook her head. "The one that's right for you. But, this time you'll make it from a position of maturity, knowing all the facts."

CHAPTER TWENTY-ONE

Jonah looked up from the floor where he and Eva Grace played with her "ponies." With two sisters, the brightly colored horses in every shade of the rainbow were familiar to him.

He'd expected Abby.

He hadn't expected Nell to be with her.

Putting down the pink pony with the electric blue mane and tail, he rose to his feet.

"Hi, Mommy." Eva Grace barely looked up from the pony she had 'galloping' across the hardwood floor.

"How about me?" Nell's tone was teasing. "Don't I even rate a hello?"

Eva Grace looked up then and flashed a smile. "Hello. Me and Jonah are playing ponies."

"I see that." Nell placed her bag on the floor, then crossed the room and crouched down. "What would you think if I took over for Jonah while he and your mommy went to the Market?"

Jonah shifted his gaze to Abby. This was a new twist to the day. He'd bet anything it had to do with last night.

Nell's face gave him no clue. That wasn't surprising. In the short time he'd been acquainted with the woman, he knew you didn't see anything on Nell Ambrose's face she didn't want you to see.

Eva Grace's brows drew together. "I like going to Market."

When he'd first moved to Hazel Green, Jonah had learned that the "Market" was held every Saturday in The Green. Not only a traditional farmer's market with locally grown produce, artisans set up booths to sell their art and crafts as well.

Nell stroked the pink mane of a yellow horse and a look of yearning blanketed her face. "I was really looking forward to playing ponies."

Whether it was the sadness in her voice or the yearning on her face, whatever it was, had Eva Grace's kind heart responding. She patted Nell's arm, her voice soft and consoling. "I'll stay and play ponies with you."

"Thank you, Eva Grace." Nell's expression brightened. "Maybe my pony and yours can race?"

"Mine is really fast," Eva Grace warned, her big blue eyes wide and serious.

"That's okay." Nell slanted a glance at Abby. "It's not all about winning."

Jonah shifted his attention to Abby. For someone who'd left to have a relaxing breakfast with a friend, she looked pale and tense.

What had Nell told her?

Abby was a smart woman. Surely, she'd understood that he hadn't been on a date with Ryann. Not that there was anything wrong with him dating.

Even as the justification flashed, he shoved it aside. It would have been wrong, and unfair to the other woman. Not when there was only one woman he wanted to be with…one who appeared to be on the verge of kicking him to the curb.

Eva Grace had to give him a hug and a kiss on the cheek before he left. The feel of those small arms around him had a lump rising to his throat.

He cleared his throat as they strode down the corridor

leading outside. "Where did you and Nell end up having breakfast?"

"The Green Gateau."

He reached around her to open the door. "That's the place with the green door and all the windows, just off the park."

"That's the one." As she stepped onto the sidewalk, she turned silent. Her teeth caught on her bottom lip.

The tension in his gut ratcheted up another notch. What the heck had Nell told her?

"Something upset you. It appears it has to do with me."

Her gaze jerked in his direction, surprise widening her eyes.

His lips quirked upward, but he found no humor in the situation. "Give me some credit. I am a cop."

"Nell said she ran into you last night." Though Abby's tone was casual, the look in his eyes had him swallowing a curse.

"It wasn't a date."

"What?"

"I wasn't on a date." Though he and Abby had only exchanged a few kisses, it felt like that would be the ultimate betrayal. "I didn't know that woman would be there. I was actually relieved when Nell showed up. If she said—"

Abby's soft touch on his arm had whatever he'd been about to say, dying in his throat.

"That's what she told me." She exhaled a rough breath. "She had a lot of other things to say as well."

Jonah's brows drew together. "Such as?"

"Such as there are always two sides to every issue."

"True."

"That perhaps I've judged you unfairly."

It was clear they were no longer talking about last night's dinner at the Trattoria. It also sounded as if Nell had stood up for him. Unfortunately, it was undeserved. "I deserve every bit of your judgment."

She nodded. For some reason his comment had the tension relaxing on her face.

Crisp white tents dotted the Green, selling apples, pumpkins and other seasonal produce. A tent offering stained glass caught his eye, reminding him of the house they'd seen on their walk. The yellow one with stained glass over the windows.

Abby didn't seem interested in stopping at any of the tents. She smiled and nodded to shoppers she knew, occasionally calling out, or responding to a greeting.

If she was as aware of the curious glances slanted their way, it didn't show. Though Jonah longed to touch her; to take her arm, he kept his hands to himself.

"Did you agree with Veronica about terminating the pregnancy?" Abby stopped. Resting her back against the side of the bridge, her dark eyes pinned him. "Or did you just go along with her wishes?"

It was a question Jonah had struggled with for years. Telling Abby he'd only gone along with what Veronica had wanted would likely be more acceptable to her than saying he'd agreed with his wife.

While he wanted to rebuild his relationship with Abby, he wouldn't do it based on half-truths or lies.

"I honestly don't know."

Suspicion flicked in her brown eyes. "You don't know?"

"I know it was easy for you. Despite everything the doctor was saying, you were determined to continue to protect the life growing inside you."

Her eyes never left his face.

"When I heard all the challenges the child would face, I remember feeling sick inside."

"The doctor said it *could* be a meningocele."

"As rare as that particular type of spina bifida is, that comment felt as if the doctor was tossing us a bone." Jonah raked a hand through his hair. "The fact is, Veronica couldn't have handled a child with severe birth defects. There isn't a single doubt in my mind on that."

Abby started walking and he fell into step beside her. "You didn't answer my question."

"I honestly don't know." Jonah took a deep breath, let it out. "I took the easy route."

"I don't understand." Her voice trembled slightly.

She understood, he thought. She might wish the answer different, but she understood.

"Veronica was my wife. I told myself I had to stand by her. Which, don't you see, allowed me to not take ownership?" Self-loathing filled his voice. "And, when she threatened to make your life a living hell if I stayed in contact with you, I told myself I was protecting you. But was I? Or was it that I didn't have the guts to face you after the predicament I put you in?"

"Going the surrogate route was my choice." Abby's gaze drifted to the yellow house Eva Grace had admired. "One day I'm going to give my daughter a house like that."

My daughter. The significance wasn't lost on him.

"We were the ones who approached you, dangling the money like a carrot before a starving rabbit."

Abby laughed and the sound seemed to surprise them both.

"It wasn't just the money." Abby spoke, her voice now as soft as her eyes. "It was the chance to give you a child. I knew you'd be a wonderful father."

Jonah said nothing, could think of nothing to say. Facts didn't lie. He'd walked away from her, just when she needed him most.

"I was right."

He cocked his head.

"You are a wonderful father. Eva Grace adores you."

"I love her already."

"She's a hard kid not to love." Abby's lips curved before expression sobered. "One last question."

"Anything." Though he couldn't imagine what else there was left, Jonah braced himself.

"Why didn't you come to the hospital for the delivery?" The hurt in her eyes shredded his heart. "I was alone. I was frightened out of my mind. I know you'd washed your hands of the baby--"

He flinched at the words.

"--but I thought, because of our friendship, you'd have come to be with me."

Puzzled, Jonah cocked his head. "I didn't know when you were going to deliver. And, the last time I'd seen you, you'd told me to stay the heck away from you."

"What about my call? The texts?" The moisture that filled her eyes told him, even after all this time, the memory hurt like a rotten tooth. "You didn't even have the decency to say you wouldn't be there."

"I never got a text or a call from you." Jonah stilled. "Surely Veronica wouldn't have—"

He didn't need to finish the thought.

The suspicion that rose in her dark eyes had him going silent for a moment. "I didn't receive your call or texts. I don't know how that happened because my phone is always with me. But, I didn't."

"Would you have been there?" Her penetrating gaze narrowed. "If you'd gotten the messages."

He wanted to be honest. He thought of Veronica. Of the threats. "I would have wanted to be there. I think I'd have been there. But Veronica, well, I'd never seen her so bent on punishing you."

"You act like she was calling the shots." Abby's brows pulled together. "You've never been one to let another person run you."

"She'd have done what she wanted, whether I agreed or not." He willed Abby to see the truth in his eyes. "If she decided to take you to court, she'd have pursued that vendetta without me. If she decided to take custody of Eva Grace just to put her in an institution, I'd have battled her in court and likely won. But at what cost? To you? To me? To Eva Grace?"

"How could you stay with such a monster?"

His words came out on a shuddering breath, "Because I helped create that monster."

The gate to the park where Jonah and Eva Grace once pushed their swings to the heavens, drew Abby. She opened it and stepped inside. Unlike the last time she'd been here, today the park was filled with parents and children.

Abby almost turned around and walked out. Then she spotted an empty ornate iron bench under a red maple. She moved quickly to it, her legs quivering. "What do you mean?"

Jonah didn't immediately answer, his gaze appeared drawn to a father pushing a girl who could be no more than six months in a baby swing. "I always wanted children. Not just one, but a whole houseful. A desire for a large family was something Veronica and I shared."

For a second a memory had his gaze turning distant and his lips lifting in a smile. Then, a shutter dropped. "Despite the fact that we were young and supposedly healthy, the babies didn't come."

Abby remembered how Veronica's personality had changed. They'd been friends back then. Veronica had told her the fertility drugs made her edgy but she'd refused to quit until the doctors said 'no more.'

Things had always come easily for Veronica. Not getting what she wanted, what her husband wanted, had driven her crazy.

"I'm surprised you didn't give adoption another try." Abby softened her voice, recalling the pain both Veronica and Jonah experienced when the birth mother changed her mind at the last minute.

Jonah shook his head. "Veronica saw that experience as just another failure. I assured her that she was enough. She didn't believe me. Not after all the talk of children early in our marriage. Not after the excitement over the adoption."

Abby looked at this man and remembered the boy who'd once been her best friend. What had Nell said about most choices not being black and white?

"I'm not telling you this because I'm hoping for absolution." His voice shook with emotion. "Despite everything, the truth is I didn't step up and do the right thing. That will be my shame until the day I die."

Though Abby had never been a crier, large droplets slid down her cheeks and plopped on her lap. She couldn't stop them. Didn't even know if she wanted to.

The angry knot around her heart that had kept her from breathing deeply the past five years unraveled and fell away. When Jonah arms slid around her, the tears became a torrent.

"I'm here. Don't worry." Gentle hands stroked her hair. "I'm here now and I'm not going anywhere."

Eva Grace stopped sawing into the pumpkin and tilted her head, her gaze now fully focused on her Abby. "How can he be my daddy?"

"Remember when I told you that Mommy planned to carry a baby for another couple but that didn't work out and I was so happy because I fell in love with you and wanted to keep you?" Abby had told this story so many times in the past couple of years, that despite her nerves it came easily to her lips.

She and Jonah had decided to tell Eva Grace tonight that he was her father. Although no promises had been made between them, she trusted Jonah to be here for her. And for her, er, their daughter.

Eva Grace's eyes shifted to Jonah. "Where have you been?"

"He-" Abby began but Jonah lifted a hand, letting her know he had this one.

"I've been living in Springfield." Jonah kept his tone easy, though Abby watched the muscle in his jaw jump. "It's a long ways away. I moved here because I want to be close to you."

Eva Grace thought for a moment, then picked up her pumpkin knife. "Do you think that his smile should go up or down?"

Jonah studied the pumpkin. "Up. Because he's happy."

The little girl smiled. "He is happy."

Abby waited while Eva Grace stuck her knife into the pumpkin and began to saw. "Do you have any other questions right now?"

"Yep."

"What is it?" Abby prompted.

Eva Grace turned to Jonah. "Can I call you Daddy?"

CHAPTER TWENTY-TWO

"I almost lost it when Eva Grace asked if she could call me Daddy." Jonah gave a little laugh. "I can't believe she wasn't more upset."

"She's wanted a daddy. Now, here you are." Abby kept her tone light. "Why wouldn't she be happy?"

There were lots of ways Jonah could answer that, but realized by her response, they both needed a break from the heavy discussion.

After Eva Grace was in bed, Abby had opened a bottle of wine and he picked up a sweet and savory cheese platter from Matilda's.

Jonah let the subject drop and allowed himself to relax, for what felt like the first time in five years.

When Abby turned on a romantic comedy, he sat on the sofa beside her while they drank wine and munched on a fig and apple compote, crisp crostini and an assortment of cheeses.

Sometime during the movie, his arm found its way around her shoulder and she nestled against him. The couple on the screen had just weathered a storm that would have shipwrecked a lesser couple when Jonah leaned over and brushed his lips lightly against Abby's.

She glanced up, a question in those beautiful dark eyes. "What's that for?"

"You're an amazing woman, Abigail Fine."

Startled surprise mixed with pleasure on her pretty face.

"And," he added, brushing a strand of hair back from her face with the back of his hand, "an amazing mother."

"I try to do my best," she said simply. "That's all any of us can do."

"Humble, too." He kissed her again. "Which I find incredibly sexy."

She smiled against his mouth and wrapped her arms around his neck. "Tell me more."

Jonah gazed into her eyes and what he'd refused to see for so long smacked him in the face. He loved Abby.

Not liked.

Loved.

"You're the best woman I know. Smart. Hardworking. Loving." Jonah scattered kisses down her jaw and neck.

Her soft moan had his mouth returning to her lips for a kiss that turned from sweet to hot in a heartbeat. By the time they came up for air, Jonah wanted her with every fiber of his being.

Too soon, he told himself.

He shifted, gathered her close and kissed her temple. "We should probably—"

Whatever he'd planned to say was forgotten when she pulled his face down with her hand and gave him a ferocious kiss. His control nearly shattered when Abby lifted her face, he saw his own desire reflected in her chocolate depths.

"I don't want to push you," he murmured, his control held in place by one tenuous thread.

"You're not." Abby laughed, a short nervous burst of air as color flooded her face. "I've wanted you since I was sixteen."

"Sixteen, eh?" Jonah eyed her for a long moment, his eyes boring into hers, then he winked. "I guess I better make this worth the wait."

～

Abby's heart performed a series of flutters as a look of tenderness crossed his face. Something inside her seemed to lock into place and she couldn't look away.

His fingers weren't quite steady as they touched the curve of her cheek, trailed along the line of her jaw. Abby held herself very still as the gentle touch left a trail of fire in their wake. If this was a dream, she didn't want to wake up.

"It's been a long time for me," she blurted out. "A very long time."

His husky laugh did strange things to her insides while the hand that stroked her hair soothed and steadied her. He smelled of sap and a familiar warm male scent that made something tighten low in her abdomen.

"Tonight is about the future." Jonah moved his arm so that her hand slid down to his and he gently locked their fingers together. "A first. For both of us."

Abby found herself nodding.

He brought their joined hands to his mouth, his eyes never leaving hers. "Are you protected?"

Protection. Her mind raced. "I haven't really da-dated since Eva Grace was born."

Jonah didn't push, just waited for her to gather her thoughts and get it all out.

"Last year there was someone in town who, well, who appealed to me." Her cheeks heated with stinging color. "I bought some condoms but he moved to California before we even went out."

"I'm glad he moved." His voice took on a horse, throaty rasp. He smiled. "I'm even more glad you have the condoms."

Running her hands up along his sides, Abby curled her body against him, moving seductively. "Are you going to talk all night?"

He laughed, a low pleasant rumbling sound. "That's not the plan."

Without warning, he rose and scooped her up in his arms.

Forgetting all about Eva Grace sleeping down the hall, Abby opened her mouth to shriek. Thankfully, Jonah was faster. His mouth closed over hers and the shriek morphed into a moan.

By the time they reached her bedroom, she wanted him with an intensity that surprised her. She rummaged through her lingerie drawer and heaved a sigh of relief when her fingers closed around the unopened box.

While she pulled out several foil packets, Jonah closed and locked and the door behind them.

She'd barely taken a seat on the bed when he pounced. She couldn't help but giggle. "Shoes off."

"It's a good start." He tucked a stray curl behind her ear, just before his shoes joined hers on the rug next to the bed.

Abby looped her arms around his neck and met his gaze. "Tell me this isn't a mistake."

He smiled, a boyish sort of smile that sent her stomach into flips and melted her heart. Then his expression sobered. "This isn't a mistake."

When she trembled, he lowered his lips to the top of her head. "We don't have to do this. Not now, anyway."

After the tiniest hesitation, Abby smiled. "We do."

Pulling back, Jonah stared down at her, a question in his eyes.

"If we don't, I'm going to explode."

He grinned, full-out. "I believe that's my line."

Slowly his arms lifted to wrap around her, not confining, but comfortable.

Abby gazed up at him. "I like to kiss you."

"You'll like the other stuff, too. But we'll start with the kissing."

Leaning over, he kissed the base of her jaw. When his mouth closed over hers, Abby nearly burst into the Hallelujah chorus.

He continued pressing his lips lightly to hers, teasingly, his mouth never pulling away. His hands slipped underneath her shirt, slowly sliding up and down her back. She knew what he was doing, making sure she was comfortable, not wanting to move too fast.

While Abby appreciated the consideration, she'd passed the desire for slow and sweet ten minutes ago. While it felt amazingly good to kiss him, it wasn't enough.

She wanted to devour him like one of Matilda's sweet cakes, in greedy little bites.

She longed to run her hands over his bare body, to feel the coiled strength of skin and muscle sliding under her fingers.

She yearned to feel him inside her.

When he began to undress her, she returned the favor.

Jonah was every bit as beautiful as she imagined. Long muscular legs, broad shoulders, rock hard abs and an erection that both thrilled and had her swallowing in panic.

Before the fear could take over, he was kissing her again and she was kissing him back. Her heart beat so hard she could feel the pulsing in her stomach.

He drew her to him and the kisses became more fevered and urgent. A smoldering heat flared through her, a sensation she didn't bother to fight.

When his hand closed over her breast, this thumb teasing her nipple, vibrations of intense desire shot through her. And when his mouth replaced his fingers, Abby heard herself groan, a low sound of want and need that astonished her with its intensity.

Those magic fingers moved lower to dark curls. A shock jolted Abby as those fingers found what they were searching for, the slippery friction spurring her heart into a rapid, frantic beat.

Her legs parted, wanting more, needing more.

Instead of pulling on the condom and relieving the burning need inside her, Jonah continued to kiss and explore her body with relentless determination. He worshipped her body with his mouth, with his fingers, until Abby found herself begging.

"Inside me." Desperation made her voice husky.

Though she didn't need to ask twice, he took a moment to kiss her with a slow thoroughness that left her hotter than a firecracker on the Fourth of July.

With quick, efficient movements, Jonah opened the foil packet, pulled on the condom then moved to catch her mouth in a hard, deep kiss. "I can't get enough of you."

Abby's lips felt swollen. Her body throbbed with need.

His hand flattened against her lower back, drawing her up against the length of his body. Abby pressed herself more fully to him, the action sending the heat percolating low in her belly to a full boil.

She planted a kiss at the base of his neck, then arched back as he slid inside her. He was big and she was so very tight.

With great restraint he moved deliberately back then forward, letting her body carry the momentum. The rhythmic stroking had him sliding deeper with each thrust until he was fully impaled.

With his arms braced on either side of her, he gazed down at her, blue eyes dark and intense.

Love swirled inside Abby filling her to bursting.

Love? She inhaled sharply.

No. No. No. She couldn't be in love with Jonah. Not yet. It was too soon.

Before she could react to the panic rising inside her like an untied balloon, he began to move again. The pressure of his erection had her body throbbing as the grinding rhythm continued.

In and out. In and out.

Her breath came in short puffs until the heat engulfed her. Abby's need for him became a stark carnal hunger.

The orgasm slammed into her with breathtaking speed. She surged upward and would have cried out, but his mouth once again covered hers, muffling the sound. The rush was powerful, like a wave flinging her into the darkness.

Seconds later, he drove deep, shuddering with his own release.

They laid there, joined together, neither of them moving. Abby knew she should be worried…about something…but right now she couldn't think what it was. Being with Jonah, with his arms around her, felt so right.

If anything was wrong, she would deal with it…later.

Jonah spent the night.

He planned to be back at his place before Eva Grace woke up. That didn't happen.

"You're here." Still in pink pajamas covered in penguins, Eva Grace ran into the kitchen and flung her arms around him.

"Your mommy promised to make pancakes this morning so I had to come back." He lowered his voice to a confidential whisper. "She said she'd make a smiley face of blueberries on the top."

"She does that for me sometimes." Eva Grace told him, her expression serious. She turned to her mother. "Mommy, can I have a smiley face on mine, too?"

"Of course." Abby smiled, drawing his gaze to her mouth. To her body now hidden beneath yoga pants and a green top advertising the Inn at Hazel Green.

He let his gaze travel slowly over her. Last night had been wonderful. He'd never felt so close to her. Still, he worried she might have second thoughts and kick him to the curb this morning.

Instead, she'd invited him to stay for breakfast.

After...she'd shared her shower with him. Just remembering her slick wet skin had heat rushing through his body like a runaway train. Pushing the memory aside, Jonah focused on his daughter.

"Help me set the table, Eva Grace." Jonah gestured to the silverware drawer. "You take care of the knives and forks and I'll handle plates and glasses."

Eva Grace happily did as he'd requested, even pulling off sections of paper towels to be used as napkins.

By the time Jonah had added juice to the glasses, the pancakes were ready. Though the mounds of golden cakes heavily interspersed with plump berries and topped with melted butter smelled delicious, Jonah didn't immediately dig in.

He glanced around the small table, still amazed at the blessing he'd received. Abby had generously opened her home and her heart to him, even though he didn't deserve such consideration.

She looked at him quizzically, glancing down at his untouched plate.

He picked up his fork. "Just enjoying the view."

She flushed and turned to Eva Grace. "Jonah has agreed to spend the day with us."

"Yay." Eva Grace held up her fork in a stiff-armed salute. "What are we going to do?"

"Hmmm." Abby tapped her lips with a finger. "Do you have something specific in mind?"

Jonah studied Eva Grace. "I was thinking the Lincoln Park Zoo might be fun."

The family-oriented zoo, located in the heart of Chicago, billed itself as a wildlife experience. In his mind, the best thing about it being in downtown Chicago was the three of them could explore it without running into someone they knew.

For now, Jonah didn't want to share his girls with anyone. Or answer any questions. "The weather is forecast to be mild. Not too hot or cold."

"Like the three bears," Eva Grace piped up.

For a second Abby appeared puzzled, then she laughed. "Like the porridge."

Jonah just shook his head. The two were definitely on the same wavelength. "What do you say?"

"I say yes," Eva Grace shouted her agreement.

"Indoor voice," her mother warned before turning to Jonah. "It's a good choice. I prefer to take some time before…"

Jonah nodded. Abby didn't need to finish the thought. Deciding what, and how much to tell friends, would be the next hurdle. Though he wanted to shout from the rooftops that Eva Grace was his daughter, his relationship with Abby was new.

Like a garden filled with newly sprouting plants, what was growing between him and Abby must be carefully tended. Last night had been a big step forward.

Today, they would experience life as a family.

It was a good start.

"I want to play with the penguins." Eva Grace's bottom lip stuck out and a frown furrowed her brow.

Abby had discovered at certain times of day the Zoo's penguin exhibit allowed for an up-close and personal encounter with the penguins.

"The girl that came out said the penguins were right by her feet." Eva Grace's voice rose. "I want them at my feet."

"You have to be six." Abby kept her own voice low. Although she'd already explained that to Eva Grace, it didn't help that the children coming out of the Encounter had been excitedly chattering about the experience. "Next year, you and I can come back."

"Hey, what about me?" Jonah's tone might be joking but his expression showed his unease.

"You can come, too." Abby shot him an easy smile. "If you want."

Jonah's gaze never left hers. "I definitely want."

A little thrill traveled up her spine. Though she still wasn't sure jumping into a relationship with Jonah was smart, today had been magical.

Eva Grace was at the age where she was awed by every exhibit. The African Journey Exhibit had her jumping back into Jonah's arms at the sight of the giant cockroaches. The crocodiles had fascinated the child but Eva Grace's tight hold on their hands had Jonah smiling at her over the child's head.

Over the years Abby had shared these kinds of experiences with friends. Being with Jonah was different. He was Eva Grace's father and he delighted in everything she said and did.

He was also protective. Like now, his eyes remained glued on his daughter as she skipped up to a cart selling Dippin' Dots.

"I'd like a cup, please." Eva Grace smiled at the older gentleman with silver hair working the cart.

"Well, little lady," The man glanced at Abby as she and Jonah strolled up, "I'd love to dish you up some. If it's okay with your mom and dad."

Abby stilled, then reminded herself this was one of the reasons she'd wanted to have this time away from Hazel Green. Here, she and Jonah didn't need to explain their relationship to anyone.

She didn't need to think of where they were going, indeed *if* they were going anywhere. Sleeping together hadn't been a promise of lasting commitment on either of their part.

Eva Grace turned to Jonah. "Can I have some dippin' dots, Daddy?"

Abby heard Jonah's quick intake of breath.

The hand that he placed on his daughter's shoulder shook

slightly. His voice, when he spoke, was thick with emotion. "Sure."

Although Abby tried to restrict Eva Grace's intake of sweets, this seemed a time to make an exception. Regardless of what happened in the past, she couldn't deny the love that shone in his eyes whenever he looked at their daughter.

Jonah took the cup from the man and handed it to Eva Grace. Pulling out his wallet, he handed the man a bill.

The man made change and gestured with his head to Eva Grace. "I had three of my own. There's nothing like a daughter."

"You got that right." Jonah took Abby's arm. "Thanks."

Eva Grace skipped down the sidewalk, happily eating the ice cream. Suddenly she twirled. "This is the bestest day ever."

When Jonah laughed, his arm settling around her shoulder, Abby couldn't help but agree.

CHAPTER TWENTY-THREE

"Can we go to Daddy's place and play Hisss?" Eva Grace asked as they started up the walkway to the hotel. "That would be awesome."

"I'm afraid not, sweetie." Abby pretended not to notice that Eva Grace had called Jonah '*daddy*' again. It was as if once used, the title had become permanently glued to her tongue. All the way back from the zoo, it had been 'daddy this' and 'daddy that.'

Jonah hadn't quit smiling since they'd left the zoo. Abby had to admit his happy mood was contagious and she found herself wishing all three of them could spend the evening together.

"Why not?" Eva Grace's voice stopped just short of a whine.

"I have to work tonight." Abby caught her daughter's hand in hers and gave it a big swing, just before they entered the hotel lobby. "You get to spend the evening with Matilda."

"I want to be with Daddy."

Iris, who was currently covering the front desk, reminded Abby of a hunting dog on high alert. Head up. Eyes fixed on the bird, er on Jonah.

Abby cursed the blush stealing up her cheeks.

"Did I hear someone say my name?" Matilda glided from the restaurant into the hotel lobby.

"Eva Grace said she wanted to spend the evening with her *Daddy.*" Iris gestured with her head toward Jonah. In her white damask shirtwaist, black linen skirt and tie, Iris could have stepped straight out of a 1900's schoolroom.

Matilda's serene expression never wavered. "If Abby is agreeable, I'm okay with Jonah watching Eva Grace. I have some paperwork to catch up on anyway."

The older woman shot Abby a pointed glance. "But I'm available if you need me."

Before answering, Abby shifted to Jonah and lifted a brow.

His expression gave nothing away. "Whatever you think best."

"Your daddy will watch you," Abby told her daughter, then held out a hand when Eva Grace started jumping up and down. "But he has to watch you here. You have school tomorrow."

When Eva Grace opened her mouth to protest, Jonah took her hand.

"We'll play that Squirrel game." He kept his voice easy. "That sounds like fun to me."

Eva Grace's eyes narrowed, studying him. "I always fill my acorn log first."

Jonah inclined his head. "Really? Always?"

"Most of the time," Eva Grace admitted. "I don't want you to be sad if you don't win."

"Sometimes," Jonah said in a philosophical tone, "the acorns don't fall your way. The only shame is in not doing your best. Understand?"

Eva Grace nodded. "I understand. You won't be sad if you lose."

Jonah just smiled.

"I'll run in and change," Abby told Iris. "It won't take a minute."

"Take your time." Iris's blue eyes sparkled. "It's been ages since we've talked. I'd love to catch up."

~

While Jonah and Eva Grace set up the board game, Abby changed into a blue and green plaid dress with three quarter length sleeves and a thin patent leather belt that emphasized her tiny waist.

Regardless of what Iris said, Abby didn't want to keep the woman waiting past the end of her shift. She kept her hair simple, rolling it under in a sleek Pageboy style. Conscious of time, she merely extended her eyeliner past the crease with an uptick and added some lipstick.

Abby paused in the doorway to the living room, her heart lurching at the sight of two blonde heads bent over the board. Jonah had the squirrel tweezers in hand and was making them snap.

"Like the crocodile at the zoo," she heard Eva Grace say as she stepped into the room.

"You look pretty, Mommy." Her daughter's eyes zeroed in on the Trifari necklace with its cobalt blue flowers each centered by a tiny crystal.

Jonah rose to his feet, his gaze slowly traveling down from her face to her blue peep-toe heels and back up. "Beautiful."

How was it that such a simple glance could infuse her body with warmth? "Thank you both."

Abby turned her attention to Jonah. "I believe our last guests are scheduled to check in around seven. Then, I'll put up the sign and forward all calls to my cell."

"That's okay, Mommy," Eva Grace flashed a bright smile. "We're going to be busy playing."

Leaning over, Abby brushed a kiss on the top of her daughter's head. "Be good. As soon as I get back, it's shower, book and bedtime."

Eva Grace nodded.

Abby shifted her gaze to Jonah and felt a punch of lust. This physical desire was something new and she wasn't quite sure how to handle it. Though she'd only slept with one other man, a boy back in her college years, she couldn't recall ever feeling this way.

It was as if making love after a long period of abstinence had reawakened dormant desires. Hopefully, it would only take doing it a couple more times more to get her hormones back in check.

From the hungry look in Jonah's eyes, Abby had the feeling he wouldn't mind helping her out in that area.

Though the rational part of her brain screamed at her to slow this train down, Abby told herself she had everything under perfect control.

She blinked when she realized that while her mind had wandered, Jonah had moved close.

Putting his hands on her shoulders, he planted a kiss on her lips. "Shout if you need anything."

Abby resisted the urge to touch her tingling lips with her fingers.

"Daddy, I'm ready to play."

"Coming." Jonah called out, then shot Abby a wink. "Hurry back."

Abby could still taste his lips when she stepped to the front desk. Conscious of Iris's curious glance, Abby feigned a casual expression. "How many more are we expecting?"

"Two." Iris glanced at the computer screen. "Then we're full. The man called to confirm the room. He said he'd be here in thirty minutes and that was a half hour ago, so I expect him any time. I have a note that the couple out of Wisconsin should be here by seven."

"Perfect." Abby turned the vase of flowers on the desk a half turn, then glanced at the clock. "Have a fabulous evening."

Iris didn't move a muscle, other than to lift a blonde brow that had been darkened with pencil to chocolate brown. "Daddy?"

Although Abby had hoped to not have to explain any of this until she felt more settled about it herself, she knew better. This was Hazel Green. While it technically was a Chicago suburb, it retained a small-town feel.

"Jonah Rollins is Eva Grace's biological father." If she was going to do this, Abby vowed to keep it simple. "Eva Grace now knows this and that's why she's calling him daddy."

"Where's he been all this time?"

Iris's question didn't surprise her. Her close friends all knew that Abby had been a surrogate for a couple who changed their minds because of the woman's health issues.

"He's been in Springfield, but we're happy he's living here now."

"What about his wife?"

"He's divorced."

"Is she interested in getting acquainted with Eva Grace, as well?"

"No." That was all Abby planned to say on the subject of Veronica.

Iris blinked, but dropped that line of questioning for a far more personal one. "Are you and Jonah involved?"

"We're getting reacquainted." Abby waved an airy hand even as her stomach lurched. She still hadn't come to grips with just how close they'd become. "Jonah and I have been friends since childhood."

While the comment didn't really answer Iris's question, the explanation appeared to satisfy her friend.

Iris slung her purse over her shoulder. "You look happy."

Before Iris could say more, or hopefully leave, the bells over the door jingled and a man stepped into the lobby.

Abby guessed the guy to be about her age, or perhaps a couple of years older. He wore a well-cut suit as dark as his hair. The way his piercing eyes slid around the lobby sent a slight chill up her spine.

Lean and muscular, he moved like a panther, his shiny loafers soundless on the wood floor.

He carried a small leather bag in one hand and a briefcase in the other. Setting them down on the floor, he flashed a surprisingly warm smile. "This is a beautiful place. Circa 1880's?"

His smile drew her in and the eyes that seemed so sharp and assessing only seconds before, brimmed with good humor. He possessed an indefinable knack, Abby realized, of making a person feel as if they were the only one in the room. Or, at least, the only one who mattered. Having his full attention was a heady experience.

Still, something about that abundance of charm had red flags popping up.

"The hotel opened in 1884." Abby thought Iris would slip out the door, but instead the blonde lingered. "Welcome to Hazel Green, Mr. Carlyle."

"It's a pleasure to meet you, Ms. Fine."

Abby froze but kept her voice even. "How do you know my name?"

"Nothing sinister, I assure you." He chuckled as if even the thought was ridiculous. "I checked out your website before making the reservation. Your picture and name were there."

Abby chided herself for making a big deal out of nothing, and looking like a fool in the bargain.

"The pictures and information are organized and helpful, but what I noticed was the little touches. Things as simple as the soap you choose to use in your hotel and sell on your website. It's obvious you care about the happiness of the people who stay under your roof. They aren't just customers to you." That charming smile flashed again as he pulled out a credit card and handed it to her to swipe.

"Thank you for the compliment. If you're hungry, Matilda's is open until eight." Abby gestured with her head while studying the card. American Express. Dixon Carlyle. Once the charge for the one night he'd booked went through, she returned the card to him, noticing his perfectly filed nails.

"Thank you. I appreciate the recommendation, but I've already eaten."

Abby wondered what had brought him to Hazel Green. "If there's anything I can do to make your stay more enjoyable, please let me know."

He picked up his bag and briefcase, then paused as if a thought had just occurred to him. "I realize this may be a longshot, but are you by any chance acquainted with Cornelia Ambrose?"

Though he seemed quite sincere, if he'd studied her website as keenly as he'd indicated, he couldn't have missed the picture of her with Nell--dressed as Hazel Green--in the section devoted to town events.

"As a matter of fact, I am." Some sixth sense kept Abby from admitting more.

Interest sparked in those warm brown eyes and the smile he offered oozed charm. "Do you happen to know where I could find her this evening? Or perhaps you have her cell number?"

When Abby and Iris only exchanged glances, he waved a hand. "We're old friends. I plan to stop by her law office tomorrow, but if possible, I'd love to connect with her tonight."

If this guy thought she would hand over Nell's home address or cell number to a stranger, he was crazy. She didn't think Dixon Carlyle was crazy. He was simply a man who used charisma and good looks to get what he wanted. "If you give me *your* cell number, I'm happy to pass it along."

Though his lips never lost the smile, his gaze turned penetrating as if he was taking her measure, seeing how far he could push.

When he nodded, Abby assumed he'd seen that no matter how much charm he oozed or how much he pushed, he wouldn't get what he wanted. Not from her.

Retrieving a business card from inside his suit jacket, Dixon flipped it over. Taking a pen from the desk, he wrote his phone number in precise strokes. "I appreciate your willingness to help. Thank you and have a lovely evening."

Abby made short work of handing over the key and let out the breath she didn't realize she'd been holding when he started up the stairs.

"Wow." Abby tapped her fingers on the top of the desk. "That was strange."

"Who do you think he is?" Iris spoke in hushed tones, as if worried Dixon was at the top of the steps listening to their conversation.

Something told Abby that worry wasn't outside the realm of possibility. "He says he's a friend of Nell's. I'll give her a call. She might be eager to connect."

"After the first glance, he totally dismissed me. But he was checking you out big time." Iris continued to keep her voice low. "He liked what he saw."

Abby rolled her eyes. "Puh-leeze."

"I'm serious." Iris's blue eyes were intense. "You just have Jonah on the brain so you didn't notice."

"Whatever." Abby laughed and gave her friend a playful shove out the door.

When she turned back, she brought the card to eye level. *Dixon Carlyle, Carlyle Investments.*

The address listed was on Michigan Avenue in downtown Chicago.

Who are you, Dixon Carlyle? Abby wondered. What is your connection to Nell?

Abby pulled out her phone, eager to call her friend and get her reaction. She hesitated. Though she definitely thought Iris had overreacted, the remote possibility that the man might be lurking at the top of the steps listening, had her texting Nell instead.

Dixon Carlyle checked into hotel. Says he's a friend. Wants you to call him.

Chewing on her lip, Abby considered what else to say. She wanted to ask who he was and if Nell had any idea why he was in Hazel Green. Something told her Nell wasn't expecting him.

Dixon Carlyle was Nell's business, Abby reminded herself.

She keyed in the phone number from the card into the text and hit send.

A second later the couple, scheduled to arrive at seven, walked through the door.

She learned they were from Door County, Wisconsin and in town to see their grandson, who had been injured in his first high school football game as a starter, Friday night.

"Trevor had been waiting for that opportunity." The woman, Libby George, had brown hair cut in a stylish bob. She looked much too young to have a grandson that old. "The first-string quarterback had been underperforming, so the coach gave Trev the nod. We wanted to come and watch, but Steve, couldn't get off work. Amy, that's our daughter, texted us that Trev had injured his knee. Then, this morning, she told us that doctor had decided he needed surgery. Steve and I couldn't stay away."

"I'm so sorry to hear he was injured. I'll pray for a speedy recovery." Abby glanced at the screen. "I've got you down for two nights."

"That's correct." Steve stepped forward and spoke for the first time.

Once the couple had entered the hotel lobby, Libby's husband, a burly man with short cropped dark hair, had moved immediately to the window overlooking Main Street, phone pressed to his ear.

"We would have stayed with our daughter," Libby told her, pulling out her credit card, "but they have a foreign exchange student this year. They gave Hans their guest bedroom which means either Amy and Todd would have to give us their bed and they'd sleep on the sofa or—"

"Honey." Steve stopped the rambling with a gentle hand on his wife's arm. "She only wants to confirm we're staying two nights and not one."

A flush colored Libby's ivory cheeks. "I'm so sorry. I'm just so stressed about Trevor—"

"Nothing to be sorry about. I have a daughter who has had surgery in the past. It's very scary." Abby thought back to those trying times.

"Thank you." Libby reached over and handed Abby the credit card. "I knew you'd understand."

Unlike Dixon, the couple greeted the news that Matilda's was still open with enthusiasm. In fact, Libby went to secure a table, while Steve carried their overnight bags down the hall to their room.

Abby put up the sign and forwarded any calls that would come in to her cell. For a moment she stood as memories of Jonah on the football field flood back. She could picture him in his red jersey and helmet. Springfield High Senators. While she hadn't been Jonah's girlfriend back then, she had been his biggest fan.

Now she was sleeping with him.

Her smile faded.

Things had moved so fast between them she nearly had whiplash. Still, she believed letting Jonah back into her life and telling Eva Grace the truth had been the right thing to do.

The problem was, while she felt as if she could now move on

and have a relationship with Jonah, a tiny part of her feared he would end up disappointing her again.

That worry had her holding back a piece of her heart. Was it a way of still punishing him? If so, that didn't seem fair to him. Or her.

Abby reminded herself she'd come a long way toward accepting the events of the past in a short amount of time. It might take time to fully let down her guard. But it would happen.

Somehow, some way, she believed Jonah would show himself to be a man fully worthy of her trust. When that happened, the past would truly be in the past.

CHAPTER TWENTY-FOUR

"I'm glad your last guest arrived early." Jonah sat beside Abby on the sofa, his arm looped casually around her shoulder.

While it was a little too warm for a fire, she'd had Jonah build one anyway.

"I think Eva Grace was disappointed." Abby's lips quirked up in a smile. "She wanted to play longer."

"She's a great kid."

For a second, an automatic impulse to bring up the past surged, but she shoved it down.

He'd apologized.

She'd accepted the apology.

End of story.

"When she won the third game of Hisss, she had me text you the news." He gave a little laugh then brushed his lips across her hair. "I think she was disappointed you didn't respond. By the time you got here, she had too many other things to say that I think she forgot all about it."

"Three games?" Abby raised a brow. "Did you let her win?"

"I wish I could say yes, but she won fair and square." He chuckled. "The crazy thing was, it didn't even bother me. If only the guys on the football team could see me now. They used to say I was the most competitive one on the team."

"The couple who checked in tonight has a grandson who plays for Hazel Green High."

Jonah slanted a sideways glance. "We should go to a game sometime."

"Sure. Sounds like fun."

"What about the other guest?" Jonah played with a strand of hair. "What was he or she like?"

"He." Abby thought of Dixon Carlyle. If she'd missed Jonah's text, had she missed a reply from Nell? "Hold on a second."

She jumped up from the sofa and crossed the room to retrieve her phone, then plopped back down beside Jonah.

"What are you doing?"

"Checking my texts."

"Really, it was no big deal. Eva Grace understood that—"

"Not your text." Abby scrolled down. "I sent one to Nell."

There was a reply from her friend. One word.

Thanks.

Abby frowned.

"What's the matter?"

"The guy who checked in tonight wanted to connect with Nell but he didn't have her home address or cell number." Abby went on to tell Jonah about Dixon Carlyle. "I texted Nell his information and all she says is thanks?"

Jonah's eyes narrowed. "What did the guy look like?"

"About our age. Your height. Lean but muscular. Dark hair, nearly black." Abby cocked her head. "Why?"

"Your description sounds like the guy Nell recognized at the Trattoria."

Abby nodded as Jonah described the man he'd seen and what had occurred. "That sounds just like him. Maybe I should call Nell?"

"You could."

"But?"

"I don't think you're the one she wants to speak with tonight."

Nell stared at the text from Abby. A hot flush of anger surged. She forced herself to take a couple of deep, calming breaths. Experience had taught her that mistakes occur when emotions rule.

"Who's the text from?" Leo's finger stroked up from the bare skin of her hip to stop just below her breast.

They'd just finished round two of some very energetic and satisfying sex when her phone dinged. Normally, Nell wouldn't have paid any attention to a text.

But all day, a sixth sense had her on edge. It was the reason she'd texted Leo and asked him over for dinner. There'd been no need to explain food wasn't the only thing on the menu.

For the past six months they'd been having sex. Either at his place or hers. A couple of times, they'd checked into a hotel room in Chicago, just to switch things up.

Leo wanted to date her. He'd made that clear.

She'd made it just as clear she only wanted him for sex. This was her community. She loved it and wouldn't risk screwing up what she had, over a relationship in her own backyard.

Being a red-blooded young man who was totally focused on his new position as Mayor, Leo had gone along with her wishes.

"Abby texted me." Nell turned away from him, pulling the sheet up with her. She grabbed his clothes from the floor where they'd fallen and flung them at him. "You need to go."

Leo sat up and stretched. His brown hair stuck up in several places and Nell could see a faint trace of her lipstick on the back of his neck. Concern blanketed his handsome face. "Is she in trouble?"

"No." Leo was a good guy. Nell accepted that fact, which made keeping their liaisons strictly about sex more difficult. But definitely not anything she couldn't handle.

Tonight had been enjoyable, she thought, cinching the silk robe around her waist while Leo pulled on his clothes. A wave of affection washed over her. He was a fabulous and considerate lover.

Because of their busy lives, it had been several weeks since they'd been able to coordinate their schedules. Nell had expected him to jump her the second he walked through her door.

Jumping him had certainly been her plan. Instead he'd surprised her with a Chrysanthemum plant for her terrace and take-out from the newly opened Thai restaurant.

Over dinner of Laad Naa, coupled with a nice bottle of Riesling, they'd caught each other up on the past couple of weeks. For dessert, they hopped into bed and hadn't left it since.

"What did the text from Abby say?"

Nell widened her eyes, startled by his tenacity. He knew better than to pry into her business. "Don't spoil the evening with questions."

He gave a curt nod, his blue eyes dark and unreadable.

She followed him in silence to the door leading to the garage. Before he left he pulled her to him, closing his mouth over hers in a kiss that curled her toes. Like a dog staking his claim, she thought, more than a little off-balanced when he released her.

"We'll get together again soon." His eyes met hers.

She stuck out a tongue at his retreating back. He left via the back door. Several months ago she'd given him an opener for her garage so he could park his car inside when he came over.

She knew they couldn't keep their relationship hidden forever, but she didn't want questions. There were too many secrets in her background for her to let anyone in too close.

Abby had said it best, Nell thought. Actions revealed character.

With a sigh, Nell locked the door. When she reached her

living room, she plopped down on the sofa and pulled out her phone, gazing at the text from Abby and the number listed.

She thought she'd made it clear at the restaurant that he was to stay out of her life and out of Hazel Green.

Yet he'd come anyway.

Nell pursed her lips as a steely determination filled her. This time she'd be more forceful because Dixon obviously hadn't gotten the message.

∽

"I don't trust him." Nell stabbed a piece of lettuce with her fork.

Abby cast a glance at the couple seated at a table by the window. "Who would? The man is a slime ball."

Whatever Marc said had his luncheon companion, a stunning woman in her early seventies, chuckling. Though Lilian de Burgh had been widowed three years ago, she still wore her wedding ring. When she gestured with her left hand, the large diamond caught the light, flashing a rainbow of colors.

Immediately upon entering Matilda's, Abby had spotted Marc and Lilian pouring over some papers.

Today was the first time in nearly a week that Abby had been alone with Nell. On Wednesday, the Birthday Bash committee had met to finalize details. Nell was there, arriving just as the meeting started and leaving immediately after it ended.

Abby hadn't had the opportunity to ask Nell if she'd reached Mr. Carlyle. All she knew was the man had checked out early the next morning.

She opened her mouth to ask, but Nell spoke first.

"It appears you and Jonah made up."

Abby guessed it appeared that way. She saw him every day and he picked up Eva Grace from school several times this week. "We agreed to move forward. Leave the past in the past."

Nell cocked her head. "For Eva Grace's sake?"

"That's part of it." Abby took a sourdough roll from the bread basket and absently broke it in two. "The other part is I can't keep holding onto the anger and the sense of betrayal from that time. I need to move past it."

The blue eyes that met hers held a speculative gleam. "You might *need* to move past the anger and hurt, but can you?"

Bringing the roll to her lips, Abby nibbled. "I believe so I'm not completely there yet, but I'm getting closer."

Nell's expression gave nothing away. "Word in town is that the two of you are dating exclusively."

"Word in town?" Abby gave a little laugh. "Are you saying we're the subject of gossip?"

"Did you expect different?" Nell's eyes remained watchful. "He's the new police chief."

"You're right." Abby took a bigger bite of the roll and chewed. "The only single man of more interest to the community would be Leo."

"You're probably right about that." Nell's voice remained conversational. "Heard any rumors about our eligible mayor?"

"Someone, I can't remember who, mentioned they think he's dating a model out of Chicago."

Nell nodded. "That's the same rumor I heard."

"Which means," Abby flashed a grin. "It may or may not be true."

Nell chuckled.

Once again, Abby opened her mouth to seize the opening. "Have—"

"Are you going to marry him?" Nell asked.

Abby blinked. "Leo? Absolutely not."

"Jonah." Nell set down her fork, her entire attention riveted on Abby's face. "Has he asked?"

Abby felt a familiar quivering take up residence in her stomach. Several times she'd gotten the feeling Jonah was on the verge of asking that very question.

Part of her wanted him to ask. The other part feared he'd pop the question.

Because, at this moment, she didn't know how she'd respond.

~

"Good afternoon, Chief."

Jonah pulled his gaze from the water. He'd told Abby to meet him by the covered bridge. Not wanting to keep her waiting, he'd arrived early.

"Mrs. de Burgh." Jonah had been introduced to the woman many considered one of the movers and shakers of Hazel Green at Leo's party. In her dark-colored pants and Houndstooth jacket, she appeared more approachable than she had the night of the party when diamonds dripped from her ears and neck. "It's a beautiful day."

"There isn't anything better than a walk on a crisp autumn day." The woman cocked her head, her gaze assessing. "Please call me Lilian. How are you liking our community?"

"It already feels like home." After spending most of his life in Springfield, it surprised him how quickly the town—and the community—had found its way into his heart. "I'm glad I made the move."

"I heard you and Abigail Fine share a history."

Jonah knew the news that he was Eva Grace's father had been picked up and passed along the town's very efficient grapevine. He hadn't thought the news would have made it to Mrs. De Burgh's circle.

"Abby and I grew up together in Springfield." Jonah kept his smile pleasant. "Reuniting with her and my daughter has been the best part of moving here."

There it was, laid out there. If she hadn't already heard he was Eva Grace's father, now she knew.

"Richard and I weren't able to have children." Lilian's lips lifted in a wistful smile. "Sharing a child with someone you love is a great gift."

"It is." Jonah agreed.

They chatted for a few more minutes before she continued down the walkway into the bridge.

He was grateful she'd stopped. It kept him from thinking about the ring safely tucked in his jacket pocket. Even though everything rational inside him urged him to take this slow, he'd meant what he'd said to Abby.

He loved her.

He wanted to be her husband, wanted her to be his wife. Wanted them to raise Eva Grace together, as well as any other children they might have. He wanted to grow old with her.

Jonah hoped the past had been finally put to rest. He now accepted he'd done the best he could at the time. While he'd likely handle things differently if he could go back, from this day forward he vowed to live his life in accordance with his moral compass.

Jonah believed Abby loved him. Though she hadn't said the words, he saw it in her eyes, felt it in her touch. She insisted she'd forgiven him and was ready to move forward.

He wasn't fully convinced.

Oh, he believed she *thought* she'd turned that page, but what he'd done wasn't an easy thing to forget or forgive. But the desire for them to begin their lives together had him willing to take this chance.

"Jonah."

He turned and smiled at the sight of Abby hurrying toward him, her cheeks as rosy as her red lipstick.

"I'm sorry to keep you waiting. I was orienting a new employee to the front desk and she was having difficulty catching on." Abby waved a hand, her brown eyes sparkling in the sunshine. "Enough about that. You said there was some problem with the security for the event this weekend."

Her brows pulled together slightly as she slipped her arm through his when they began to walk. "It must be serious if we had to meet in person."

"It is serious." His heartbeat hitched. "There's something I need to show you."

It wasn't just the ring, it was the key in his pocket that had him taking a calming breath. She would say yes. She'd be happy. Thrilled. Tonight, the three of them would celebrate the first step in becoming a family.

"Show me?" Her voice rose as she glanced around as they exited the bridge. "I'm sure we don't have any activities planned on this side of the bridge."

Jonah led her down a path to a gazebo several yards from the walkway. The structure, often used for small weddings was surrounded by beautiful foliage. He'd hoped no one would be here mid-afternoon and his luck had held.

"I love this gazebo." Abby touched the white lacquered wood and smiled. "I had Eva Grace's five-year pictures taken here."

"Abby."

Just saying her name had her smile fading.

"What's the matter, Jonah?" She turned and placed a hand on his arm. "You look so serious."

"I love you."

She blinked.

"I think in some ways I've always loved you." Jonah let out a shaky breath as a wave of emotion swamped him. Dear God, he wanted so badly for her to say yes. "You and I, we just fit. I remember the first time I saw you. You were barely older than Eva Grace."

He smiled at the memory. "You had such attitude."

"All I did was tell you, since I found your ball, you should let me play." Though she smiled, the watchful look in her eyes remained.

"We spent years never being available at the same time." Jonah decided to not to bring up the surrogacy. "When I moved here and saw you again, all those old feelings rushed forward."

He dropped his gaze to his hands for a second. "Before, I was alone. I never realized just how alone. Now, I'm whole."

Her eyes were now as large as saucers, but he appreciated that she didn't interrupt.

"I love and respect your honesty and willingness to be true to yourself." Jonah kept his gaze firmly fixed on her. "You make me want to be a better man. A man worthy of you and Eva Grace."

She took a step back and when he stepped forward to take her hand, he found himself speeding up the speech he'd prepared.

"I will love you and Eva Grace until the day I die. I will do everything in my power to make you happy."

Her face went white. "Wha-what are you saying?"

Jonah flipped open the ring box and dropped to his knee. "I'm hoping you feel the same way and want to spend the rest of your life with me. Will you marry me, Abby? Will you let me be a husband to you and a father to Eva Grace?"

CHAPTER TWENTY-FIVE

Abby gazed into Jonah's brilliant blue eyes and her heart rose to her throat. She couldn't bring herself to look at the ring, fearing she might be tempted to put it on her finger.

She tugged him to his feet, her gaze never leaving his. "First off, I love you, too. I know I haven't said it before, but I do."

Relief flooded his face.

"But I can't say yes. Not yet." She lifted her hands and the words tumbled out. "It's too fast. I'm just getting used to loving you. Eva Grace is getting used to you being her father."

"Is this—" His gaze searched hers. "—because of the past?"

She wanted to be honest. Had to be honest if their relationship had any chance of long-term success.

"I don't think so. I believe I've put it in the past." She spoke slowly, her heart clenching at the hurt she saw in his eyes. "But again, everything has happened so fast. I need time. This isn't no. It's a not-right-now."

She watched him slip the ring back into his pocket, saw him force a smile.

"I understand." He tugged her to him and she wrapped her arms around his shoulders. "I'll wait as long as it takes for you to be sure. I want you confident that I'm someone you can trust and love forever."

She rested her head against his broad chest and fought the urge to weep. "You said you had something to show me."

"That's for another time." His arms tightened around her. "You're shivering. Let's get somewhere warm."

She kept her arm looped through his as they strolled back across the bridge. But he was right. A deep cold had permeated every inch of her body.

She loved him. She wanted to be his wife. But something inside her wouldn't let her accept his proposal.

His phone rang when they reached the opening of the bridge leading to the Green. He pulled it from his pocket and frowned.

"Who is it?"

A muscle in his jaw jumped. "Carole Devlin."

Veronica's mother. Carole, a news anchor for a Minneapolis station, had raised her daughter alone.

Abby remembered how she and Veronica had bonded over the fact they'd both grown up without a father. The phone continued to ring. "Answer it."

Jonah shook his head. "I'll call her back."

"It must be important for her to call you." She told him. "Seriously, I don't mind."

"Are you sure?"

Abby nodded.

"Carole. Hello." He glanced at Abby. "Yes, I can talk. You sound upset."

As he listened, his fingers tightened around the phone. "What's her condition?"

After a few seconds, he expelled a breath. "That's good news."

Something had happened to Veronica, that much was clear. But what, Abby wondered?

"Why me?"

He listened and, although he held the phone tight against his ear, Abby could hear the urgency in the woman's voice.

Jonah's brows slammed together. "Emotionally married? What the heck does that even mean?"

He stopped and closed his eyes for a moment. "I'll think about it. I'll get back to you."

It was apparent by the strident voice on the other end of the conversation that wasn't an answer Carole was prepared to accept.

"I'll get back to you," Jonah repeated. "I'm not able to give you an answer right now. Yes, I understand the importance. But we're no longer—"

Abby watched the red creep up his neck.

"Yes, I'm a man who believes in doing the right thing." He glanced at the stream to the right of the walkway as if ready to lob the phone straight into the water. "I'll be in touch. Good-bye."

He shoved the phone back into his pocket, his jaw tight.

"Something happened to Veronica." Abby stated the obvious. "Is she okay?"

"That's debatable." He met Abby's gaze. "My place is close. We need to talk about this. Come with me?"

In answer, she took his hand.

"Veronica attempted suicide." Jonah's voice broke. "Although I don't love her, and I'm not sure I ever did, it makes me sad to think she was hurting so much she preferred death over life."

"Her mother found her in time. Perhaps now, she can get the help she needs." Abby handed him the cup of cocoa she'd insisted on making and sat next to him on the sofa. She reached for the remote. One touch had the gas log blazing. "Did Carole say why?"

He wondered how she'd take him talking about Veronica, but he wanted no secrets between them. "She said Veronica felt like a failure after the divorce. She hadn't been able to give me a baby. That mattered so much to her."

Nodding, Abby sipped her own cocoa. "Veronica was a perfectionist."

"Carole alluded to that fact." Jonah gazed into the flickering flames. "Veronica is in a private facility, receiving counseling. They've diagnosed her with Generalized Anxiety Disorder."

"Sounds serious."

"I guess." A hard knot formed in his gut. "Carole says the counselor feels that Veronica is still emotionally married to me, whatever the hell that means."

"She can't let you go."

He met Abby's gaze. "It isn't her choice."

"Why did Carole call?"

"She wants me to fly to Minneapolis and participate in family therapy." He set down the cup he hadn't touched and raked a hand through his hair. "Carole insists I need to be there to help Veronica move on."

"What do you think?"

"The Birthday Bash is this weekend."

The past week there had been lots of talk over the dinner table. They'd all been excited for the event.

"Eva Grace will understand." Abby kept her tone reasonable. "We'll tell her that an old friend of yours is in the hospital and needs your help."

"You said she'll understand." His gaze searched hers. "What about you? Will you understand?"

Instead of answering, Abby placed her hands on either side of his face and gazed into his eyes. "What do you believe you should do?"

"I should go."

She smiled and brushed a kiss across his lips. "Stay as long as you need. Eva Grace and I aren't going anywhere."

∼

"Fabulous job, Abby." Lilian de Burgh, dressed in an iridescent Victorian gown that appeared lavender in one light, blue in another, stepped forward.

The older woman gestured with one gloved hand to the large room that had been transformed into an early turn-of-the-twentieth-century ballroom. "Hazel Green would have approved."

It was high praise and Abby appreciated the kind words.

"Thank you, Lilian." As the woman strolled off, Abby let her gaze drift around the ballroom decorated predominately in silver and blue, Hazel's favorite colors.

While rich jewel tones or light pastels were popular in the 1890's, the gowns in the ballroom were every color of the rainbow. The men wore black tails with white shirts and silk bow ties in either black or white.

Most of those who'd chosen to attend this event were in their thirties and older. The Millennials were celebrating Hazel Green's birthday with a Beer Bash at a lake on the edge of town. For the youngest residents a carnival, complete with a Bounce House castle, had kept Eva Grace and other children busy this afternoon.

Abby wished she could have stayed home with her daughter tonight. That hadn't been an option. The Chair was expected to be visible at all the events. She'd stayed at the lake only a handful of minutes. Just long enough to make sure everything was under control.

The loud and energetic band by the water had the crowd up and moving. If the number of people dancing was any indication, adding the Beer Bash had been a wise move. Abby had noticed several of Jonah's officers mingling with the crowd, confirming security was firmly in place.

Jonah would be pleased with their performance.

Abby's heart twisted.

He'd called every night since he'd left, always speaking first to Eva Grace and then to her. Always ending the conversation with, "I love you."

Having him gone made her realize just how completely he'd become a part of their lives.

"Abby. I'm so glad I ran into you." Liz's pale-yellow gown was the perfect foil for her dark hair and hazel eyes.

Abby's heart stopped. "Are the children okay?"

Liz's mother was keeping both Sawyer and Eva Grace overnight. Abby wondered if it had ended up being too much for a woman, considering Sandra had only recently completed radiation treatments. But Liz had assured her that her mother was strong enough and really wanted to do it.

Abby had told herself it wasn't as if Liz's mother had to entertain the children. And, she hadn't dropped off her daughter until four.

"They're fine." Liz assured her. "I just spoke to Mom and she was reading them a book before bed."

Abby released a breath. "I hope she knows how much I appreciate her watching Eva Grace."

"Having her and Sawyer there tonight was good for her, too," Liz said. "She didn't feel strong enough to come to the party, but she loves children so it's a win-win."

"I'll pick up Eva Grace first thing in the morning."

"Not too early." Liz laughed. "Mom has pulled out her Mickey Mouse waffle iron and has a special breakfast all planned."

Abby grinned. "Eva Grace will love that."

"I'm so sorry Jonah couldn't be here." Concerned darkened Liz's hazel eyes. "You mentioned an issue with his ex-wife?"

"She's having some health issues." Abby kept it vague, knowing it wasn't her story to tell. "Her mother asked Jonah to come."

"Are you okay with that?" Liz asked.

"I am. It was the right thing to do."

"Good." Liz turned to go, then pivoted back. "Oh. I keep forgetting to give you this."

The reporter opened an ornate purse covered in sparkly beads and pulled out a picture. "We didn't end up using it for the article in the paper but I thought you'd want it."

It was the picture of her and Jonah, watching Eva Grace at the cake walk.

Abby studied the photo for a second before slipping it into her bag. She gave Liz a hug. "Thank you."

When the music from the band ended and Leo took the stage, Abby held her breath. Nell, in full Hazel Green persona stood beside the young mayor. For tonight's event, Hazel wore a gorgeous Worth gown that reflected the influence of the Art Nouveau movement with black velvet tendrils on ivory satin.

Hazel smiled as a large multi-tiered birthday cake was wheeled out. Elegant was the word that came immediately to Abby's mind. The ivory frosting matched the satin on Hazel's dress. It had to be five feet tall with gold bows and beading interspersed with layers of pink roses.

Though candles had been used on cakes in the 1890's-- especially in the homes of the wealthy— they'd been left off this cake.

Nell stepped to the microphone as everyone cheered. She lifted a gloved hand and waved to the crowd. Instead of performing tonight, Hazel had been instructed to offer a short remark of her own choosing to the crowd.

Hazel's gaze swept the partygoers.

When Nell hesitated for a split second, Abby turned. The tiny hiccup in that sweep wasn't long enough that anyone who didn't know her well and wasn't watching intently, would notice.

Abby searched the faces in that section of the ballroom. Dixon Carlyle stood at the back, a half-smile on his face.

When Abby glanced back a second time, he was gone.

"Thank you all for coming to celebrate my special day with me." The voice, the intonations and vocal variance, were classic

Hazel. If seeing Dixon upset Nell, it didn't show. "I arrived in this community an outsider and you welcomed me. Without hesitation. Without questions. As a child, I traveled frequently. I never felt a part of anywhere I lived. Until Richard brought me here."

Once again, Nell's gaze swept the crowd, this time without interruption. "From the bottom of my heart, thank you for becoming my family. I love you all."

She stepped back to stand beside Leo as everyone cheered.

Abby watched Leo give her hand a squeeze, the gesture definitely not part of the script. Hazel didn't even glance in his direction. A second later, she lifted that hand to wave to the crowd.

Because of her popularity, Abby didn't have a chance to congratulate Nell on the brief comments. They'd been perfect and came off as completely heartfelt.

By the time the party ended at eleven, Abby was exhausted. After confirming the clean-up committee members had everything under control at both venues, she headed home.

Barely a second after she'd collapsed onto her sofa and kicked off her shoes, her phone dinged indicating a text from Jonah. *Can you talk?*

She responded by calling him. "Hey, you."

"I wasn't sure you'd be available."

Simply hearing his voice had everything in her relaxing. Abby put the phone on speaker and began to pull the pearl tipped pins from her hair. "I just got back to my apartment."

"I wish I could have been there." He expelled a breath.

"How's Veronica?"

"Making progress. I'll be back tomorrow. I'll tell you all about it."

"You sound tired."

"It's been a grueling couple of days." He offered up a laugh that contained little humor. "I confessed I'd sent money to you for years. It felt good to come clean. I never liked lying to her."

"How did she react?"

There was a long silence. "She was upset, but I think she understood. She carries a lot of guilt for her behavior back then. The counselor is having her write down what she'd have done differently."

Abby frowned. "What's the purpose? It changes nothing."

"I believe it's a way to show we learn from past mistakes." Does that make sense?"

"I guess." Abby gave up trying to unfasten the multitude of buttons on her dress while having a conversation.

"I did something similar in one of the letters I sent you." Jonah cleared his throat. "For me, reflecting and putting it down on paper helped."

"Well, then, I hope the exercise helps her." Abby's insides began to jitter. She didn't like thinking about Veronica, much less talking about her. "Tell me again when you'll be back."

It surprised her just how much she'd missed him. In a short time, he'd become an integral part of her life.

"I've got a five-a.m. flight. It should get in around six thirty." He paused. "I'd like to see you and Eva Grace first thing."

"Eva Grace is spending the night with Liz's mother. But I'll be here." The wariness in his voice had Abby injecting additional warmth into her voice. "I can't wait to see you."

"Good." He blew out a breath. "That's good. Sleep tight, sweetheart."

"I miss you," Abby murmured, but too late. He'd already hung up.

CHAPTER TWENTY-SIX

At two o'clock, Abby gave up trying to sleep. She rolled out of bed, pulled on an old chenille robe and padded to the kitchen in search of milk to warm. When she opened the refrigerator door she realized milk couldn't begin to quiet the questions tumbling in her head.

Without giving herself a chance to change her mind, she returned to her bedroom. Opening the closet door, she jerked a large bag from the top shelf. As the satchel only contained letters, it wasn't overly heavy.

She took the bag into the living room and dumped the letters addressed to her onto the kitchen table.

Another woman might read the letters in random order. That wasn't Abby's nature. She poured herself a glass of wine and set about putting the envelopes in postmarked order.

By the time she finished, her wine glass was empty.

She poured herself another and slit open the first envelope. It was dated within a couple of weeks after the visit in the doctor's office.

Dispassionately, she read Jonah's letter—really more of a note

—telling her how much he regretted putting her in this situation. Blah. Blah. Blah.

Her fingers tightened around the sheet of paper as the fear and anger from that time flooded back.

Stuffing the letter back into the envelope, Abby took a gulp of wine and moved onto the next.

By the time she reached the month before Eva Grace's birth, Abby detected a difference in the letters. Guilt had set in. While he still tried to explain away his actions, she could see he had doubts.

Tossing the envelope aside, she forced herself to read the next, sent shortly after Eva Grace's birth. In this one he spoke of wishing he could have been there when the baby was born. If he'd gotten her messages, it didn't show.

Abby continued to read. When she found herself reaching for the bottle to pour a third glass, she stopped herself.

Taking a few calming breaths, she methodically made her way through the years. Guilt and regret practically jumped off the page.

Part of her rejoiced at his pain. The other part hurt, understanding she wasn't the only one who'd suffered.

When she reached the letters sent earlier this year, she discovered what he'd alluded to in his conversation.

"I've accepted that I can't undo my past behavior," he wrote. "It's done. But I will tell you again just how sorry I am. If I could go back, I'd have stood up for you and my baby in the doctor's office that day. I'd have made it clear to Veronica that if she pursued legal action against you, not only wouldn't she have my support, I--and my family—would fight her every step of the way."

Tears filled Abby's eyes and spilled down her cheeks. She brushed them away with the back of her hand and continued to read.

"I have wronged you. I have wronged my daughter. I want to make it up to you. I want to make it up to her."

Abby sat back, taking a moment to collect her thoughts. Was Jonah's relationship with her and Eva Grace only about atonement? A sick feeling churned in her stomach.

The next letter informed her he'd applied for the Chief of Police position in Hazel Green. The one following that he'd been granted an interview. The next informed her he'd been offered the position. And, the last, sent shortly before his arrival, gave his starting date.

Dropping the letter to the table, Abby sat back in the chair and closed her eyes. Reading the notes had been a month by month review of the past five years.

She must have fallen asleep, because a knock at the door startled her awake. Her head rested on her arms and eyes felt gritty.

A second knock had her glancing at the Felix clock. Seven thirty.

Abby stumbled to the door and opened it without checking the peep.

"I made it here in record time." The smile on his face disappeared at the sight of her. "What's wrong?"

Abby supposed she did look a mess. She'd taken the pins out of her elaborate coiffure of the night before, but had done little else with her hair. Undoubtedly, she had a sleep crease on one cheek from the envelopes she'd slept on. And the pink pajamas with pigs and faded chenille robe wouldn't win any couture awards.

"I'm fine. I fell asleep at the table." Abby reached around him to shut the door. No need to scare any children that might be in the hall. She pushed back at her hair and gestured with one hand to the table. "I read your letters."

Moving to the sofa, she dropped down on the cushion, regretting that second glass of wine. Her head felt thick and fuzzy. Although, some of that may have been from crying.

Jonah glanced at the table and a muscle in his jaw jumped. Instead of sitting beside her, he took a seat in a nearby chair. His gaze searched her face. "It appears we've both revisited the past. What did you discover?"

"You really didn't know I called?" It was a piece of the puzzle she couldn't reconcile.

His brows pulled together. "When?"

"Right before Eva Grace was born." Abby rubbed the bridge of her nose with her thumb and forefinger. "In your letters you said you wished you could have been there. But you didn't respond to my call or texts?"

"Ah, those messages."

Disappointment flooded her. "You did get them."

And obviously ignored them.

"Veronica brought them up during one of the sessions. She deleted them." His gaze never wavered. "Apparently I'd left my phone at home."

"You didn't know before this weekend?"

Jonah shook his head. "For what it's worth, she feels guilt over deleting the texts and voice message."

Abby didn't know what to say to that so she said nothing.

He finally broke the silence. "Did you learn anything else from the letters?"

"I discovered I wasn't the only one suffering." Abby expelled a shaky breath and steeled herself. "Is this thing between me and you, some sort of atonement?"

"No." He shook his head, said again more forcefully. "No. Absolutely not."

The tight band around her heart released at his adamant reply. "I didn't think so. I hoped not."

Without her realizing how it happened, he was on the sofa beside her, her hands in his. "What's happened between us is about friendship and love, not some way to make up for the past. Because that simply isn't possible. If I learned anything this past few days it's that I need to accept the past and move on."

"I want to move on."

A watchful wariness filled his beautiful blue eyes.

She looped her arms around his neck and kissed him lightly on his lips. "I want to move forward with you."

Jonah placed his hands on her shoulders and held her back at arms' length, his gaze searching hers. "What are you saying, Abs?"

Abby had thought she'd be scared, but she wasn't, maybe because she'd never been surer of anything in her life. "Your letters showed me you're the kind of man I knew you to be. You made mistakes. So did I. The time has come to leave the past in the past."

Hope flooded Jonah's blue eyes.

"What I'm saying is yes. Yes, to a life with you. Yes, to children. Yes, to everything." Her lips trembled with emotion and her voice grew thick. "I want it all, Jonah. I want it with you."

Then, she was in his arms and she was kissing him with all the love in her heart.

The sun, which had been hiding behind clouds, came out to stream in through the window, promising one fine day.

EPILOGUE

"Where are you taking us?" Abby gazed up at Jonah, her arm linked through his as they made their way through the covered bridge.

Thanks to the snowfall last night, the grounds of the Green were a wonderland of white. Abby had bundled up when Jonah had asked her and Eva Grace to walk with him, telling them he had something to show them. The word 'surprise' had the little girl pulling on her coat, hat and boots in record time.

Abby admitted to being curious, too. But Jonah remained tight-lipped.

"You'll see soon enough." He flashed her that smile that never failed to make her heart beat faster.

"Does it have to do with the wedding?" All the plans were in place. The ceremony would be held at Leo's home over Eva Grace's winter break, with close friends and family in attendance.

The plan was for Eva Grace to return to Springfield with Jonah's parents while Abby and Jonah headed for the warmth of the Caribbean. Everything had been well thought out, including having Matilda oversee hotel operations while Abby was away.

"Look at her." Jonah gestured toward Eva Grace and chuckled. The little girl had dropped down onto a bed of white and was busily moving her arms up and down, making a snow angel.

Abby smiled. "That's our girl."

"Eva Grace." Jonah motioned to their daughter. "Let's go. Your surprise awaits."

The child, bundled in a snow suit able to withstand arctic temperatures, scrambled to her feet, brushing off the snow with her mittens. "Where are we going?"

Abby looked at Jonah. "That's what I've been asking your Dad. He's being very secretive."

"We're here," was all he said.

Abby glanced around the neighborhood and gazed at him in puzzlement.

Jonah extended one hand in the direction of a large Victorian home with the yellow siding. "Behold, our new home."

Eva Grace's eyes widened. "Are we really going to live there?"

Jonah nodded.

"I love it." Without missing a beat, Eva Grace opened the black iron gate that enclosed the yard and raced up the walk to the porch.

Abby stared at Jonah, as wide-eyed as Eva Grace. "Are you serious?"

"It's my wedding gift to you and Eva Grace." When she didn't immediately respond, his brow creased. "Don't you like it?"

Tears pushed at her lids. Before she could speak, Abby had to clear the thickness in her throat. "When I was a little girl, this was the kind of home I dreamed of one day owning. I never, ever, thought my wish would come true."

"You deserve all of your wishes to come true." Jonah waited for her to step into the yard then closed the gate behind them. "Would you like to see the inside?"

"Absolutely." Abby had to stop herself from racing to the door. She paused at the base of the steps leading to the front porch.

He tipped her finger up with a gloved finger. "What are you thinking?"

"What's going to happen to my apartment?" She knew she shouldn't be worrying about that right now. Shouldn't be giving it a second thought. "It's just that it holds such special memories. I can't imagine simply turning it into more hotel rooms."

"I've got an idea."

Abby stared up at him.

"What about a coffee shop? I realize the space isn't large but it would make the perfect intimate gathering spot for those looking for conversation, coffee and community."

Long ago, those had been the words on her business plan. What did it say that it didn't surprise her he'd remembered?

Abby suddenly felt quite breathless. "You really are determined to make all my dreams come true."

He grinned, a quick flash that lit up his face. "I aim to please."

Flinging her arms around him, Abby pulled his head toward her for an earth-shattering kiss. "I love you, Jonah Rollins."

"Mommy. Daddy." Eva Grace called out from where she stood on the porch, peering through the front window. "This place is awesome.

Abby turned in Jonah's arms to face their daughter.

"The yard is humongous," Eva Grace continued, flinging out her arms. "It's even big enough for a dog."

"It appears I'm not the only one with dreams." Abby lowered her voice, for Jonah's ears only. "I wouldn't mind a puppy."

Jonah winked. "Eva Grace. What do you say to a puppy for your birthday?"

In answer, Eva Grace squealed.

Her father grinned. "I believe that's a yes."

Abby tightened her arms around her future husband's neck. "What about your dreams?"

His head lowered, his mouth a breath away from hers. "Mine

came true when Eva Grace called me 'daddy' and you said you'd be my wife."

~

It was a rocky road for Abby and Jonah, but I have to admit I cheered when they found their happy ending. Not to mention, I fell in love with Hazel Green and all the wonderful people who lived there. And wasn't Eva Grace a hoot? I'll let you in on a little secret…I have three little granddaughters who I drew on for inspiration to make Eva Grace come alive on the page.

If you enjoyed this book, I know you're going to love Leo and Nell's story, ONE STEP AWAY. In that uplifting story you'll not only get to learn more about each of them, but you'll get to see more of Hazel Green and all its wonderful traditions. Grab your copy now or continue reading for a sneak peek:

SNEAK PEEK OF ONE STEP AWAY

Chapter 1

Tonight, Nell Ambrose would embrace the daring nature she normally kept hidden.

"I could have met you at the church." Nell slid into the passenger seat of Leo Pomeroy's BMW roadster.

The two-seater Z4 was an impractical car for northern Illinois, but that was part of the reason Nell enjoyed riding in it. Not that she availed herself of the opportunity very often. The last thing she wanted was for anyone in Hazel Green to think she and the mayor were "involved."

"Since we're both heading straight to the hotel after the wedding rehearsal, driving separately doesn't make sense." Leo, a handsome man with hair the color of rich Colombian coffee and vivid blue eyes, waggled his brows. "Shall I book us a room after we eat?"

Nell only laughed.

She might have agreed if the hotel was a large one in a city like Chicago, rather than an intimate ten-room vintage hotel owned by her best friend. After the rehearsal at the church, the dinner was being held at Matilda's, a farm-to-table restaurant inside the Inn at Hazel Green.

Leo put the car into first gear and pulled away from the curb. "You'll wound me eternally if you say you're not the least bit tempted." He hesitated for several seconds. "It's been a while, and I've missed…it."

Smart man. He'd learned not to say he missed *her*. And Nell was careful not to say words that would tie them together in any way other than physically.

"I am tempted." It had been several weeks since she and Leo had spent any time between the sheets. He'd been busy running the city. She'd been swamped with legal cases and with prepping for a platform performance as town matriarch Hazel Green. "But I won't sleep with you in the hotel owned by the bride."

Daring was one thing. Foolish quite another.

What Leo suggested would be terribly risky, especially since she was determined to keep her relationship with the mayor private.

Nell couldn't keep her lips from curving as a thought struck her. "What do you think about disguising ourselves one day soon and checking in under assumed names?"

It would be difficult since the staff at the inn were well acquainted with both of them. But if they could pull it off…

Escapades were her weakness. When she was young, she'd learned that being bad could be exciting and getting away with things could be addictive. Being very bad, well, that was thrilling.

Leo gave a good-natured chuckle. "Would you really do it?"

"Yes." She shot him a wink but could see he thought she was teasing.

She was dead serious. Which showed he didn't know her nearly as well as he thought he did. If he had any idea of the things she'd done before breaking free of her family…

Well, no matter. If she had anything to say about it, he'd never know all her secrets.

Because, if by some fluke, her past *did* catch up with her, the only house of cards she wanted tumbling down was hers. She would not let Leo, or any of her friends, be caught in the fallout.

"What's the matter?" He reached over, and before she knew what he planned to do, he brought her hand to his lips and pressed a kiss in the palm. "Cornelia Ambrose never looks stressed."

"True." For Nell, the importance of maintaining internal and external control had been drilled into her as soon as she'd been old enough to speak.

"It's been a busy week." She went on to tell him, in very general terms, about several of the cases she'd been working on and about a recent Hazel Green command performance.

"It was at the Palmer House?"

By his tone, you'd have thought she'd jetted off to Cairo instead of simply taking the train into Chicago.

Hazel Green was at the end of the Metra commuter rail. It had taken less than an hour for her to arrive at the front door of the turn-of-the-century elegant hotel off Michigan Avenue.

"It was a luncheon meeting of the Gold Coast Historical Society." Nell's brows pulled together when he turned into the church parking lot. How had they gotten here so quickly?

She enjoyed this alone time with Leo and wasn't ready for it to end.

They never went out together. Granted, there were a number of functions they both attended, but always separately. Tonight, as maid of honor and best man, it made sense for him to pick her up and for them to arrive and leave together.

She pushed open her door while he was rounding the front of the vehicle. "In doing research on their group's history, they discovered that Hazel Green once spoke to their society."

Leo stood next to the car. Even dressed simply in gray pants and a blue striped shirt, he looked every inch the successful businessman he'd been before running for elected office. Like her, the young mayor appeared in no hurry to rush inside.

Nell shut her eyes and lifted her face to the sun. When she opened her eyes, she found Leo staring. "I was remembering the meal. We had turtle timbales, kingfish and bonbons."

The flash of surprise that skittered across his face told Nell she wasn't the only one who found it an odd combination. "Lucinda Covert, the group's president, announced quite proudly that these same three items had been on the menu when Hazel Green originally spoke to the group."

Leo chuckled, seeming to find amusement in the comment. "I assume you gave the same speech to complete the déjà vu moment?"

His sharp mind was only one of the many things Nell liked about him.

"Hazel did a performance as Susan B. Anthony that day, so I spoke as her. Then I switched back to my Hazel Green persona and spoke about the importance of the arts."

"Two personas in one day." Leo appeared both awed and amused. "It's a wonder you can recall who you really are."

Nell wondered what he'd think if she told him she'd had a lot of practice playing different roles. Wondered what he'd think if he knew Cornelia Ambrose wasn't even her real name.

Though Nell knew she should hold back, tonight she didn't stop herself. After a quick glance to make sure they were alone, she gave in to temptation and brushed his lips with hers.

His lips were warm, and the citrus scent of his cologne teased her nostrils. Everything inside her yearned for the honest closeness she could never allow. "I'm enjoying being me this evening. Being me...with you."

"That's how I like it." His voice held a curious intensity.

The look in his vivid blue eyes had Nell shifting focus. She lifted a hand to his cheek and brushed her knuckles against the scruff.

Leo's tactile nature made him an amazing lover. The simple touch had the desired effect. Heat flared in his eyes.

"Are you growing a beard, Mr. Mayor?" Nell cocked her head and spoke in a teasing tone. "Or did you forget to shave this week?"

"That's two days' growth." His eyes never left her face. "I was thinking about letting it grow a little longer. What do you think?"

"Will it be scratchy?"

"If it is, I'll shave it off."

The coquettish smile she shot him was worthy of Hazel Green. "I don't mind it rough."

"Nell." Leo surprised her by taking her hand, tightening his fingers around hers. "Let me come home to you after the dinner tonight. We can—"

"I can't." Genuine regret filled her voice. "We're doing a girls' night at the hotel."

"I could rent a room." His tone turned persuasive. "You could sneak away and join—"

The sound of an approaching car had Nell jerking her hand free. A second later, a red sedan driven by a pretty blonde with a mass of curly hair rounded the corner and swung into the lot. "Looks like Jonah's sister is early, too."

"Think about my offer." Leo's devilish smile could tempt a nun to doff her habit.

Though she and Leo loved to banter, they were both conscious of their positions in the community. Or rather, *she* was conscious of Leo's position. Not only as mayor, but his position as part of what she thought of as the Pomeroy dynasty.

The Pomeroy family was one of Hazel Green's founding families. Jasper Pomeroy had been Richard Green's closest friend.

When Nell socialized with Leo in character as former town matriarch Hazel Green, it was as if she was part of the inner circle. Her lips curved at the thought.

"I can see you're tempted." Leo's low voice was a pleasant rumble.

She met his gaze, and her heart lurched. Truth was, she was always tempted by Leo. Nell had learned from the best just how fun it could be to take what you wanted. But, like the toys of childhood, she'd done her best to leave that life behind her.

However, sometimes that past came calling, even when not welcomed. She narrowed her gaze at the black Land Rover pulling in beside Jackie's sedan.

What the heck was Dixon doing here?

Dixon Carlyle cut an imposing figure as he stepped from the ebony vehicle. From his stylishly cut hair—dark as a raven's wing—to the tips of his Italian loafers, everything about the man screamed wealth and privilege.

Thankfully, Nell had learned from an early age that appearances could be deceiving. In Dixon's case, she knew for a fact his persona as a successful wealth management adviser was a false front.

She knew his past.

Worse, he knew hers.

Nell still hadn't discovered the real reason Dixon had come to Hazel Green. He'd arrived out of the blue last fall and never left. Supposedly, he had an office in Chicago on Michigan Avenue, but that could be simply another lie he'd spun.

Ever since last month, when he'd taken an apartment in Hazel Green, Nell had done her best to keep her distance. She'd insisted he keep his—but he'd never been good at following orders.

"What's he doing here?" Annoyance laced Leo's words.

"I have no idea." Nell kept the irritation from her voice. Any sign of displeasure would indicate Dixon's presence mattered. *That* was definitely not the impression she wanted to convey.

When he walked over to Jackie and flashed his charismatic smile, Nell knew the groom's twin sister didn't stand a chance.

Jackie Rollins had arrived last week, surprising everyone by announcing she was moving to Hazel Green.

The blonde emitted a full-throated laugh. No doubt Dixon was dazzling her with his charm. Something he possessed in abundance and knew how to use to his advantage.

She felt, rather than saw, Leo staring at her while her gaze was riveted on Dixon and Jackie.

Nell surprised Leo, and herself, by looping her hand through his arm. "We should say hello. Jackie doesn't know many people in town yet."

"Appears she's getting acquainted." Leo slanted a glance at her. "Tell me again how you know him."

"College friends." Nell kept her tone offhand. "Eons ago. Or at least it feels that way. Do you remember a lot from those days?"

"I remember some, but like you, it seems so long ago." An easy smile lifted Leo's lips. "Were you and Dixon ever romantically involved?"

"No." Nell nearly shuddered at the thought. "He never appealed to me in that way. Now, you, well, let's just say you captured my attention from day one."

"Good to know." He shot her a wink, and together they crossed the short distance to where the couple stood talking. Deep in conversation, Jackie and Dixon didn't turn immediately. When Dixon did look up, he glanced at the hand she rested on Leo's arm. One of his dark eyebrows rose imperceptibly.

Nell caught the gesture only because she knew him so well. Her chin inched up just enough to tell him she didn't care what he thought.

Irritation surged as amusement danced in Dixon's slate-gray eyes.

"Jackie." Nell greeted Jonah's sister, then made a great show of widening her eyes when they landed on Dixon. "And Dixon. This is a surprise. What are you doing here?"

"Frank Partridge came down with the stomach flu." Dixon

pasted a sympathetic expression on his face. "I'd been consulting with Pastor Schmidt on several church financial matters. He knows I'm a pianist, and when Frank canceled, he asked me to step in."

Jackie smiled warmly at Dixon. "That was sweet of you."

"Frank Partridge?" Nell paused. "The mailman?"

"Postal carrier." Dixon's lips quirked. "That question tells me you don't attend services at Hazel Green Community. Frank is at the piano every Sunday."

Leo studied the man through curious eyes. "I didn't realize you played."

Dixon shrugged. "I'm not a classical pianist, but I'm accomplished."

"It was kind of you to step in and help." The grudging quality to Leo's compliment had Nell hiding a smile.

"What can I say?" Dixon winked at Jackie. "I'm a nice guy."

It took every ounce of control Nell had not to roll her eyes when Jackie giggled. Instead, she gestured carelessly with one hand toward the church doors. "We should go inside. I'm sure Abby and Jonah are wondering where we are."

Just before they reached the entrance, Henry Beaumont roared up on his Harley. Henry—known as Beau—groomsman and son of the editor of the *Hazel Green Chronicle*, would walk down the aisle with Jackie.

Nell knew the attorney-turned-trial-consultant superficially and had no intention of becoming better acquainted. From a young age, lawyers and police officials had been on her list of those to avoid.

Thankfully, because her practice specialized in child advocacy cases, her interaction with law enforcement was minimal. Her contact with other lawyers, well, that was often unavoidable.

Like now.

Chapter 2

"Tomorrow, I get to scatter real rose petals." Eva Grace Fine, daughter of the bride and ecstatic flower girl, spun in a circle and favored Nell and Jackie with a blinding smile.

For tonight's rehearsal, Eva Grace had chosen to wear a red tulle skirt with a sparkly top covered in poppies. Her curly blonde hair was held back from her face by a thin red satin band.

"If I didn't know better," Nell said to Jackie, "I'd think you were her mother." When Nell had first seen Jonah's sister, she'd been shocked at the resemblance between Jackie and her young niece.

"That's quite a compliment." Jackie smiled. "Since I think Eva Grace is adorable."

Nell was careful who she let into her inner circle. Even those closest to her—such as Abigail Fine—were not privy to her secrets.

Still, she found herself cautiously liking Jackie Rollins. She sensed the woman hid her own secrets behind that sunny smile. Uprooting herself from Springfield, where she'd lived her entire life, to move to Hazel Green didn't make any sense.

Especially when, other than her brother and Abby, Jackie knew no one in town.

"I'm so happy you're both here." Abby stepped into the bride's waiting room and gave each of them a hug.

As was Abby's habit, she'd chosen a vintage dress for tonight's event. The sleeveless brown and white polka dot A-line dress with the white patent leather belt had been popular in the 1960s. It was perfect for someone with Abby's cute figure and big brown eyes.

"I love the dress." Jackie stepped forward and gave her future sister-in-law a hug. "You have such interesting clothes."

"As a merchant in a town that promotes itself as a place where history comes alive, it's practically a requirement." Abby jerked a finger in Nell's direction. "I'm still trying to convince that one to add more vintage to her closet."

"I'm an attorney, not a merchant." Nell ran her fingers through the blonde hair she was in the process of growing out. "I have quite enough vintage in my closet, thank you. Not to mention an entire Hazel Green wardrobe."

For a second, Jackie appeared confused. Then she laughed. "I keep forgetting that Hazel Green isn't just the name of the town. She was a real person."

"Wait until you see Nell in her Hazel Green persona." Pride filled Abby's voice. "You'd never guess it was Nell."

"The first time I saw her, I thought Mommy had made a new friend." Eva Grace quit twirling. "I asked Mommy who she was. When she told me it was Aunt Nell, I said, 'No way, Jose.' But it really was her."

Nell laughed, charmed by the childish chatter. No matter what persona she took on, it was a source of pride that she never broke character. Her mother had once dubbed her a chameleon, able to blend in no matter the surroundings.

"When do I get to walk down the aisle?" The six-year-old's pretty face pulled into a frown as she fixed her gaze on her mother. "Daddy told me if he knew I wouldn't have real flowers to toss, he'd have brought some for me."

"Daddy" was Eva Grace's biological father, Jonah Rollins. Abby had been a surrogate for Jonah and his then-wife, Veronica. When doctors warned the baby would likely be born with severe birth defects, Veronica pushed for an abortion. Abby stood firm and continued the pregnancy, breaking the surrogacy agreement. Eva Grace had challenges, especially during those early years, but none as severe as the doctors anticipated. Abby had spent the first five years of Eva Grace's life as a single parent before Jonah was back in the picture.

"Tossing real petals tonight would be a problem. Instead of leaving right after we finish rehearsing," Abby placed a hand on her daughter's shoulder, "we'd have to stay and pick each one up."

Eva Grace wrinkled her nose. "Oh."

"You're good at pretend." Abby smiled. "We'll see those petals even though they aren't there."

Nell knew the truth behind the statement. Most people saw what they wanted to see, not what was right in front of them. Perception, she'd learned from an early age, was everything.

Eva Grace appeared uncertain, but at that moment, Liz Canfield rushed into the room.

"I'm so sorry. The train was late and, well..." Liz paused. "Anyway, I'm here now."

Liz, who'd once been a reporter for one of Chicago's largest newspapers, was part of Nell and Abby's circle of friends. Nell liked the divorced mother of one, admired the strength she'd shown when her once happy life had unraveled.

Shortly after Liz's marriage had collapsed, her mother had been diagnosed with cancer and the newspaper had eliminated her position. The pretty brunette had appeared to take it all in stride. Cool confidence was the face Liz presented to the world.

"Jonah's parents are here. They walked through the door with me," Liz informed Abby in a low tone. "They stopped to speak with Jonah and Leo. I told them we'd be out momentarily."

Abby nodded and kept her voice equally soft. "I don't want Eva Grace too wound up before the practice."

Nell understood. This was exciting stuff for the six-year-old.

Liz nodded her approval. "It's important we all remain calm and focused."

The former reporter had taken on the task of wedding coordinator. A job she appeared to take seriously, if the directions she began barking out were any indication.

Twenty minutes later, Nell had to admit the woman had a talent for keeping everyone on task. Though it was only natural that Jonah's parents needed to be properly welcomed back to Hazel Green—even though they'd just been in town last week for a wedding shower—Liz cut the reunion short, announcing everyone could catch up at the rehearsal dinner.

This was Nell's first time as anyone's maid of honor. Unlike many young women her age, she'd never even been a bridesmaid. For most of her life, Nell had avoided close friendships.

Practically from the moment Abby had arrived in Hazel Green, she'd refused to let Nell keep her at arm's length. For that matter, neither had Liz. Or Rachel. Instead of no friends, Nell had a gaggle. She was truly mystified by how that had happened.

"Nell, listen up."

Blinking, Nell refocused on Liz, paying careful attention to the instructions on where to stand once she reached the front of the church. Huffing out a breath, Liz positioned her and Jackie at a slight angle.

"You are to remain evenly spaced. Never stand with your full back to the guests." Liz put her hands on Jackie's shoulders and made another slight adjustment in the bridesmaid's stance. "Bouquets are to be held in both hands in front of your body."

Liz scrutinized them with the intensity normally reserved for drill sergeants. Nell found herself holding her breath.

"Good." Liz gave a nod of approval. "We need to practice walking out. Remember, keep twenty feet between you and Abby."

Though Nell would be exiting the front with Leo, Liz insisted that she and Jackie get their parts perfect while the men watched from a nearby pew.

Leo smirked at her as she walked past. She couldn't help sticking her tongue out at him.

"Eyes forward, Nell," Liz called out.

Once the recessional was done to the drill sergeant's, er, to Liz's satisfaction, they moved on to the processional.

Abby and Jonah had chosen to follow the Midwest format where couples entered the ceremony in pairs. That suited Nell just fine.

After Jonah's mother had taken her seat at the front of the church, Jackie and Beau made their way down the aisle.

Liz nodded her approval at the pace.

Leo, standing at Nell's side, held out an arm to her. "Ready to do this?"

As Nell gazed into those clear, blue eyes, she had the odd sensation that she was about to step off solid ground onto shifting sand. Which, she told herself, was absolutely ridiculous.

She and Leo were practicing walking down a church aisle. Nothing more.

To the piano accompaniment of Pachelbel's "Canon in D Major," she started down the aisle.

Dive into this wonderful page-turner and find out the rest of the story!

ALSO BY CINDY KIRK

Good Hope Series

The Good Hope series is a must-read for those who love stories that uplift and bring a smile to your face.

GraceTown Series

Enchanting stories that are a perfect mixture of romance, friendship, and magical moments set in a community known for unexplainable happenings.

Hazel Green Series

These heartwarming stories, set in the tight-knit community of Hazel Green, are sure to move you, uplift you, inspire and delight you. Enjoy uplifting romances that will keep you turning the page!

Holly Pointe Series

Readers say "If you are looking for a festive, romantic read this Christmas, these are the books for you."

Jackson Hole Series

Heartwarming and uplifting stories set in beautiful Jackson Hole, Wyoming.

Silver Creek Series

Engaging and heartfelt romances centered around two powerful families whose fortunes were forged in the Colorado silver mines.

Sweet River Montana Series

A community serving up a slice of small-town Montana life, where helping hands abound and people fall in love in the context of home and family.

Made in the USA
Middletown, DE
01 July 2024